Grimes' Retribution

Paid in Full

Written by

H.A.L. Wagner

Edited by

Troy McElvoy

©2019 Forker Media

I'd like to thank my parents and a couple of my friends. I'm also thankful for being laid off.

H.W.

Published by

Grimes' Debt: A Paid In Full Novel © 2019 H.A.L. WAGNER ISBN: 978-1--942657163

The Grimes Collection:

Grimes' Punishment A Blood, Sex and Brawls Novel
Grimes' Retribution A Debt Paid in Full Novel
Grimes' Reckoning A Waking the Dead Novel
Grimes' Redux You Only Die Twice Novel

Debts, I had a few

The sun hadn't risen, even though it wanted too. The black night held on for an hour more. I hadn't moved from the metal folding chair in seven hours. Four hours ago, I had to pee, three hours ago my kidneys flopped like fish, and an hour ago I went numb from the bellybutton down. I was beating the odds; I was up ten grand … I-was-on-a-roll. For the first time in a long time, I was winning. Then, Marcus Riley called.

I brushed my shaggy hair away from my eyes and bent my two cards back against the green felt table. Looking up at me was the eye of the queen of hearts, and she had with her a ten of spades. Then I looked at Marcus for any *tell*. He was a fat guy, curly top head with a few random large moles on his face. He was sweating, we were all sweating sitting on the back deck of the house. The house was owned by Azad Aziz. The Arminian businessman came to town a few years ago and bought a notorious dive bar known for loose bartenders called Bald's Place. Locals called it Baldy's. It was the kind of dive no one went to, but everyone had been there. Blood stains on the carpet and bullet holes in the ceiling. How he managed to own a multimillion-dollar beach house could only come through less than legal dealings. This card game was one.

Aziz was out three hands ago, while I still had a stack of blue chips with a white stack doubly large. He sat now at his custom thatch and bamboo tiki bar in a high back stool sipping from a sweating glass. His thick black hair was slicked back but the high humidity had pushed his hair out at the sides, accentuating the receding hair line indentures above the temples. With bushy black eyebrows and intense amber eyes, he watched the game while twirling his diamond pinky ring.

1

The third player at the table was Smitty. He has one name, first or last, I don't know. I've known the white haired sixty-something handicapper a long time. He had a tanned rugged look about him, like he just got back from hunting Jaws, but when he smiles, he's all granddad. Smitty taught me to play the dogs and always had a tip on which Jai Ali player was about to be deported, that's the guy you bet. He was a numbers guy running numbers from way back. He came up in a time when there was still a mob in Daytona Beach.

"Oh, I believe that'd about do it for me." That was Smitty, half granddad and half mobster. There was always a wad of cash folded in his pocket and a gold bracelet on his right wrist.

Smitty just folded.

Marcus looked at me with the frozen stillness of a mannequin. I knew what I had, a ten matching the dealer's ten of hearts for a pair. Lady luck was going to plant a big wet kiss on me, I could feel those lips puckering up. That little tingle deep in my bowels, climbed higher in my chest, making it tight so I couldn't breathe. My fingers raked through my beard waiting for Marcus to fold.

Marcus belched softly, blowing hot remains of chicken parmesan my way. His cards flipped to show me two deuces that went along with a third in the dealer's row. My stomach sank as I gnashed my teeth. I couldn't help but make eye contact with those amber globes buried deep in Aziz's head. His bushy eyebrows went up and down then arched into points. I now owed him eighteen thousand dollars.

If you've never really won at anything, can you ever really have a losing streak? I pondered that as Aziz's man, Boghos, pressed a large furry hand down on my shoulder, keeping me in my chair. The urge to urinate came back with a vengeance.

Boghos was in a damp black silk shirt with the sleeves rolled up to his girthy forearms. His nails came to a well filed point just past the fingertips. Stubble from being awake for twenty-four hours began to blur the lines of his finely shaped beard outlying his wide jaw.

I let his hand hold me in my seat. Boghos was bigger than me, but I knew I could take him in a fight, well, I could have three months ago. Since then, I hadn't been taking care of my body, mind, or spirit, unless you count drinking spirits as medicinal. Glutton for punishment, I guessed, for what I did, killing those people. They were all bad people so in the end I wasn't going to hang myself over it. I ended up with a nice payday out of it. So nice in fact, I decided a professional gambler was the life for me. The last of it just went to Marcus.

What promise I had in a new career as a private investigator vaporized after my first big job finding the missing daughter of a powerful lobbyist. After that, it was a rapid descent as I began to ignore all the calls from my only employer, Willis Sanford Esquire, here in town. Instead, I took my hush money from that job and focused my talents at the kennel club, handicapping dogs with Smitty. When the excitement of losing wore off, I made the move to the poker room. I wanted more action than they could provide. Smitty got me into private games like this one, with higher stakes. Azad's games were supposed to be the best in town. My only friend left in this world, Billy, warned me they were fixed, said, no one walks out of Aziz's game a winner. "You win tonight," he said, "You'll pay tomorrow." He was right.

Marcus ran his fat fingers over the table and scooped up the last of my streak. He peeled his round frame from the chair and flipped the dealer a couple blue chips. Of the four stacks of chips, Marcus took only half of one, turned and nodded to Aziz who nodded back, and walked out with the half stack. In the other room a man would exchange the chips for cash. I figured he left with four grand out of the forty something he had on the table. Everyone owed Azad sometime.

Smitty got up, drained his glass then nodded to Aziz. On his way out, he paused to look back at me. The wrinkles around his mouth wiggled as his lips parted, but he said nothing. He turned and left. I expected more from the old man.

I was the only one still at the table. A sweat bubble had rolled down through the black strands of my temple, but I couldn't move to wipe them. Instead, the bubble collided into others and rolled on down my neck absorbing into my t-shirt collar.

The two fans spun on high, but the air remained stagnant, even on the beach the air tonight was dead calm. Out past the slack low tide heat lightning flashed silently in the clouds. Just off the screened porch a static charged blue light lured unsuspecting bugs to their immediate death. There was a good chance I would be next.

"Mr. Grimes," Aziz said as he made his way over to the poker table, "Seems you have run quite a considerable amount of debt in a short time. Most men, they spread things out, a little at a time. Not you, no you show up a few weeks ago with twenty G's, cash, and want to play cards. I take your money. Then you want to borrow more, so I lend it, but eventually you lose that just as fast."

Boghos's grip tightened. There was no way I was going without a fight, but I fully expected to go down. As far as the criminal element in this beach town went, I knew who most everyone was. There were your biker gangs, running shine, drugs, and guns. The street gangs, mostly 3rd Street, I already tossed with and walked away. And then there were drifters trying to make a buck while getting a tan.

"You don't gain access to these private events without me knowing something about you." Aziz reached in his front pocket and pulled out a vape pen. He huffed and blew out sweet vanilla vapor. I felt like I just licked the inside of his nostrils. He continued, "But ask about Roger Grimes, there's just rumors and conjecture. This, intrigues me greatly." He vaped again then walked back to the bar.

His back was to me and Boghos. His arms spread wide as he gripped the teak. I could see the dark sweat soaked armpits and other spots on his back. "I do not like to be intrigued, Grimes. I want to know things right away. So, because of this, this not knowing who you are, I am extending the limits on your loan. You have ten days to pay me half. If you do that, you get another five days for second half. This is very generous of me."

That was it, there was no ultimatum. A man sure of his power didn't need to give one, people could fill in the dead space on their own. I was thinking about my own dead space.

"That's probably a good idea." I said flatly. If wanting to avoid pissing my pants was my plan, I failed.

Aziz turned, the amber in his eyes was replaced with a deepening red, a building fire that consumed his face, "Get him out of here!" he shouted and threw his glass past my head. It shattered on the terracotta floor behind me.

Boghos snatched me by the neck, forcing my head down and forward, pulling me from my chair like an out of line child. As I bent at the waist, I felt my bladder pinch like a water balloon about to burst. The urge to fight was blocked by what little reason I had left, allowing Boghos to shove me through the door, across the burnt red patio and down the grey wooden steps to the white sandy beach.

I pulled my face out of the sand and stood upright to feel the pressure drop to the bottom of my bladder. My pelvic floor muscles were strained near the breaking point. I thought I made it; I saw a leafy sea grape tree in a dune and knew I could finally relieve my burden. Then Boghos hit me. First in the kidney and I felt the dribble in my shorts along with the pain. Then as my spine arched back, his large furry hand came around and hit me in the stomach. That was all my pelvic muscle could take and a warm wet flow darkened the front of my grey shorts cascading down my legs into my size twelve Vans slip-ons.

Boghos scoffed and walked back to the house, never looking over his shoulder.

Rock bottom just fell on me, and I was trapped in its rubble. It was time to stand up, shake the piss off my legs and go back to being a private investigator.

Chapter 1

My friend list was short. My friends with money list, even shorter. Driving up to the CBR Building off US 1 twisted my guts. The knot tightened with every step across the marble entrance and tighter still up every floor until I got to the seventh floor.

Inside the office carpet was a cream Berber. On one wall hung two Zulu spears with a zebra hide between them. A few chromed frame chairs surrounded a coffee table covered in magazines. Straight ahead was Monique's desk. Beyond the large wooden double doors was Sanford's office. She sat relaxed with her feet tucked up under her butt as her long nails tapped away at the keyboard.

"Hi Grimes," she said while still typing.

"Hey, boss in?" I said slowing but not stopping at her desk. I wanted this meeting over with.

Her long eyelashes fluttered as she glanced up then back to the monitor, "In court."

"Oh, right." I stood there looking at the large wooden doors. Relief washed over me as I exhaled.

Monique looked up at me again and held the stare until I turned for the exit.

"You doing alright?" Her perfectly shaped eyebrows pinched together.

"Yeah, just peachy." I turned to leave.

"I'll tell him you stopped by."

"Sure. Thanks." I left without a loan. Strike one.

That took all my nerve to make my way up to the law office. Willis Sanford still had me on retainer, payment for being the lone solider in his army to rid the streets in Daytona Beach of the rats and the bugs that kept a permanent black eye over an otherwise beautiful beach town. I saw firsthand when a good man and friend died of a drug overdose and then saw it again with the first case Sanford put me on. I never planned to kill anyone, but that's what I did. The drug dealers, pimps and child molesters that called these sandy streets home now had something to fear in the dark. Just as they were coming alive, so was I.

Willis applauded my efforts from his stuffed leather chair as he read the news headlines, nonviolent crime was down; drugs, prostitution, and theft, but violent crime saw an uptick. *Imagine that* he'd say with a smile and dancing coffee-colored eyes behind steel rim glasses. We had a secret spreadsheet, stolen from a drug dealing pimp that led us to the top of the heap. The cops weren't moving fast enough for Sanford. He wanted me to go after them. I had seen and done enough and walked away.

I was done, my wounds hadn't healed into scars yet and I kept getting more. I should have stayed a thief, now I just need to stay away.

***

Seated in an antique wooden desk chair everything in my body was tight. My jaw was clenched, my shoulders held heavy thoughts. Hands on the clock grew larger and crashed into the next minute like a dump truck through a brick wall. I stared down at Beach Street from my second-floor office window. Traffic was nonexistent, not even in the parking spaces along the road.

My office wasn't anything like Sanford's. His was a block west of mine and seven stories, of which he was on the top. From my second-floor office, I could see the Halifax River and Jackie Robinson Stadium, so it was a nice view. Sanford, from the seventh floor of his building could see both the river and the ocean beyond that.

His office had a marble top wet bar, fully stocked with liquors I couldn't afford or pronounce. I had a mini fridge with Miller High Life in it. I also had an old couch with burlap cushions colored in orange and brown. I leased an apartment on the beachside, but most of my time was spent here in the office on that couch.

My mind was wrapped around travel plans to get out of the country, somewhere down in South America, maybe Uruguay. I hadn't come up with one cent to pay Aziz. I wasn't ready to go up against him over this debt. I knew I could fight what was coming, I just didn't want too anymore. I stood my ground before, fighting with my fists and with guns to make wrongs right and a lot of people died. I had been running from only myself since then.

I called Smitty.

Not long later, he sat across from me, his legs crossed, hands folded in his lap. His twitching grey eyes calmed and narrowed as I told him what happened after he left Aziz's place.

"Yeah, I know, yeah it was dumb. Do you have a job for me or not?"

"This isn't like you kid." Smitty usually called me kid. "I should have noticed it sooner. I mean, hell you look sick. You've lost fifteen pounds and you look soft, not the same hard Grimes I know." He crossed his arms and studied my face. "Is your mind, right?"

"Sure." That was a lie. If my body looked rough my mind was somewhere between that dump truck and the brick wall.

"Is Billy available?"

"No, no way. I won't ask him. He's gone legit same as me."

"Yeah, I stopped by his auto shop the other day, got an oil change." He looked around the office,

"Smitty, I can work a job alone. You know how good I was. Besides you got me into this mess." I tried to stop that last sentence, but that train was too fast.

"Sorry your *legit* job don't pay your debts." Smitty was getting annoyed with my pleading. A few months ago, he wanted Billy and I for a job, I turned him down, refusing to even meet with him. It wasn't like me, but I've changed. I wouldn't call it grown, just changed. Billy Horseblood and I had been car thieves and bank robbers. Smitty pulled us up into a life of high-end theft. Then a couple years ago I quit. He didn't like it one bit, but instead of catching hell, he just smiled his grandad smile and said it was okay.

"I need you to procure something for a client." Smitty went on to describe the job. I listened to the old criminal talk with words you read from a pulp novel, words they used when he was still with the mob. Escaping his verbal barrage, my mind wandered back to the plan of escaping to a Uruguayan beach.

The gangster in him faded when I heard him say, "Yeah kid, it should fix you right up." And he was grandpa Smitty again.

A knock at the door got me up. Smitty went on talking. As I opened the door my nose filled with lavender, I drew it deep into my lungs. A repressed memory of her rushed forward causing momentary blindness as all I could see was flesh and tears. How I chased her around town and fought off all challengers to be with her, all that time and alcohol wasted. The nights spent tossing and turning on the couch, wondering if she was coming over and the dawning realization that she wasn't. Young, dumb, and full of, well, angst. I called it love, never being sure of what she called it. Then she left.

Now Crystal Johnson was back and standing there just staring at me. I left the door wide to let her in and took up my seat behind the desk.

Crystal walked slowly in red heels and black skintight jeans to the edge of my desk, leaning slightly against the edge, leaving an indent at the top of her thighs.

"Smitty, you better go." I said, cutting the man off from whatever offer he had for me. In the moment, it didn't matter.

"Okay kid, have it your way, but time is not on your side. And get a haircut you damn hippy." Smitty said then gave Crystal the once over. I heard him mutter *dames* as he walked out shaking his head. Strike two.

I never heard the door close. I was lost in a sharp pair of hazel eyes, taking me backwards eight years. The good times pushed up, before the sleepless nights, to times of laughter and passion, so much passion.

"Kill Oliver Lean or I will."

Her words spun my stomach and put images in my brain. Things I tried to bury, but had stayed with me, lingering, creeping up on me in the middle of the night. Their faces appeared in my dreams, turning fun into horror as I killed them over and over night after night. Sometimes the dreams were reversed. All of them, the ones I killed were there, just faces in the dark coming closer and closer. I had no choice but to shoot but the damn trigger wouldn't pull. The gun fell apart and just as they rip me to pieces with their bare hands, I awake.

My eyes snapped into focus, narrowing to take into view her smooth porcelain face, shoulders ending in a tiny waste and rounded hips she couldn't hide. Her arms crossed as she cocked those hips to one side. She was serious.

"I'm serious."

"You're nuts. That's not what I do." I felt the anger well up inside me, pumping my veins full, swelling my muscles taught. Damn her and that stupid idea. Stupid talk like that was why we split. But there she was, all dolled up and needing my help. Her good looks had done her in again and she needed saving, someone to reach down and pull her up out the black muck she always seemed to fall in. I walked away from her years ago, I should now, but damn, we had some hot times. When I fall for a girl, I always fall hard.

"But ya' could." She ran a long finger tipped with blood-red polish along the edge of my desk as she came around to where I sat. "I know you could."

Trapped in the fog of memories I said, "Yeah. I'll do it." It turned my guts over to say. The fog lifted, and I remembered the lives I took so violently. I filled the void with drinking and gambling, escaping the faces that found me in the night. Everyone thinks it's the righteous kill or the vengeful kill that you can walk away from, maybe so, but I was hired, coaxed, and conned into it. And none of it sat right with me since.

The dame bounced into my lap, lashing out with hugs and kisses. They weren't the same hugs, they weren't the same kisses, but I let her body heat warm me.

I patted her on the ass and motioned to stand. I stood over her, holding her at arm's length. "On one condition,"

Looking up into my steel blue eyes she smiled and nodded, she would do anything to get Oliver Lean dead.

"You stop fucking around with these shit bags. I mean it. No more." When she smiled again, I pulled her in. I wanted to feel the depth of her breasts smashed up against my sternum. My nose was positioned perfectly atop her head to smell her hair. I allowed myself to be transported back to a time when my next move would have been unzipping her jeans. That was a long time ago and she had made no indication that would be happening this time around. Still, I pictured it happening.

She pulled away, her eyes finding mine, "I'm not stupid, he always called me stupid, said I could never be anything then spit in my face. No really, hocked a loogie and spit it right in my face." Her eyes became slants and the corner of her mouth curled. "But I'm not stupid. He's the dummy." She laughed. As the smile faded, she grabbed her arm and in a way that was hugging herself, adding, "That wasn't the worst of it." She went to explain in detail some more of Lean's failings as a man, especially those in the bedroom and how violent he would be afterwards.

"And all his pals. A bunch of slime balls always touching me and grabbing my ass, right in front of Ollie. Who, the hell, would let his friends grab his girl like that? I know you wouldn't Roger. You'd break all their necks, especially that Juan. Out of all of them, he was most obsessed with me." Her eyes narrowed as she thought back to whatever indignities they put her through.

"He had that look you get, you know the one, like a caveman." She said cracking an obsequious smile that brought her back from where she had gone in her memories to a safe place here with me.

"Huh," I quit listening; all I could think about was how damaged she was. This wasn't the same Crystal Johnson I knew; the one I saw at parties in a circle of laughing drunks as her goofing around would keep them rolling. It helped she had nice tits, a cute face and tiny waist, but it was her ability to cut up and enjoy life that attracted the moths to her flame. That light was gone, stomped out by a piece of shit that would think about what he did as he sank to the bottom of the river. I would make sure he thought about it.

After a deep breathe, my head cleared, and I chalked taking the job up to a nice imagination. I couldn't take this job.

"Give me two weeks." *What did I just say?* I could never kill for money or for anything or anyone ever again. That was in my past and it in my present nightmares.

"Two weeks and you'll cool off." I said trying to be clever, and back pedal out of whatever this hate for Oliver she had. Like a three-day waiting period for a gun, and hopefully she would cool down and forget the whole thing. If not, I would either be in Uruguay or fish chum floating past Aziz's beach house.

"Two weeks? No way Roger, I can't wait that long. I won't be alive that long. If he finds out…if he suspects…" the hazel in her eyes turned red as tears began to rain down her cheeks. "Roger," Her eyes hung like wet rags, "You're just the strongest man I have ever met." Her eyes tightened at the corners as she rolled them over my body with a familiar stare, like I was a picture in a dirty magazine.

"Can't I just rough him up, roll him. Maybe put him in the hospital. You'll have time to get away. Daytona has been nothing but trouble for you, now is your chance."

Crystal shook her head 'no'. The tears made another appearance. "He's got to die. I'll just do it myself Roger. Is that what you want, to see me go to jail for life?" The red-eyed tears began to turn to red embers, "You know I'll get caught."

I let out a string of swear words under my breath. I knew the next words would be breaking all my rules, "Unless you have ten thousand dollars, I need more time." She popped up on the balls of her feet as her arms swung around my neck. Even the kiss on the mouth and warmth of her body pressed against mine was not enough to erase the regret filling my stomach with acid. *What an idiot.*

As my senses began to return, I said, "It's got to be ten. Can you get that in three days?" An easy way out of a job you don't want to do is to just overbid. It was a win either way for me, if she paid it, I could put a nice down payment on my debt to Aziz. If she didn't, I was that much closer to finding out what Uruguay was like in the winter.

Crystal crinkled her brow. I had seen that look before. It was not a good one to be on the receiving end of. There would be more water works coming and I was all out of tissues. There was no way a girl like Crystal would have ten thousand to drop on a hit. I was in no position financially to do a job like this. It took planning and lots of extra costs. This was a small town, not like Chicago or New York with people going missing all the time and murder rates as high as Bagdad. This was Florida. To properly dispose of the body, you take him out to the swamps with bone digesting gators.

"I'll need half up front."

"Okay. I can pay that." Crystal tried to keep a straight face, but the smile came out anyway. It was crooked with her eyes pulling tight like a twisted jester about to get one over on the king. The smile washed away quickly. "I don't have it all right now. Later, tonight maybe?"

I nodded. She went in for one more hug. I peeled Crystal away once more. "I've got to get started. You can drop the other half in three days." I hated reminding her she had to pay but I had to eat. Being a lazy PI with a taste for whiskey was not congruent.

"I knew you would be there for me Roger." Crystal smiled. She ran a well-manicured hand through my black hair. Just like old times. Damn if she still didn't have me by the balls. Hell, I already said yes to kill a man I never met.

She reached up and touched the whiskers along my square jaw. Her lips parted ever so slightly, and her warm breath exhaled. I couldn't control my hand as it slid down her side over her hip. I could have kept going but she pulled away.

"When it's over, Roger, when it's all done, I'll be free."

For me, the realization that I was just played peeled away her beauty mask that quickly left the coke head smiling before me. The crow's feet were deeper than I had remembered, and her tooth was chipped. Her waist was thicker, and her butt settled lower than it used to. I blinked a few times confused as to how she had gone from the girl of my memories to one I wouldn't have looked twice at.

Crystal walked out with nothing more to say. I should get cash payment in my hand tonight, but buyers are liars. There was time to back out, but I never went back on my word. I had gone straight a few years ago and even put the skills I learned on the street to use becoming a private investigator. Back then I was heading down the path of a career criminal. Traveling across the state, hitting banks, jewelry stores and occasionally boosting cars, with Billy, my criminal mentor by my side. Together we built a good system we could live well from. Smitty fronted a number of heists and we all made a nice little thieving trio.

I wanted to go straight, for some time. When I became a PI, I got mixed up with a benevolent do-gooding lawyer named Willis Sanford. He had started a crusade and tried to convince me I was his *White Knight*, sent to clean up this beach town. Sanford had lost faith in our justice system. Too many were getting away with too much. In in his pursuit for higher justice, I took a few lives while breaking up a child sex trafficking ring. Good for me, good for the city, but I didn't feel so swell about it.

All of that seemed so important then. Now, money is what I needed, so I plotted the assassination of a man I never met based on the line Crystal fed me. If I was anything, I was a planner. From jewelry heist to bank robbery, I planned them all, but I gave that up. Thinking some more about killing, I decided rage would be a nice excuse, maybe the conviction to save a friend, but neither was true. The memory of unrequited love for Crystal was all there in my face but I wiped it away to see her for the self-centered woman she was. If this guy, Lean, smacked her around and she was still with him then she stayed for more than love. Wanting Lean dead meant there was someone bigger waiting for Crystal and Oliver Lean was in the way. Lean must have some leash made of diamonds to keep that bitch tethered to the point of getting wacked.

I tilted back in my chair trying not to be disgusted with what I had become. The spiral drilled deeper down, and I was not jumping off anytime soon. The end was coming up fast if I didn't take control of it. There was still time to turn around and climb my way out.

My phone was open, and I hit up social media sites looking for Lean. The guy was familiar to me, but it had been a while since I saw him last. I had no idea what he looked like now and there were more accounts for an Oliver Lean than I expected. The plan was to contact Lean through this phony account I made for a chick named Sophia, a twenty-three-year-old Columbian girl who liked to go to clubs and get her hair done. It would have him hooked; guys are all the same, dumb. He would respond.

I wasn't on the site long when the office door opened. Only minutes after Crystal left and I was already getting sloppy. I grunted getting to my feet. *No new cases*, I thought as I walked around my desk towards whoever was walking in.

The man was not tall. His jaw square, his eyes like two little black marbles. A tight-fitting black t-shirt covered the body of a man who liked to lift but also liked to eat Whoppers afterward. "You the PI?"

"Yeah," I said leaning against my desk.

"I'm Oliver Lean, and someone is trying to kill me."

My senses went crazy. Was he here for me? What did he say? Did he know? Was he going to force this fight here, I wasn't prepared for this, not in my office, not so soon? What a mess, there would be with the blood and the noise of a gunshot or maybe use at knife. I didn't have my knife on me, or my gun. They were both in the desk drawer. I would have to beat this Lean guy to death with my own hands.

Lean's eyes grew round and glassy. He pinched them shut. "Someone's trying to kill me." His mouth opened and was full of stringy spit, he looked pathetic.

My brain emptied of crisscrossing thoughts leaving a blank stare on my face. The first thought after a mind sweep like that was being punked. Crystal had to be playing a joke. *Where's the camera*, kind-of thoughts. I expected her to come through the door laughing and we all go grab a beer and catch up like we should have done originally.

Air traveled through my hanging jaw and forced its way into my lungs. As hot breath escaped out, I decided no one would get killed today.

In my absence to speak, Oliver Lean looked around and took a seat on the well-worn couch. The burlap cushions rubbed against the man's darkly tanned skin. Lean chose to stare out the window than look me in the eyes. Crying was not something Lean wanted to do or let me see him do, but it had been a long week for the man. It all started four nights ago at a bar, Baldy's, the dive owned by Aziz. It's the kind of place with multiple health code violations, not for the roaches or mold. The violations came because the barmaids kept taking their shirts off and served shots from between their held-up sagging boobs. I remembered back to the first time I was there. Without explanation or clean up, the men's bathroom floor was covered in blood. It was *that* kind of place.

Oliver Lean continued with his tale of murder attempts. He was at the bar when the roughriding bartender said, "Hey Ollie, that guy been asking about you."

Lean looked back as the man left his table for the door. The man was tall and thin. He kept his head down and wore a ball cap. Not being a tough guy on his own, Lean waited for his crew to show. If the man came back, Lean would beat the truth out of him, with his crew behind him.

Lean bragged about his crew, Juan Carlos, Kyle, and his cousin Chester. They were all tough guys and connected to organizations I never heard of. Eventually they showed, and they drank as the bartender delivered shots wedged in her cleavage. Lean forgot about the stranger and made the mistake of taking a phone call outside. The crowbar came in hard, but Lean was able to fight his attacker off and soon his crew came running. The would-be assassin ran off into the night. They drove around looking for the man, but never found him.

All the usual questions were thrown at Lean, who could it be, why would he attack, who'd you piss of this time? Oliver Lean had no answers.

His story went on. The next night, just before midnight, Lean was finishing dinner with his side chic, the one Crystal knew about. The girl was short with big tits and a big ass and a face that was hard to watch in motion, and it was constantly in motion. She never stopped talking, even with her mouth full. Lean didn't care, it allowed him time to think which wasn't often. A normal person wouldn't be able to think with constant chatter in their ear, but Tammy hardly asked questions, and when she did, they were more rhetorical than direct. So, Lean just thought about other stuff, sex mostly, but cars too.

Lean and Tammy lumbered across the street after their full meals. Tammy kept talking, going on about her job as a server and how stupid the public was and how this lady never tipped but this one tipped well. Lean had heard the story twice that night already, so he was good and zoned in on what he planned for Tammy as soon as they got back to her place.

No one could have heard the car over Tammy's yap, a dog maybe. The engine roared as the tires squealed for traction. Lean turned his head in time to see the blinding headlights. He said he pushed Tammy out of the way of the speeding car, but I believed it more likely the other way around when he said Tammy took a header into the gutter. Tammy was alive but wouldn't be waiting tables for a while with a broken pelvis.

I took a seat after the story of the last attempt. Two possible coincidences in a row were beginning to seem less coincidental as Lean started his third story on escaping death. This time he was at his house with Crystal. Seems like a good alibi for Crystal.

Lean lived in a town house on beachside. It was a nice little community but beachside always attracted drifters and opportunists looking for a quick buck. Usually, it was a car left unlocked or a bike in the yard. It never amounted to more than the homeless or young punks looking to make a start in the life of crime. I had been through that stage, it just lasted fifteen years. Lean's condo was nice, it had a gate.

It was another late night on the couch with Crystal and the glow of the TV. The back-door knob jiggled. Lean claimed he jumped up and grabbed his pistol, which he never kept far, and went to the window to investigate. So far, I believed most of what Lean had said, there was little reason not to. But what Lean said next made all his other stories begin to mix and mottle with the truth leaving me to sort it out. Questions were now raised, and answers would take time.

Lean looked me in the eyes then looked away. "The tall man was back, and he had his gun out. So, well, I shouted for him to get the fuck outta my yard or he was dead." Lean was flushed and breathing heavy. "The guy came at me. So, I shot him."

I mulled it over before saying, "Through the door?"

Lean cocked his head, "No. He was, well, he, ran and I shot at him. But ah, he just kept going."

"So, you missed?"

Lean crinkled his brow and his lips curled up in excitement to hear his words aloud, "If I'd a got him I would 'a just buried him there or dumped him in the river." His smile faded through the silence then he said, "No cops, I fucking hate 'em." Lean smiled again as if that identified him in the same club as I, which he was not. Besides, being mostly a loner, I don't join clubs. I didn't have a problem with cops, they had a job, and I had a job, so what. Though I had a legal PI license it seldom held me to a code or standard. The license was a way to work within the system to achieve my goals. Willis taught me that, he used me for that as well.

"Anything since?" I asked.

Lean rubbed his sweaty palms along the stylish jeans he had squeezed into. He shook his head *no,* then went on to tell me he thinks his condo may have been broken in to.

"You *think,* but don't know?"

"I might have left the window open. I don't remember. Nothing I noticed was taken but just, stuff was a little out of place." Lean shrugged so I shrugged. A good thief could pull a job like that, in and out with nothing out of place. The victim wouldn't know for days or more if there was indeed a break in.

All of it could be in his head. The tall thin guy from the first go around could have been one of Crystal's exes, there was a long line of them. How far down the list was I?

I made Lean wait as I stared off running scenarios through my brain. As I neared the least likely, a memory returned of Boghos punching me in the gut and the warmth of urine down my leg. Take the 9-millimeter out of the drawer and shoot Lean right now. Hell, I haven't even got the down payment yet. Better still, where to dump the body? A drive down some back roads would lead to gator infested waters. Taking the contract on Lean would only cover half my debt with Aziz. What was Lean willing to pay? Take Lean's case and the money then shoot him and feed the gators. Or take Lean's money and actually investigate who wants him dead. Having another hitter could create serious problems for me. The professional in me had to find out who the other killers were.

Crystal was the obvious culprit but why hire me now? The spiral turned some more.

"I can pay you." Lean said answering a lot of questions piling up in my head. He stuck his leg out to reach in the back pocket of his skinny jeans and pulled an envelope. The envelope was so thick the flap couldn't close.

I became thirsty. My eyes locked onto the fat envelope and wanted to know how much was in it but knew I couldn't ask. Between Crystal's payment and Lean's, it could be enough to set me straight and pay off my debt with Azad Aziz, and maybe even purchase some real surveillance equipment. The kind of equipment that would help grow the business from strong-arming dead-beat dads for child support to catching cheating wives in the act and insurance fraud cases. The spark inside me began to catch fire as imagined possibilities exploded.

There was no way Crystal could even come close to matching that. What if it was Crystal? Could I turn her in? "Who else knows about these attempts?"

"Well, my girl that was with me. That side chick, she wasn't so sure it weren't an accident. My buddies they saw him the first time."

"Okay so you haven't answered the question, why does someone want you dead?" I had already heard Crystal's reasons.

Lean put his elbows to his knees and looked me in the eyes. "Do you know who I am?"

I shrugged.

Lean sat back into the couch. His fingers twisted lose brown and red fibers of burlap. "You don't *know* me." Oliver Lean's dumb bro accent faded, his annunciation improved and suddenly he became very convincing. The change in tone and manner must have registered on my face because Lean paused and said, "Yes, I'm not the Jersey shore reject I pretend to be. I'm or was a computer engineer and a few years ago, I kind of got into hacking and that led to money laundering for a, well a big player in town. I'm just a computer nerd not a mobster. Now I'm stuck. I figured I would come up with a backup plan to get out any time I wanted. Well, I haven't. I thought I was too brainy for these thugs."

"Brains can be bashed, Ollie." I sat up in my chair. "Now tell me how 'he' became 'they'?" This revelation made the envelope significantly lighter.

"You haven't said you would take my case."

"No, and I won't until I know what I'm jumping into. And before you throw more cash at me, I want to know everything then I will decide." I laid it all out for Lean. The guy's story had taken a turn. Inside I felt a change, a fire burning my bones and twisting my guts. My head was lighter, and my eyes became wider as Lean went on. Something was welling up inside and whatever it was, I knew it could only be excreted through long nights, risk taking and careful thought, in other words, hard work. It had been a long while but now I had a real case, and I was eager to delve in. This was something more, something to get me going again, and something I had to do.

"You see, Mr. Grimes, I can't just go to the cops with this. I thought a guy like you, wouldn't mind making my problem go away." Lean pulled his broad shoulders back and flipped his head side to side cracking his neck. "Look I got money and I got connections back home that could make this disappear real quick, but I need this problem to go away quietly. You know what I mean?"

I nodded. I knew what he meant but wasn't buying what he was selling.

"I gotta go, but ah, lemme know what turns up." He spun the envelope on the desk then extended his hand with a knowing smile.

I nodded and shook Lean's hand, with that, the secret was safe for now and I was taking the case.

Chapter 2

Repeated calls to Crystal went to voice mail. I sat spinning in my desk chair, staring up at the ceiling when I felt my hair brushing past my temples. If I was going back to work the hair had to go.

A few minutes later, I was down the hall in the Men's Room with the clippers, rinsing the sink of my hair trimmings. When I got back to my office, I had a text from Crystal: *You can't call.*

I texted back: *Cooper's 11?*

Crystal responded fast: *I'll meet you at Cooper's at 11. Delete this and those calls.*

I was impressed. I underestimated Crystal, thinking she was stupid. Wouldn't life be great if it was Crystal this whole time and I was just the next ex-boyfriend to sit in a bar and wait for Lean? I had never been that lucky. Still, I stayed optimistic.

Cooper's is an Irish pub, heavy on the dark wood décor and served up a variety of fried concoctions that passed for bar food until 3 a.m. So, it was a kind of an after-hour's pub, but also a popular spot to pregame as well, leaving eleven to midnight a dead hour. That's why I picked it for our meeting and the wide variety of craft brews available would help me while I waited.

Being a block from my office I went there often. The bartenders were generally good with one in particular, Alysa. She was a gorgeous girl, with the right mix of everything, looks, attitude and personality. We got to know each other after I moved into my office. Nothing beyond, bartender and patron, but she made drinking much more enjoyable. After Sanford and I broke up the sex trafficking ring, things went dark for me. Drinking more, eating less, doing nothing but spending the blood money Sanford deposited became my daily routine. She saw the change and not liking it, cut me off. I said some choice words and stumbled off to drown myself in a bottle alone, without her gorgeous green eyes judging me or the sounds of her good advice to contemplate.

I hated myself for a while. I thought she hated me too. Once the tired numbness faded, I came down to Cooper's, but Alysa had moved on. That's the way it was around here, just when you meet the bartender of your dreams a new bar opens, and they are off. Like modern day cowboys, slinging drinks and herding customers, they follow the herds to the new watering holes. Judging by what I was looking at inside Cooper's, I didn't blame her.

I got there about ten-thirty and watched as people met up with their packs. A few guys would high five as chicks walked around hugging friends. They would drink a beer or two and then leave for a trendier bar or club. I stuck to the oatmeal stout and an order of onion rings.

Just after eleven Crystal walked in with a friend. The girl had short black hair, shaved on one side. Her face had dark eye liner and several piercings: nose, lip and more up the side of one ear. The dark maroon lipstick made her look angry, like she needed to be kept on a leash, I thought as I finished the last of my stout. Crystal on the other hand, looked done up with blown out hair and high heels on, giving her a slightly unstable walk. She had a never budging smile and tightness about her that told me she was coked out.

I waved the pair over. The friend smelled of cigarette smoke and hairspray. Crystal overdosed on the perfume I had found so alluring earlier that day.

Crystal looked around the bar and then at me, "This is my friend Sunrise Palace."

I nodded, not letting the ridiculous name show on my face. I put an onion ring in my mouth and chewed.

"Is it cool if she is with us?" Crystal uttered then wiped at her red nose.

Crystal didn't care and I didn't care, but Sunny Palace cared for all three of us. She wanted me to have a problem with her. Her intense stare was unwavering. The black hoodie and jean cut-offs with leggings going down into black boots screamed for attention just so she could scream back to be left alone.

"Okay Crystal, I got a line on the guy. Give me the half so I can do my job." I said without making eye contact with either girl. I noticed Sunrise never took her right hand out of the front pocket.

Crystal looked over to Sunny who kept her stare going, "No funny ideas." Sunny said through gritted teeth.

"I'm no comic." That one went over both their heads. "Anyway…" I let the words linger trying to move things along.

Crystal swung her head scanning the room once again. She was looking for someone who was looking for her. It could be a little nervous paranoia or maybe she was looking for a tall thin guy in a hat. I wanted eyes in the back of my head just then. Eyes or sixth sense, either way it was too late. The cold steel muzzle of a gun pressed against my neck in a downward direction.

A woman's voice trying to sound gruff came from the booth behind me, "Pass your gun under the table to Sunny."

I moved only my eyes. "Crystal, what did you get me into?"

"Sorry Roger," Crystal whispered, "they just don't trust you like I do."

Sunrise Palace piped up, "Don't you look at her. Hand me your gun."

I felt her fingertips brush past my knees. The urge to reach out and snatch her fingers and make them bend in a way they were never intended was restrained. That cold steel against my neck would warm up fast if I did. Maybe it was my need to call a bluff or maybe I was being a misogynistic male who just didn't believe the lady behind him with a gun could pull the trigger. Either way I was not going to be held at gun point.

"Here." I said. When I felt Sunny's fingers straighten out to receive the pistol, I grabbed two of them and bent them back. She let out a screech as I twisted. Next, I slipped out of the booth to face down the pistol.

A pair of frightened round eyes looked back at me, and the pistol quickly retracted behind the booth. I played it right; she wasn't going to pull that trigger no matter what. I jerked Sunny out of her seat twisting her fingers some more. The pain put her on the ground uttering a few choice words.

"Hey, you, we got a problem here?"

I turned around to face a bar back that must double as a bouncer. He was neither abnormally large nor threatening. The only thing to worry about was the unwanted attention if I busted the guy's face on the table.

"Nah, just my boy here with an attitude problem." I said looking down at Sunny.

She swore again and got to her feet.

"Boy? Looks like a real sissy."

"Yeah, I gotta toughen up the little bastard." I tried a slight smile.

"Well next time do it at home where people won't call the cops on ya." The bouncer walked off.

I grabbed ahold of Sunny's collar and tossed her back in the booth. I remained standing, so I could see all three of them. "You, get over here." I waved the would-be gunslinger over.

She got up out of the booth. She was a tall girl, about six feet, but looked taller with the ball cap riding high holding in all her hair. She had dull skin with plain brown hair and hazel eyes. The tall girl tucked her long coat as she took a seat where I had been. I slid in next to her.

Sunny started running her tough gal voice, "Yo, what the hell did you do that for, yo? Shit man that hurt, you nearly broke my damn fingers."

"Yeah, I bet your girlfriend would be really disappointed." I wasn't in the mood to fool around after having a gun pressed to my neck, I was more inclined to kick the shit out of all three of them and then let Oliver know who was behind the attempted hit. Three uncertain faces stared up at me. Their plan had gone awry, I had stolen their next move. The disappointed faces forced a tiny feeling of pity inside, then I quickly squashed it.

Sunny looked over to the tall would-be shooter, "Dang Abby, you should a' shot his ass."

Abby said nothing. She folded her hands in her lap and looked down at the table.

"Just what the fuck do you amateurs think you're doing? Who's leading this trio of chaos?" I looked at all three of them like an angry parent looks to their bastard children. This job had turned into a convoluted mess all because I was caught up in an old memory that would never be again. "Crystal what is going on?"

Crystal kept a close watch on the table. She refused to lift her head. "I, I had to Roger."

"Crystal no." said the tall one. Sunny Palace was shaking her head no, as well.

"If you don't tell me now, I'm walking outta here and spreading the word all over town you tried to hire me to kill Oliver Lean." I leaned into the table. I was ready to breathe fire and spit lava. I had been played again by an old flame that needed to be extinguished. Crystal just had that hold over me, the kind that cannot be explained or even explored. Even as I sat fuming at her, I wanted to reach out and touch her hand and caress her face. Then I remembered why I was there.

Crystal couldn't avoid eye contact any longer. "He put my sister in the hospital, nearly killed her."

Sunrise started to bark. I put my hand in her face, muzzling her. "Your sister? I never met any sister." I had known Crystal for years. I searched through all those memories for a face, a kid, a story of a kid sister. Nothing came to mind. Only memories of how things ended, the lies, the cheating, the bad. Just one more reason for me to walk from this case now before I walk in handcuffs later.

"You never met her. I, I never told you about her. Let's face it, you hung around some scry people back then. I'm the older sister, the protector. You know a little about how I grew up Roger, all of mom's *boyfriends*." Crystal grew up fast. She was forced to see things and hear things no child ever should. Her mother wasn't anything more than a smack addicted prostitute who would trade anything to get high. Around that same time, I was experiencing similar adolescence. A father who was never home and a mother who worked hard and partied harder. It set up the illusion we knew more about each other than we did and set up the lie I was her protector.

"She was why I could never leave home. My sister Tara is eight years younger than me. I fought hard to make sure she never had to do the things our mom made me do. DCF kept taking her away, but mom would sober up and get her back, she had something over the judge for sure. I was home the day mom and Tara came back from another hearing." Crystal went on to tell how she got Tara out of the house. It wasn't hard. Her mom left and came back six hours later drunk. When she sobered she got angry. Crystal took the beating. She lifted her shirt and showed everyone the scar under her left breast. "I never told you how I got this Roger."

I shook my head. This case just got deeper. The emotional flood gates were about to burst. The three broads would sob and bond over the tragedy of Crystal's sister Tara, whatever her fate may be. Lean could have killed her, messed her up, got her hooked-on drugs, it didn't matter. I was expected to get pissed and want vengeance for poor Tara too. The truth was I didn't care. Crystal was a mess and sometimes it's just hereditary. The apple doesn't fall far and all that.

"So, what'd he do?" I asked as I signaled the waitress for another round. Crystal went on with her story. When the waitress brought the new round, I had enough.

"Is she dead or what?"

"Man, you better cool it." Sunrise snapped.

I snapped back, "Listen you little firecracker, one more pop outta you and I will drag you out by the hair and smash your face with a brick. Got it?" I waited for her to reply then I looked back at Crystal.

Crystal picked at the paper napkin, "He got her hooked-on drugs and things spiraled out of control. She's in a mental hospital now." Crystal started to cry. Her friends offered handholding and comforting words. I sipped my stout.

"It would have been better if he just killed her. I don't have the money for one of those nice institutions. The place she is in is a dump and the guards, oh those are the ones that need to be beaten." Crystal wiped away the tears as anger replaced sorrow. Her nose was running. She threw back her drink and smiled.

I felt heat rise in my chest and creep out of my collar. There was a look I had in my eyes, letting her know the hook was in and no matter how big and strong I was I became submissive. Something about those guards messing with her was generating the hate I needed to carry on with this job. She had me, dammit.

"Why have you been dating Oliver?" I said usurping common sense to override my caveman instincts.

"To get close to him." Her eyes narrowed. The thrill returned as thoughts of killing him circled in her mind, the first time she tried to kill him. She stood over him with a knife as he snored away. Laughter tickled her throat as she traced the blade along his chest ready to plunge it deep. But she didn't follow through. Now, that same thrill was sneaking back, climbing her leg, passing between her thighs. This time images of me killing him, my large hands around his neck, cutting off his last breath, stoked her fire. The heat forced her legs apart stretching the limits on her skirt, forcing it higher up her thighs. She was looking across the table at the man that would finally kill Oliver Lean, and I would do it good. There was no doubt about that.

"You're not going back to him, understand?" I said then emptied my pint. Her thighs slammed shut and she crossed her legs, clenching them tight. She had picked the right man for the job.

"Whatever you say Roger." Her fingers dug into the old green vinyl bench seat. She wanted me, needed me to fill her with hope she hadn't felt in a while. Here it was on display. She knew I was strong. I had never been beat in any arena I chose to fight in. My hands were all the proof required, large veined and scared. She watched as I laid my palms down flat, talking, my fingers danced with each word. Crystal bit her lip, using the pain to keep control.

"So, you and this crew of yours needs to cool it with the cloak and dagger shit. Hey!" I jabbed the tabletop. Crystal snapped out of it.

"Yeah, yeah. We'll stay out of your way Roger."

"So how many times have you three tried to kill Oliver on your own?" I looked each of them in the eye. They did their best to lower their eyes and look elsewhere.

Crystal looked back, "How did you know?"

"I don't rank high on your bailout list and with what you idiots pulled tonight makes me think you already tried to off Lean."

"Twice," Abby mumbled. "Once at a bar and then again at his house. That's it, at least on my end." She looked over to Crystal who nodded in agreeance.

"So, he'll be waiting, puts me in a nice spot." I was disgusted. I scratched my two fingers on the table, like signaling a dealer for another card. "The money." Crystal reached in her purse and pulled out a wad. She slid it across the table.

"What the hell Crystal." I shook my head.

"See," Sunny said with spit. "I told you to wrap it and keep it neat."

"Look, Roger, do it quick okay? Ollie is getting real suspicious, of me and everyone."

"Yeah, he is." I smirked then caught my slip. "I'm sure he is." Stupid beer brain. I saw the look in her eyes that I had said too much. Her sister, Tara, would have to be investigated before I pulled the trigger on Lean. I was finally crawling out of the ditch I laid in for the things I did. I never wanted to kill again. If the face value were true, the guy was more than a drug pushing abuser, he was intentionally destroying lives, then I would have to do it. I hated to think that way, that I was only good for one thing, but man I was good. With Aziz on my ass, principles died first.

Chapter 3

All day the air-conditioner struggled to get my office cooled down. I sat at my desk typing key words into Google hoping for the right information to pop up on Lean, Crystal or Aziz. After a few more beers I looked up Whispering Pines, the place that housed Tara. I was smack in the middle of this tale with Tara. There were two halves of a story before me, one from Crystal and the other from Lean. If I was doing the math, I thought it might only add up to one, but those two were liars and I knew it. I needed to know it all.

With a name and an address, I settled in on the burlap couch with a pillow that needed a wash. Then I got a call.

"Hello."

"Tick tock Mr. Grimes." The Arminian accented voice hung up.

My eyes refused to stay closed long enough to dream. There was no comfortable position on the couch tonight. Eventually, yellow sunbeams made their way into the second-floor office, ensuring me no chance of sleep. On the street below, the morning commute had tapered off giving way to retirees and kids fresh out of high school meandering about Beach Street. I rolled off the couch and slipped into a pair of board shorts and pulled a faded t-shirt over my tanned and tattooed hide.

Just as I slipped the shirt over my shoulders a knock sounded at my door. I stood frozen until my eyes found the black pistol on the desk. I slipped it in my waste and went for the door.

Through the frosted glass was the distinct outline of the building manager, short and stout.

"Mr. Grimes, Mr. Grimes you asleep in there? I told you-"

The door swung open.

"No, nope, not sleeping." I sputtered groggily. "I just got to work, Roberta." I said. She looked me up and down. My t-shirt was wrinkled, and I was missing my shoes.

"Better not be staying the night." She twisted her curly topped head around peering in my office. Roberta jingled as she stepped in with her orthopedic shoes with the key to every door in the building clasped to her belt.

"I just keep strange hours." I shrugged.

Roberta nodded, "And you keep a mini fridge and a coffee pot too. Don't think I don't see you leaving the bathroom ringing water out of your ear from a sink bath." She huffed and then jingled on down the hall.

I did treat the office more like a studio apartment. With a couch, a desk and chair and a TV on a bookshelf, there weren't many reasons to leave.

After my usual morning routine of coffee and microwaved breakfast, I decided to add three sets of push-ups and pull –ups. It was something I used to do way back when I was unable to finish the third set. I checked the surf and fishing report. It was too hot to stand around fishing. A tropical depression offshore was kicking up some decent sets. After a flat summer on *Lake Atlantic*, I didn't want to miss the late August swell.

I dusted off my 6'10'' fun shape and grabbed some wax. I was halfway out of the building when I remembered I was still driving that shit box Honda I traded for a handgun and $200. My C-10 had been shot to pieces months ago and I needed something that ran and was legally registered in a hurry.

I stood in the parking lot in my baggies holding my board looking at the neon red Civic. The fifteen-inch gold and chrome rims stuck out with spacers and the window tint was bubbled and peeling. The windows were left down because the AC never worked, and the white sheepskin seat cover was damp with morning dew.

There was no way I was going to get that board into that car. I put my board away and went to see Billy.

After my C10 had been shot up, I limped it to his shop, blowing steam and leaking oil, and left it there in the parking lot, no call or note to explain. The key was in it. I knew Billy would do something with it. We spent a lot of time, sweat and money on that truck. We dropped in a new LS1 motor, lowered the suspension, and slapped a limited slip in the rear end. The body was straight black primer with a grey roof. I had planned to patch the small rust bubbles on the cab corners before the cancer grew.

Sanford set up a chain of events that left Billy and I not talking for a month. I let another month go by before I sent a text. We talked, I stopped by, but it wasn't the same. There were still some things left unsaid, that we just silently agreed would remain unsaid.

It was time to make peace with the old redskin warrior and bury the hatchet. I knew what Billy did to me wasn't his fault, he was coerced into giving me up to Willis. We've had a long relationship both as friends and thieves. I was on my own now and we never talked about what that meant for him. With our last score, I helped him start up the garage he ran, it wasn't my fault he was struggling with it; that he couldn't find a decent tech or balance his books.

Friendships, like any relationship, expand and contract. I was headed in my own direction without him as mentor. Right now, I was headed in the direction of his shop.

I pulled the little rattling POS into the parking lot of Billy's auto shop and parked it in front of the last bay door. I headed out of the sun and into the blackness of the shop.

Inside, Billy's only mechanic Jose, had a 1973 Cadillac up on a lift. He was reaching up into the car's underbelly when he caught sight of me.

"Grimes, what's up?" Jose said with both hands raised above his head as he wrenched down on a bolt.

"Nothing. How you been?" I said putting up a hand to rest on the suspended Cadillac.

A door close behind me and I turned to see Billy coming out of the office, red rag wiping off grease from his fingers. He stood just under six feet but had long thin arms and legs that made him look taller. He was wearing a faded denim button up shirt with his black braid snaking over his left shoulder.

"Well, that's a real nice rice burner you got there." Billy chuckled. There was a slight tension forcing more of a laugh from nervousness than actually thinking he was funny. Nerves were never something Billy had to deal with. He was a racecar driver and we used to steal hundred thousand-dollar cars for kicks on weekends, so now the nervousness was not something I had heard in his voice.

"Yeah, I'm hoping you can help me with this thing. I need a ride I can put a surfboard in." I said as we stepped out from the shade of the garage bay and into the blinding white sun together.

"You know how to get into any car on the road. Just go pick yourself out a new one." Billy's smile faded a little. He reached back and ran a hand over his long black braid. "But I guess you don't do that no more."

We stood in silence. I was prepared to move past the new divide in our relationship and work on getting things closer to the way they used to be, us sitting around drinking cold Miller High Life and laughing about old times and looking forward to new ones. I wanted that bond back and standing humbly at his feet with this ridiculous car was a good start.

"Smitty stopped by my office." I said to which Billy nodded. He had had the same visitor.

"Yeah," Billy crossed his arms. "I told him we don't need you to pull the job. He also told me who you owe money to."

"I'm working a couple of cases and should be out from under that debt soon."

Billy lit a cigarette and took a long first drag. With smoke coming out of his mouth he said, "How long is soon? We can get this job done in three days. It will cover your debt."

"That much money, huh?" I hadn't stolen anything in years, I was rusty, my hands were steady, but it was my mind I worried about. And it wasn't just me I worried about. We were all getting older.

"Do you really want to go back to work for Smitty?" I said knowing all the work Billy put into starting this shop.

The cigarette dangled between his lips so loosely it could have been held by a string. "This job aint so much about me and what I need. All I'd be doing is driving and covering your ass like usual."

Getting the band back together had a welcoming feel. My life so far as an upstanding citizen was anything but. Being a PI was a new direction I needed to stick to no matter how unfamiliar. I shook the temptation out of my head and focused on my short-term need, "I need wheels. I've got this car and $1,500.00 towards something more my style."

"Alright c'mon back here with me." Billy turned and I followed him through the bay, past the lift and Jose`, then out to the back where a six-foot-high chain-link fence lined with razor wire bordered a gravel lot with sporadic leafy green weeds. There were several antique and classic cars in various states of disrepair. There was a 1987 Buick Grand National, a couple of 1971 Ford Mustangs (both Cobra Jets), a Nash Metropolitan, a lifted F-150 on 38's and a few more cars from Detroit.

We walked towards one GM I recognized. My 1982 C10 pickup was sitting in the sun, baking away while the salt air oxidized the exposed metal from the bullets that punched through the steel and settled in my radiator and oil pan.

It looked lame, like a lion run through by a rhino, laying on the Serengeti, struggling to breathe as blood poured out of every hole. A lot of man hours and beers went in to getting that truck right. Though the body wasn't complete, underneath, where it matters, was perfect.

I went up to the front fender and stuck my pinky finger in a rusty bullet hole. The hood was off, laying in the bed. I peered into the engine bay. The top of the motor was off, leaving the block exposed, green coolant lay in the visible channels.

Billy leaned in next to me, "I pulled the valve cover and found a lot of shavings. Then I found the bullet hole. You drove in minus two cylinders, not to mention the lack of oil and coolant. The motor is toast, burned up brother."

When I didn't speak or move my eyes, Billy kept talking, "There's still some value here, things we can save and fix. I started in on it right away, after you dropped her off. Then well, I just wasn't sure it was what you wanted. But I got a line on a new motor. A guy up in Jacksonville has one he's willing to trade for some of those Mustang parts. I was hoping to get it all swapped before you came back."

"That's alright Billy. I didn't leave it here for you to fix her up. I'm actually not sure why I dropped it off." I said looking at him, with my hand over my brow blocking out the penetrating sun. I moved to the cab door and swung it open. Inside the bench seat was stained a deep rust from where I had bled. I had been shot three times. The body armor took two and my body took one. The wound still fresh, puffed and pink. I am lucky to be walking considering where I was hit.

"I can hook you up with some wheels while we figure this thing out." He said slapping the fender. "But before we go knuckles deep on her, don't forget about your true love." Billy pointed to the only carport in the lot. Partially out of the sun, a rectangular shape was covered by a threadbare and faded blue car cover. We walked over the crunching gravel making our way closer. My heart picked up beats as we neared. I remembered what it was and ashamed of myself for forgetting.

Billy reached out and pulled off the cover. Under it was my 1978 International Scout II. She leaned to the right due to a flat tire and had a rough light-green glaze of pollen over the once sparkling copper metallic red paint. The black soft-top was ripped in the rear corner and all three of the plastic windows were permanently fogged. I pushed in the chrome square button on the door handle and yanked back. The door squealed open, and a rush of hot vinyl air filled my nose. Everything inside had a film on it but otherwise just how I left her.

Billy grinned at me, "I kind 'a figured you wouldn't want to build that C10 again when we could get to work on this."

Billy sucked on his cigarette. As he spoke the smoke followed every word. "I wasn't sure what kind of build you wanted but I was under the hood the other day, changed the oil and coolant and put in a fresh battery. She cranks." He flicked his ash and folded his arms. "Still has that lifter tap and a miss. I think it could be she jumped time."

That lifter tap was the reason I parked the Scout. Stealing was paying off, with all the work Smitty was throwing at us it felt like it would never end. Billy convinced me tearing into the motor and touching up the rusty spots was the perfect project needed during the down time, to let things cool, and break from the stress in between jobs. I agreed and parked the Scout where it sits now. A few months later I was pinched and spent nine more months in jail. Then all the private eyeing got in the way, and I never came back to her. It was time.

"Will my fifteen hundred get us started?" I asked knowing it would just scratch the surface.

"How much do you want to do yourself?" Billy smiled. He finished off the cigarette and flicked the butt. A grease-stained hand slapped my shoulder, turning us around, he said, "I can part out what's left of the C-10 this week, then see what we got to work with. I think I got a ride for you in the shop."

We walked back into the dark cave of the garage bay. As my eyes adjusted to the dim light, I saw, I hoped, what he was going to lend me.

"The key's in it."

I pulled the door open on the 1966 Oldsmobile Cutlass. The paint was a dull original GM Silver Mist with a black convertible top. Sitting in the black bucket seat, I pumped the accelerator one time and turned the key. The car fired right up. The dual exhaust rumbled through the shop. Jose strolled over with a big grin on his greasy face. He wiped his hands on his blue work pants and went around to the hood and popped it open.

I got out and joined him under the hood, looking down at my reflection in all that chrome. The original Rocket V-8 was replaced with a Chevy 350 Performance Ram jet. The mechanic went on to say it puts out about 350 horsepower and is fuel injected so I wouldn't need to pump the accelerator to start it. How was I supposed to know?

Billy leaned in and flipped the switch to take the top down. "You should be able to fit your board in now."

I got behind the wheel and settled into the black rolled and pleated bucket seat. I said gesturing to the Honda, "The title is in the glove box, sell it or scrap it or do whatever you want with it." Then I said, "When do I need to bring this one back?"

"November."

"Turkey Rod Run." I said knowing he planned to sell it then. Thanksgiving weekend in Daytona Beach is host to one of the biggest classic car meets in the country.

"Yep, so try not to get shot in it." Billy slapped the top of the door as a sendoff.

"When I wrap up this case I've got, I'll have more to throw down on the Scout." I rolled out into the parking lot and then lit the tires as I slung the long Olds coupe out onto US 1.

A stop over at the office and I left with the surfboard stuck out the rear seat. I laid a towel down so any bits of sand wouldn't scratch the interior. I drove up A1A, looking between beach front hotels, out to the blue-green ocean beyond. I swung into a couple different different beach approaches. I passed up Daytona all together and made my way into Ormond Beach eventually stopping at a little park near a Lifeguard tower.

After rubbing on some fresh wax, I made my way through tiny, crushed shells speckling the white and pink sand. The water was a perfect aqua blue and clear to about two feet. A school of small pompano darted past my ankles as I waded out to the waist high surf.

The sets rolled in steady and smooth. With the fun shape board, it was nice to just get up and ride the wave, nothing fancy. I stayed through a few sets. Sitting with my legs startling the board waiting on the next wave to pick up I spotted a white Toyota Sequoia, lifted on twenty-two-inch rims and noisy mud terrains roll up to the parking lot. Before the occupants even got out, I started paddling in.

The soft sand fought me with every step as I trekked up to the parking lot. I watched the three olive skinned men circle the silver Oldsmobile. The largest of the three touched the fender and nodded with approval. The middle-sized man shrugged. The smallest man, who got out of the driver's seat didn't move.

I climbed the wooden stairs to the concrete sea wall and onto a frying pan of black asphalt. I leaned the surfboard against the wooden railing above the sea wall.

"Nice ride Grimes." Aziz said. The big man, Boghos, nodded.

"Piss pants." Boghos said with a snicker. I smiled and held the laughter, which would cause a fight. He was staring me down, looking menacing, as he tried to causally walk behind me, but I wouldn't allow that. I began to long for the time when I could dismantle the hairy man's bearded face.

"I think it would repay your debt nicely."

"By double, but it's not my car."

"That's not my problem. My problem is the eighteen grand you owe me. Try to understand it my way, Grimes. If you don't repay me exactly what you owe, why should anyone else repay me? See where this is going?" Aziz ran his finger along the hood of the car and flicked at the hood ornament.

"I have nothing Aziz, so there is nothing you can take from me." My eyes narrowed; I slowed my breathing to compensate my rapid heart rate.

Boghos took a large step and covered the distance needed to grab a hold of my board. I was too far away to get between him and the board. He looked to me and grinned.

"Valuables are not always measured in cash, Mr. Grimes. Take that surfboard for instance, or perhaps this classic American muscle." Aziz turned his back to me without a care or second look.

Boghos pulled his fist back and let it fly, punching a hole in my surfboard. He laughed and dropped the board, then his face went straight. His shoulders bowed as he inflated three times his size. Saliva mixed into his thick black beard hair leaving glistening streaks in the bright yellow day light.

The anger was hard to suppress but now was not the time to give in to the beast inside.

Aziz continued to run a finger along the fender as he walked around the classic muscle car. He leaned and pressed two hands on the hood. All I could think about were the rings on his fingers and the scratches they would leave.

"I have done my research on you Grimes. What I didn't know when I leant you the money, I know now. You want to repay me? I have a job for you."

I said nothing.

Aziz sneered then said with a more relaxed face, "I need you to steal something for me."

"I'm no longer a thief."

"You will always be a thief, Grimes. It's who you are. This however is not that *kind* of a job. It is more in line with your new career."

"I'm busy."

"Save yourself the heart ache and do this job and your debt will be cleared." Aziz came off the hood and fiddled with his rings. He looked me in the eyes then down at the hood. *Not the original paint*, I silently screamed. I couldn't face Billy with a scratch down the hood.

I moved. Boghos was quick to come at me. I returned his fury with a swinging kick just above his left knee. He braced and my foot glanced off. Boghos threw a wild bear paw at my head. I blocked and slid into it, letting the meaty hand glance off.

Tucked and twisted, I released like a spring, slinging my left up and out into his stomach just below his ribcage. I could hear the air escape as he blew spit, absorbing the blow.

Boghos staggered back. He squared his feet and roared. I was ready, I wanted him to get angry, the angrier the better. He was going to know what my fist tasted like as I rammed it down his throat.

Aziz lifted an open palm. Boghos immediately began to calm his breathing, though he kept the fire in his eyes stoked.

"Oliver Lean has something I want. Steal it and we are even."

Before I could comprehend what, he was asking, a squad car called out.

Boowup! Boowup! A shiny white Ford sedan with red and blue flashing lights from behind blacked out tinted windows rolled up.

"Boghos!" Aziz shouted.

Boghos used a few remaining seconds to stare into my eyes, daring me to attack. I remained still, only my chest rising and falling moved. Then Aziz called again. This time Boghos lowered his arms.

I turned to Aziz who was looking around at the few beachgoers watching our brief exchange with wide eyed fright.

The car door opened, and all five feet seven inches of Deputy Camp stepped out. With a smile forcing more wrinkles in her bulldog face, I almost didn't recognize her. Her deputy uniform was a pressed forest green. On each sleeve was something new, a yellow chevron.

"Don't stop on account of me. I'm sure one of you deserves it." Deputy Camp said, looking at us through reflective sunglass lenses.

Aziz waved his hand then turned and walked back to the ridiculously lifted Toyota. The driver scurried ahead and fired up the truck. Boghos got in still staring at me.

I picked up my surfboard and stuck my fist through the hole. The board was ruined.

"Roger Grimes." Camp called out as she approached.

"Deputy Camp." I said with a half-smile and nod.

"Shark attack?" Camp said trying to make a light sarcastic remark, but it fell flat. I wasn't smiling any longer.

"Any way," Camp continued, "I made corporal thanks to a tip about a human trafficking operation in town. I'm sure you know all about that," she cocked her head to the side and waited for me to fill in the silence. When I didn't, she went on, "It was in all the papers. Not my promotion, I mean the bust. A Daytona Beach officer was caught up in it too. He was running protection, firing him was just a slap on the wrist. Top brass didn't want the department under a microscope. I'd have made sure he went to prison, every last one of them."

Turned out Deputy Camp was talkative, maybe I just have one of those faces, I don't know. Either way she wanted to show her gratitude for something she wasn't entirely sure I did. Camp followed me as I walked back to the Olds and stuffed the busted board into the back seat.

"Well, that bust really shook up this town and all the way to the capital. Some heavy hitters were tied to this thing. Not to mention the wake of bodies left behind. I can't say they didn't deserve what they got a thousand times over." Camp wiped a palm across her forehead and flung sweat away. Her radio crackled, and she reached without looking to turn it down.

"Lieutenant Gibson from FDLE was appointed special investigator by the state's attorney. He's hell bent to catch the guy or guys behind the killings. Whoever shot up that pool hall did one hell of a job." Camp said. She was sniffing around. Though I handed her a promotion, she was still a cop and I was still a criminal. That would never change. My blood was on the scene and if the crime scene crew were worth anything, they would find it. There would be no match, but if I were to bleed anywhere again it would be a needle in my arm and the forever sleep.

"Yep," was all I had to say. I stood there, still dripping with saltwater, letting the sun dry me off. As the ocean water evaporated off it left salt clinging tightly to my skin and put a crunch in my hair.

"It was probably some rival traffickers, no way it was one man." Camp looked at the pink puffy scar on my side then out at the soft waves rolling in. She was waiting for me to follow social protocols and say something, anything. I didn't. She looked back at me and nodded, knowing I wasn't speaking. Once back in her squad car, the flashing lights went off and she rolled out.

I stayed in the parking lot and watched her go. The waves crashed behind me as seagulls screamed at each other, passing along a message, a warning to be on the lookout. A special investigation was going on because of the can I opened. One more thing I had to worry about.

Chapter 4

Sand shook from my flipflops onto the pristine polished marble hallway as I walked to my office. Crystal said Tara was being kept at Whispering Pines, so I decided to change into something more professional before I checked it out. I slipped into some khaki Dickies and a short sleeve button down. Looking like a working stiff would get me in more doors than looking like the beach bum I was. Today though, my wallet was stuffed with cash, a half payment to kill Oliver Lean. The easy way out was right there. All together it was not enough to pay Aziz back fully though. Maybe I could use the cash to just run, finally get out of the vortex that traps people to this town. You never leave Daytona Beach, people are caught on a boomerang here, just circling. They leave and come back. There're other beaches to live on, like in South America, so maybe one day I'll go.

Whispering Pines was a half hour drive from my office. Tucked in the corner of a strip mall, it had forty rooms and about one hundred residents. The math was not hard to do. The place was an assisted living facility not a nut house like Crystal had described. The drugs must have really done a number on Tara's brain for her to wind up here. I pulled my sunglasses off and walked through the heavily tinted glass door. Inside the smell of antiseptic overwhelmed me. The reception area was small and manned by a thin, black-haired Latina in a set of pink scrubs and name tag that read Rosa.

"Are you here to see a resident or a doctor?" Rosa said without looking up from her phone. She pointed at the clipboard then went back to texting on her phone. Her features were sharp, a pointed nose slightly turned up, her eyes deep brown, were perfect almonds. With high cheek bones and wide jawline, she could pass for a Soap star on Telemundo.

I waited without writing anything. After a few seconds Rosa realized I was staring at her. She took the clip board and looked up at me. "You don't look like a pharma rep, so who is the resident?"

"I'm here to see Tara Johnson." I smiled.

"Name?" Rosa asked looking to her computer screen.

"My name? George Nolan." I didn't know where I grabbed the name from.

"I don't see you on the list for admittance. Sorry."

"Oh, are you sure? Is there a phone I can use to talk to her?"

Rosa squinted and leaned into the monitor. She whispered under her breath reading the notes on Tara and then finally looked up.

"That's not possible." Her face hardened. There was a tight lid on Tara.

"Why is that?"

"I'm not really sure but her visitor list is flagged, so that means no one is to see her but a select few."

"Oh, that's too bad," I frowned. "I drove all the way down here to see her and now I can't go in. I'm from New York. I'm in advertising up there." I smiled and leaned in on the counter closing the distance between us.

"Yeah? Like that Mad Men show?" Rosa put her elbows up on the desk and clasped her fingers together. She had finally looked me in the eyes.

"Something like that only without all the mid-day cocktails."

"Do anything I might have seen?" Rosa was leaning forward now too.

"Let me think. I mostly do local stuff up there but nationally I worked on a commercial for a jewelry story." I made it a point to break the eye contact only to look at the door to inside the facility.

"Oooh diamonds, huh? So, what do you do exactly?"

"Casting. I had to pick the right hands for the spot." I reached out and touched her light brown hands. Taking one of her hands into both of mine, I flipped it back and forth and ran two fingers over her palm. She took a deep breath and held it until I let go.

"I think I could work with this." I said smiling.

Rosa leaned back in her chair, puckering her lips as if to whistle, she let out all her breath. Using a manila envelope, she fanned her face. "You just crazy."

"Hey, I see something I like and get it. It's my job." I looked at the door once more. "I work so much up in New York I just haven't been down in a long time. Now I've finally come all this way." I put my face in my hands and gave Rosa the sad eyes. It was over the top, but she somehow found it endearing. I found her stupid for it. None the less, she pressed a button and the door unlocked.

"Room 305 and take this visitor's badge." Rosa was all giggles as I took the badge and clipped it on.

The halls were filled with the clacking of walkers being shoved around. The air was stale and the lights fluorescent and bright. All the windows were tinted making it impossible to see the weather or the time of day. The sounds of blaring televisions bounced off the black and white checkered linoleum floors and bare white block walls picked the sound up again and into my ears. Nurse's aides walked around in scrubs. Some pushed carts with pills or DVD selections and books. Others were glued to their phones as they dodged the elderly wanderers like a skier through the slalom.

As I searched for the room, three aides rushed by followed by a fourth man in a blue dress shirt with a stethoscope around his neck. A loud beeping was coming from the room they all rushed to. Next a woman in a white lab coat dragged a crash cart. I stood just outside the room as the man with the stethoscope shouted orders. The beeping went to a constant ring. I waited there until I saw the EMT's jogging down the hall pushing a stretcher along. It was over for the girl in 305.

I watched them wheel out the body of Tara Johnson, her face covered with a respirator. Her hair matted with vomit. I tried to think back to a fond memory of Tara as a child when I would go to pick up Crystal for our dates, but I didn't have any. She hadn't existed in my world until last night.

She had just been a figment of my imagination. A girl Crystal talked about, but I never saw. My mind created an image, similar features to Crystal but with braces and a few zits. Tara was permanently frozen in my mind as a teenager. She had never grown up, never met Oliver Lean. For all I knew she went off to have a happy life. Now here she was, being wheeled out on a stretcher.

I wouldn't get any information out of Tara today. I looked around for an exit other than the front door. There were no side exits to this place, a security feature to keep the old from getting out. I would have to walk past Rosa on the way out. Just as I neared the exit a man in a cheap tweed sport coat stepped out from a room. The man was heavy set with rosy cheeks. His brown hair was wispy on top due to thinning and he had a bushy mustache. The man did a quick one eighty and turned shoving a pistol deep into my ribs. The guy had the drop; there was no point in fighting him off. "This way."

The two of us turned left, in step, before the exit door. We walked past a few open doors then went into an office with nothing more than two desks and a calendar on the wall. "Take a seat." I did what I was told.

"Alright," the man heaved his pants up then slipped the pistol into the holster under the coat. "I'm Sargent Jennings, let's see some ID."

"You want to tell me what the hell this is about?" With his gun holstered I had more leeway. I knew I could get to the man's wrist and keep that pistol covered. I decided against it and put my wallet on the table. The private investigator's card was front and center.

The man looked down at it and then back up, "Shit. Who hired you?"

"My phone call."

Sargent Jennings took a seat at one of the desks. "Honestly, I don't give a shit if you talk with me or not. This is a federal case.

A US Marshall is gonna be coming through that door any minute to ask you and they *will* find out."

Federals? I shifted in my seat. "So, if I tell you can I walk?"

"Nope." Jennings picked at his fingernail with the other nail making a clicking sound. After he split the nail and bit it, he said, "How much do you know?"

"Oliver Lean."

Jennings scoffed. "That little shit stain? I hope he's not your client." Jennings went back to clicking his nails together. "The guy fucked up. But hey it's out of my jurisdiction. Is Lean your client?"

"He's the reason I am here."

"I tell ya what," Jennings leaned in on the desk looking through squinted eyes, his glare was conjuring an idea. "I'll let you outta here now, before the Marshals get here if you promise to tell me what he hired you for."

"I never said he hired me."

Jennings leaned back in his seat. He pushed his lower lip up into the upper and frowned. "Roger Grimes." Then he flipped my wallet back at me. "Get lost scab." His head pop towards the door. I got up and left.

At the front desk Rosa was busy with EMTs so I just dipped my head and walked out into the sun.

It was hot. Opening the door to the Olds and blurry heat waves poured out of the black vinyl seats. I took off the button-down and slipped into the oven. I fired up the V-8 and pulled away. The AC was blowing hard but not cold. It needed to be charged but I didn't want to go back to Billy's shop for another car.

I hoped to get this case over and done with, get my Scout back on the road and enjoy what little money I had left over. Half the payment was resting in an envelope in the top desk drawer, money I accepted to kill Oliver Lean and money to help keep Oliver Lean alive. Now it seemed to be money I would have to return. Tara Johnson was probably dead, and Oliver had something to do with it and the US Marshals were already involved. There is no way to kill a man when the Marshals have him under surveillance. It explains Lean's paranoia. Not only was Crystal trying to kill him, but the marshals were following him all over.

The cell phone on the passenger seat lit up. The number wasn't programmed in the phone, so I let it go to voice mail. The phone rang again and again it went to voice mail. After the third time I decided to call back and hang up. I didn't want to talk, and this person was pissing me off trying to make me talk. The number called back. I answered and hung up. Then the voicemail notification chimed. I listened to the message. "Answer your phone ass, Crystal is missing. Call me back."

I wasn't positive but thought it was Sunny on the voicemail. I watched the phone light up as I thought about Crystal missing. It had only been twelve hours since we met face to face, that can hardly be called a missing person. The nursing home probably called her about Tara, and she rushed out. Cell service is always bad in a hospital. I drove on. Questions were piling up. Was Tara's death a murder? Who else wanted Lean dead? The AC was blowing but not cooling. The sun was just too overbearing to put the top down. I felt the sweat roll down my sides and collect at the waist band.

The heat was sucking the breath from my lungs. A check of the digital gauges showed me the engine temp was climbing dangerously high. Something was wrong with Billy's latest build. Gremlins always find a home in a new build. Fixing the overheating issue, myself was an option that grew more and more likely. Working with my hands would allow my brain the freedom to wander and the lesser used sections would be free to piece things together.

Inside the auto parts store it was much cooler. The soda fizzed as I sucked it back. I bought a thermostat on a whim and some coolant. The next stop would be to Billy's house. There I could find shade in his garage to work. I could also be alone with my thoughts. It would all get done faster that way.

The house was an old Florida home built in the Mediterranean Revival style most people call Spanish. It was white with a square flat roof and a red garage door that was raised up. Billy was standing off to the side of the driveway flushing a four-core aluminum radiator when I pulled up. His cigarette was nearly all ash and when he waved, it finally broke and landed on his navy-blue shirt.

Billy was a wiry guy who, through a lifetime of turning wrenches in the Florida sun, had a permanent greasy stained look about his skin. He was older than me by a good ten years. The Cherokee blood ran deep in him, especially when he had his black hair pulled back in a tight braid, which was almost always. His dog's name was Dog. Billy loved that dog; they shared a bed and even a plate sometimes. When Dog died, he just shrugged and said, 'It was his time.' And a few weeks later he brought home another Dog. That's the way Billy was, salt of the earth, people often said about him.

"Well, what's up Roger?" Billy went back to the side of the house and shut the water off.

When he came back, I said, "I didn't think you would be home." I got out and popped the hood. "She's been running hot, so I thought I would stop by here and take a look."

Billy nodded, he said nothing leaning over the hot motor, all smiles like he was looking down on a baby's crib. He wafted in the gasoline vapors and hot oil as he looked over the motor he built and installed with pride. The coolant bubbles fizzed as the engine cooled.

I went into the garage and came back with a cold beer. I sat on a stool near the work bench and sipped the beer.

"Don't you ever keep anything but beer in your fridge?"

Billy pointed to the hose, then said, "Gonna let her cool a minute." He went back to his radiator, tapping it to drain any extra water and then joined me in the shade of the garage. "Hot on a case, huh?" Billy stuck a cigarette in his mouth.

I shrugged. "I have two clients actually."

"No leads?"

"You remember Crystal?"

"The one who screwed you up while screwing others, yeah. Hope she aint back in your life."

"She's, my client."

"And   the   other   one?"
"Her boyfriend Oliver Lean."

Billy didn't say anything. He picked up the radiator and went back in the garage to the work bench.

The beer was cold on my lips, the shade a break from the sun on my skin. I stood in the garage reading through the texts Sunny had blown up my phone with. She was worried about Crystal and posed theories of where she was and how Lean killed her. All of it outlandish, the girl had a vivid imagination. Once I was done here, I figured I would get in touch with Lean and find out if he was with Crystal. For all I knew one or both of my clients could be dead, and so could I if I can't pay Aziz.

Billy was standing at the work bench fitting hose clamps over the two new radiator hoses he would be installing. He put the screwdriver down and said, "Ollie Lean, I kicked the shit outta that guy a few years back for messing with my sister Jeanie." He chuckled and went back to what he was doing.

I nodded without comment. They were half siblings twenty years apart on his Cherokee side. So, it made for a weird older brother/father relationship. Billy would be there to protect her or give her advice, but he would also buy beer for her. Jeanie left the tribe in South Carolina at seventeen and ran down to Daytona Beach. Like so many others, she got a job at a bar, got sun burnt and made bad choices when it came to men. She was one of the lucky few to escape the vortex because she had her strong-willed brother to make damn well sure she left.

When Billy kept fussing with the radiator, I went to work inspecting the motor in the Olds. I was not under the hood long when Billy came over and brushed past me. He pointed out that the wire on one of the two electric fans was frayed and probably not working. He told me to flip the key to 'on'.

Billy called it right as only one fan was turning. I got out to join him leaning against the front fender. Billy accused me of using him to do the work and we laughed. It felt good to share a laugh without the nervous tension that had us by the throat every time we saw each other.

"There's some electrical tape in the top right shelf." Billy said pointing with the cigarette at the toolbox. "Should ought to hold it until I can replace the whole wire."

I came out of the garage with the black tape and asked, "What'd he do to your sister?"

Billy was under the hood again. His face emerged twisted in thought about my question and said, "Tried to take nude pics of her or some shit. He got nasty, so I got nastier." I could tell Billy wasn't telling me the whole story, but the man had a right to protect his sister's integrity by keeping quiet.

"Where was I when all this ass kicking took place?" I said wondering why he didn't ask me to help.

"It was a couple of years ago."

I nodded. I knew where I was, sitting in county jail on a trumped-up charge. The judge had seen me walk too many times on technicalities and had his chance to make sure I had a record. The vortex nearly swallowed me in there, but when I got out, I became a private investigator.

The taped wire worked, and the fan came on to cool the motor. I gave Billy my thanks and pulled away. I didn't mention Aziz's offer to wipe the debt if I stole for him or anything about the case. Trust was not the issue with Billy, in fact, there were no issues. I didn't associate with people who had issues. Talking was not my strong suit. Everything was played close to the vest even if it meant the long way around. Billy probably could have filled in some details on Lean or what Crystal had been up to lately, but none of it would be information I wouldn't find out soon enough.

Back at the office I milled around without any direction. There were things to do, procedures to follow, things they taught me in my courses that I should be doing. My brain built a wall and blocked any methodical thoughts from proceeding. Deep in the hollows of my skull, back past the nuts and bolts and the gears that kept me running, my brain was working the case. There was no cognitive reason to back that up other than my current lack of focus. My mind wandered, I thought about getting a dog and played that out until I was convinced it was a bad idea. Then thought about a girlfriend and that ended with me having too much to do, too much attention to give. Then I remembered I have an apartment, with a TV.

The third-floor apartment was a typical old Florida apartment with white tile floors throughout. It had a partial view of the Halifax River. The two-story house across the street blocked most of the river from view, a reminder I was poor, and they weren't. The place was sparse, a couch, coffee table and TV. Walking in, the apartment was an orange glow as the setting sun bounced off the brackish water. I closed the blinds and lay on the couch. Flipping through the string of texts from Sunny I grew tired and fell asleep.

I woke a short time later to my roommate, Brock, walking in. The guy was nice but loud and used the word *Bro* too much. His hair was light brown and long but not long enough for a ponytail, so it was always in his face. I greeted him as he came in, kicked off his flip-flops and grabbed the remote.

He started talking as he channel-surfed. His words weren't making an impression in my mind, just a slight buzzing sound that was growing more and more irritating. Shut up in my own lonely world left me unable to come down from my isolated mountain top and talk to the villagers. I wanted back up the mountain. That's the problem, I seek solitude, then the longer I enjoy it the harder it was to adjust back into normalcy.

The texting with Sunny started up again coming in fast and furious. The alert sound was worse than my roommate's voice.

"Bro you're blowing up." Brock said with a smile. I just looked at the guy. I grabbed my keys and phone, then headed for the door.

I sat in the Olds and read the texts. Sunny was demanding half the money back because it had been hers to help Crystal. Now I had to respond.

I sat in the Olds and sent her a text.

Me: *I've tried to contact Crystal too*

Sunny: *Finally! ASSHOLE now I threaten to take money back you respond.*

Me: *Sure. I'll let you know when she gets back to me*

Sunny: *DICK*

Me: *Thanks*

Sunny: *That's not a compliment*

Me: *Sure. By the way Tara is dead.*

The next text didn't come through for a minute.

Sunny: *WHAT?!? Does Crystal know?*

Me: *Probably.*

I didn't receive any more texts from Sunny.

The office was dark when I went in, and I left it that way. The chair was facing the window and I stared out at the street and the river beyond that. The bridge was lit and so were the cars passing over it. This case had folded in on itself. Why she came to me with that ridiculous request. Could Sanford have put the word out I killed people for a living now? Was he somehow involved? I didn't like the possibility of that being a yes to either question. Killing Lean would get fast money from Crystal, but it wouldn't be enough. Getting them both to pay was the real mystery I needed to solve.

A gun in my hand would kill him fast. A knife would be quiet. Brass knuckles would make it painful. A chill broke across my body as sweat soaked into my shirt. My psyche wouldn't allow me to kill a man for nothing more than the word of a coked-out ex-girlfriend. Without finding the other killer or killers would mean leaving a loose end and that's how I wake-up to a barrel pointed in my face. Solving that question would generate a paycheck from Lean and then killing him would get one from Crystal. Even better would be if I could wait for the other killer to do the job and then tip it to the cops and get that bastard locked up and still collect from Crystal, assuming she wasn't behind the other hitter. It felt good having options.

Then there was whatever Aziz wanted me to find. It would cover my debt so why fight it? I was still new at being a PI but I had some cases solved. It's what I wanted to do, what I got a license from the state to do.

The easiest thing to do would be to call Lean and tell him to meet me at the office in an hour to go over what I found. So, I did. If Crystal really wanted the money back for not killing Lean, I figured I would oblige. Lean's money was good, and I didn't owe Crystal anything for the memories she conjured.

An hour later, Crystal still hadn't responded to the text. Cell signal in hospitals can be tough to find. With the active police investigation, she would have a lot of extra paperwork on top of what there normally was. It made perfect sense that Crystal hadn't responded.

Someone knocked on the door.

In a few strides I was at the door. I twisted the knob and let it swing open and Lean walked through. He took a seat on the couch. I sat down in my desk chair incredulous, staring at the man I was hired to kill.

"What'cha got for me Roger?" Lean was dressed in a white fishing shirt with many pockets. He had khaki shorts and flip flops on.

"First, any more attempts on your life?"

Lean smiled, "Not one."

I slid open the top desk drawer and laid my hand on top of the nine. "Tell me about Tara Johnson."

The smile was gone from Lean's face. His eyes shifted landing everywhere except on mine. After a strong exhale he said, "She's a mess. You know who she is already if you're asking. I'll tell you what I know. She was a girl who used to hang around with the wrong crowd; I used to hang around with the wrong crowd too. We met at Baldy's, she was a bartender there. You know the place?"

I nodded.

"Then you know what kind of girl she is. We hooked up and next thing I know she's mixed up with some number's runner. Gambling and debt collection kind 'a stuff. Not sure why she was hanging around that crowd. I was never in the trade myself, I mean, I was, well fuckin who cares who I was, nobody does anymore." He finally made eye contact with me. Then he looked at the hand in the drawer and swallowed.

I slid my hand out, in it was a pint of booze. I unscrewed the cap and put it on the table. "Get a glass."

Lean nodded and retrieved a glass from the counter against the opposite wall. I poured a large amount and he drained it in two gulps. He wiped his mouth and started talking again. "Thanks. So, I don't see Tara around much and I go down to Baldy's and start asking around. This guy Eddy. Young guy, kind 'a heavy but solid. So, he comes to me and says Tara is going on a trip and won't be back maybe ever."

"Who the hell is this guy to tell you what to do?" I poured myself a drink.

"Right," Lean said excitedly, "he said he was doing it because he liked me. He works at Baldy's, does odd jobs; fixes things and bounces, stuff like that. He's the owner's lackey."

I sipped the whiskey. "And you have no idea what she was doing other than working for your numbers guy?"

"I heard rumors what she was doing and where she was, but I tried to push her out of my mind." Lean sat back in his seat.

"Then what?"

"Well," Lean shifted in the cushion, "I kept asking and I get a call from my boss to stay out of it."

"Your employer, Armenian?"

Lean nodded. Armenian meant only one man, Aziz Azad and he was involved in my life more than I wanted. I stopped mingling with outlaws, years ago. Now this new heavy hitter was in town, getting his hands into everything and currently had a heavy hand on me. All that killing to rid the city of bigtime criminals had left a vacuum and Aziz thought he could fill it.

It made Lean feel tough, being associated with a man like Aziz. A man with a growing reputation for violent ends. As much as Lean liked to walk around like he was a tough guy was all due to protection from Aziz. It seems that protection was pulled which is why he kept a lower profile lately.

I continued, "Any reason he would want you dead?"

Lean bit his lip and creased his brow. "No. I don't work for him anymore. He's more of a partner now. Even when I did work for him, I just moved accounts around online, cleaned money. I made everything legit, on the surface. I never screwed up or stole." He kept thinking, his brain was a fried egg, sizzling and popping, as he searched deep. "Besides Tara."

There she was again, at the center of this whole plot to kill a man. She was connected; Crystal either didn't know or decided not to tell me how deep Tara was in all this. Loners like me don't join clubs or organizations and the mob, syndicate or cartel was nothing more than that. Back in my criminal days of robbery and theft, I was often approached by organized gangs like 3rd Street, who ran the biggest car theft ring in the central Florida, to pull a heist for them. I would always decline. Working alone or with one or two others was enough. Once you agree to do a job for Aziz, he owns you, hell, I was proof of that. 3rd Street wasn't so bad. They knew me well enough to leave me alone. It takes guts to turn your back on Aziz. Lean didn't have it but maybe Tara did.

"There's more than one person that wants you dead." I poured another round into Lean's glass.

"Who?" Lean sucked back the golden painkiller. He was on the edge of his seat.

I shrugged. "I haven't got that far."

"Dammit." Lean ran his fingers through his hair pulling it apart from the gel that held it together. There was one other line of work that he was not telling me.

I sat in patient silence as Lean grew the balls to cop to whatever it was, he left out. I knew it had to be the juice, something to quench my thirsty curiosity. Crystal's story was lacking something that revenge for a junky sister just didn't have. Cops were involved and if they hadn't moved then Lean wasn't what they really wanted. Someone somewhere was after Lean to kill him, present company excluded.

"Out with it Lean." I wished I still smoked. It would be a nice three-minute distraction while Lean coughed it up.

"Okay, is there some kind 'a client privilege?"

"No. Tell me or get out."

"Shit." Lean looked side to side to make sure we were still alone in my small office. "Glory Catz 24 dot com." Lean looked down at the floor. I continued to stare. Obviously, it was a website and by the name I guessed it had something to do with sex.

"Google it." Lean said, lifting his head. "Catz, with a *z*."

"Tell me what it is."

"It's mostly a webcam site. Average people, men, women and couples, groups, anyone with a webcam basically has their own site and they do porn. Customers love it because they can interact. Ask the chicks to do stuff they wanna see. People pay big money for participation like that." Lean reached out for the bottle. I slid it just out of his grasp. I pointed to the chair and Lean sat back down.

I pulled a tablet out of my desk drawer, clipped it into the keyboard and searched. Clicking out of the popups I navigated the site, scrolling through bios of bare breasted chicks and dudes with hard cocks. A trend started to stand out, all these people looked average. Sagging skin, stretch marks, people over thirty, all just average people. Any one of them could be your neighbor, bag your groceries or flip your burgers.

Besides moving money for a criminal enterprise, Lean operated an online business that really paid the bills and took little effort. Oliver Lean peddled porn. Glory Catz played short videos to tease horny bastards until they throw down a credit card and finish watching the video. Webcams for those of you who want it simple. Girls, couples and dudes set up webcams and logged in to paying customers who then instant messaged them, and they chatted as the girl or couple got it on. Socially, he never revealed the true nature of his cash flow, instead tried to say it was *family* money, like *connected family*, from up north. There was a sense of power behind the myth that the title of porn king could never bring.

"This lady looks like my third-grade teacher." I said noting the woman's mid-40's age and short hair. She sat spread eagle on the edge of a Lazy Boy. Behind her was a typical suburban home. A China cabinet with knickknacks and a tacky owl wall clock. They all looked so average. One or two girls stood out as pretty, but the more popular cams were couples or older ladies. The more *Middle America* they looked the more likes and comments they got.

"She could be. These people are from all walks of life." Lean said as he began to nibble on the corner of his thumb nail. He spat out what little piece he got and continued, "People are sick man, they want the average housewife and her, hairy blue-collar husband to bang on the kitchen table. Why, when there are so many hotties willing to take it off? Because they identify with it. Knowing they are real, turns my customers on more than the same old plastic chicks with the Hollywood backdrops out at a pool too big for these schlubs to ever take a dip in."

After thoroughly searching the site for faces and other body parts I may recognize, I asked, "So who is it? I assume you pissed off one of these amateurs. Angry husband or jealous wife?"

"No, I really don't know. That's why I hired you."

"It would be helpful Oliver, if you told me about this sooner. I already wasted two days looking in to shit when this big elephant was in the room." I stood up. The images of body parts slapping together and fluids exchanging flashed on the screen of the tablet. I shut it off and walked around to the other side of the desk. There were thousands of uploads and millions of subscribers. Any one of them could be the other hitter, pissed at something Oliver did or maybe didn't do like take the site down. Tara was the linchpin holding the identity of the would-be assassin.

"How did Tara end up a vegetable?"

Oliver Lean had spent the better part of his twenties trying to become something he didn't have the guts for. A tough mouth with a weak spine didn't amount to anything for Oliver. His mouth got him in the door with Aziz, but they must have quickly realized he was no use and found his pretty girlfriend Tara to be of better use. His stint as a gangster ended with getting his girlfriend addicted to the drugs and shipped off for some reason. That reason cost him his job and maybe his life.

"When she came back from wherever it was, she went, she was into drugs. I mean, everyone in this town is on one drug or another but she had it bad. Then one night while messed up she said she wanted to do a cam show for me."

"Tara wanted to do porn? Her idea, not yours?" After what Billy told me about his sister's run in with Lean, I doubted Lean's story.

"I wouldn't call it porn, per say. It was all her idea. She *demanded* to. It was her show all the way, all I did was set up the camera. I posted it and it took off. She eventually sobered up and swore she would never do that again and asked me to take it down, but it kept getting hits. She did this thing with a…" Oliver looked up at my blank stare, the kind that made Lean feel like he was already a corpse. "Anyway, the next time I got her high I got the webcam out. It took a third time and all the profits to get her on board. But her ass brought all the boys to the yard." He was smiling by the end.

"So, she overdosed?"

"Yeah, but before that, Eddy showed up again and said Aziz wanted me to take her down, something about being too recognizable. She was still working for him. I don't really know for what. It came down to her having to keep a low profile. If one of Aziz's men spotted her so could the cops." Lean shrugged then his eyes drifted back to the bottle. His mind wondered off as his gaze intensified. I slid it over towards him. Lean jumped up to catch it before it fell off the desk. He chugged and then came up for air with a smile across his face.

"Thanks." Lean searched for where he left off. Once he found it, he started again, "A low profile wasn't enough. I was ordered to make her go away. I created the problem and I had to fix it. Keeping her drugged up was easy, expensive but easy. Her fans raged but gradually people stopped watching and one day I just filled the syringe a little too much, but I didn't account for her tolerance.

"It all worked out for me. I didn't actually kill her, and my business partner was content she was gone." He smiled once more though behind it his mind traced the steps that lead him there. All the, *what if's* and *should 'a dones* piled up like the sweat beaded on his brow. He took another swig. The bottle was now empty.

"See how much better you feel when you get it all off your chest?" I bent forward in my chair. With my elbows on my knees, I looked down at my hands. My next move eluded me. Crystal had her reasons but who else? Aziz would have Lean dead by now if he wanted.

"Okay. Go home." I didn't look up.

Lean sat still for a moment then he stood and made his way through the door without saying anything.

In the distance a foghorn sounded as the Main Street Bridge dropped the flashing red crossing bar and prepared to open. The mast of a sailboat drifted north towards the bridge. Both sides of the bridge were pointed high in the sky as the mast sailed through. Once the bridge came together again the mast was out of site.

A shrill groaning accompanied rhythmic slapping. I was alone on the second floor of the building. The office across the hall was for a tax lawyer who always left at six even during tax time. Following the sound, I put my ear to the desk. I pulled the tablet back out. I hadn't closed out of the website, and it started another video on its own. A brunette with black eye liner running down both cheeks was looking up at the camera as the guy with the tribal tattoo behind her gyrated faster and faster. I paused it before the guy could finish. I studied the scene once again. This couple was fit, and the background looked staged, like a high school girl's bedroom. Even with a hard life the girl in the video was not in high school. Her muscle tone, fake tits and spray tan just didn't have the fresh youthful appearance of a teenager.

Sitting in the old wooden chair with the tablet clenched in both hands my eyes darted along the tiny images of videos yet to be seen. It was going to take some time and a box of tissues but somewhere in there among the countless uploaded and streaming videos was the person that wanted Oliver Lean dead. It was time to get to work.

The first forty minutes went by fast. I didn't even notice the time as I skimmed each video skipping through the longer drawn-out ones. I got up and went to the mini fridge and came back with a cold beer. I popped the cap off and sucked it back. Hydrated, I started back at it. The next hour started to drag. My eyes were beginning to get sore and every time I closed them, I pictured scenes from the videos. Some of them were good and I didn't mind, then there were the strange ones. Cosplayers came up time and time again. People dressed up like their favorite superheroes performing sex acts on each other. Something about mixing warm childhood memories with sweaty sex organs didn't sit well with me.

When all the free previews were used up the site asked for a credit card. A text went out to Lean, *Get me a login to your sites. I think the person I am looking for is in there somewhere.*

Lean sent back a few texts with questions but eventually the idea of giving free porn seemed a lot less expensive than dying. I then called Billy.

"Hey, want to help me with a case?"

Billy shouted a few excited swear words then asked what he would be doing. When I explained what I needed help with Billy shouted again. Then he asked, "Can I do this from home?"

"Yeah. Just make sure you are paying attention. Look at viewer submitted stuff not the produced videos. And you're going to have to search the guys too."

Billy swore again but he agreed to do it. I gave him the password and reiterated what to look out for. We agreed to touch base in two hours.

An hour later I was growing tired of the perverse nature of these people. I saw things I couldn't un see and things that made me question had I been doing it all wrong this whole time, and do girls really like that? I had enough. Doubts of this new lead crept in, making me angry I lost time the way I had, and now all I wanted to do was go down the street to the bar and pick up a girl and try out something new on her. That would be a waste of time as well.

I sat in the dark weighing my options and reviewing my dwindling bank account.

The bar was a block down, and I needed out.

I walked past Cooper's and went two more blocks to Baldy's. There was a lackey there I needed to talk to.

It was still early for Baldy's to be overly crowded. Out front a row of choppers with various customizations lined the curb. Nothing too fancy, a sign they belonged to a club. Real bikers don't spend thousands on custom work to their bikes or they do it themselves and it shows in the welds or the oil under the frame. The Harleys were ridden hard by even harder men. I liked this bar.

Inside, I caught a waft of piss and stale beer. The bar started on my left and ran most of the length of the wall. On the right were a couple of high top two-seat tables. An archway led to a room with two pool tables. Past that was a jukebox that had no power to it and a couple of dart boards on the wall. The walls were mostly lined with old vinyl beer banners. A girl in a bikini holding a football and a girl on the Harley holding a beer. Neither advertisement appealed to my nature.

I made eye contact with the bartender, a slender thirty-something with stringy brown hair and wrinkles around her mouth from too many cigarettes. She wore a white bikini top and jean shorts she failed to fill out in the back. At her bar were three bikers that owned the choppers out front. All in their leathers with their colors sewn on their backs. Each dude had weathered-wood beards from thousands of windblown miles. Another of their kind was shooting pool alone.

They all carried knives and guns for sure, and so was I. In a place like this everyone knows everyone is carrying. Here, words are chosen carefully, and fights are seldom, a criminal Cold War exits, ensuring mutual destruction for anyone that steps out of line. In a way it's the safest place in town for a guy like me as long as I treaded lightly, they would leave me alone as long as I don't hold eye contact for too long.

The bartender took her time to come over and ask what I wanted. This was not the kind of place you order a water. I had to order a beer, but I didn't have to drink it. The bottle went up to my lips, the fluid cold, but it never seeped into my mouth.

The voices of the customers echoed from the yellowed plaster walls as each of the road warriors grunted to communicate. It was too quiet to start asking questions. The cover of 80's rock music would do the trick.

I plugged in the juke, and it lit up purple and pink. The echoed voices softened as eyes drifted towards me and my music selection. Shoving a five-spot got me six plays. Punching random letters and numbers got me guitars shredding through the blown speakers.

From the bar a skinny biker with tanned arms ending in black leather gloves got up heading my way. I changed the grip on my bottle from forward to backward so I could crash it across his already scarred cheek if need be.

"I totally dig this band man." Sounded the crusty biker as he began to shred along with an air guitar rendition.

I nodded and went back to the bar. The bartender came over and asked if I needed another.

"Nah," I said. She turned away from me, so I spouted, "You seen Eddy around?"

"Yeah," was all she said. Her hand went out and she leaned on it. We stared at each other for a few seconds.

"Is he here?"

She shrugged.

"Okay, well, I owe him some money and I got it for him." I turned and looked at myself in the mirror behind the bar.

"He'll be in soon. You can leave it with me."

I laughed, "No. I guess I'll be back." I turned on the stool for the door.

"Let me check when he gets in." she rolled her eyes and walked off.

She went down the hall, past the bathrooms to the office. The song ended and the voices echoed once more for a few seconds as the next song kicked on.

The bartender came out of the low-lit office and got back behind the bar. One of the bikers asked for another round and she went to work for them. The way I nursed my beer, she knew I was not spending another dime.

She got down to my end of the bar and said, "He aint coming in today."

"Thanks. Got any idea when his next shift is?"

The bartender thinned the whites of her eyes and puckered her lips, "You ask a lot of questions."

A couple of bikers stopped conversing and turned their attention down my way. I avoided looking right at them.

"Just trying to pay the man back." I shrugged and left it alone. If any of those leather clad bikers caught wind of a pig, I would get fried.

I got off the stool and made my way out.

Once around the corner I headed for Coopers. Foot traffic was light on Beach Street, cars passing by were nearly as scarce. I caught sight of a black silhouette somewhere behind me. I kept my pace and didn't look back. Just up ahead was an alley, too narrow to pass a car through. I dipped in and pressed my back against the brown bricks. The alley was filled with the hum of window AC units kicking on and off, all of them dripping water down and splashing into tiny moss-covered pools along the coquina rock road.

My hands were out, fingers loose, waiting to pounce on whoever turned that corner. Shuffling tennis shoes scraped along the cement. I controlled my breathing while listening to each step get closer. Then the scraping stopped. My breathing stopped, and my eyebrows pinched together.

A car slowed and stopped. The door opened and closed. The car throttled away.

From outside the alley, I watched an early 2000's Honda sedan round the corner. I couldn't see who was in it. I slapped the brick, working the stored energy from my arms. I was a trap all wound up ready to spring, but the rat didn't take the bait. There was beer at Cooper's.

Still energized from the tail I missed; I blew through the doors at Cooper's looking for a drink. I might as well have been greeted by chirping crickets. There were enough empty barstools for me to pick from. At the end of the bar would let me see the back door and the front door. The place glowed with neon beer signs and flickering TV's hanging in each corner. There were two bartenders on tonight. Dina, knew my face and my beer by now, but not my name. She was a cute round-faced brunette with a full sleeve of tattoos down her left arm and jiggled all over when she walked. She was good at her job, talked to everyone like a regular, like she was your friend, but outside a good tip she could care less, so I tipped well. The other bartender, Chastity was big in an athletic way, like you'd want her on your roller derby team. She was bi-racial with mocha skin and kinky, copper hair and light amber brown eyes. She neared forty years old, giving her a more straightforward demeanor. She always mistook me for someone one else. She would ask, *Hey, you were here two nights ago right with your friend.* And I would say no but she would swear it was me. Then she would ask what she could get me, even though Dina was already pouring the stout.

The only other company tonight was a couple out on a date night sitting at the other end and two guys in their sixties sat in the middle of the bar. The old guys were discussing the regatta that was on one of the TV's. Both men wore ball caps button down short sleeve shirts, shorts and deck shoes. Their tans were thick except around the eyes and just below the collar of their shirts. The jewelry was nice and so were the Scotches they sipped.

"Drinking alone man?" Dina asked as she set the stout down on the coaster.

"Looks like it."

"What is it you say, I'm alone not lonely?" She smiled as she wiped up the bar top with a rag.

"Sort of. Don't mistake my being alone for loneliness." I couldn't help but smile back. She was good at her job alright. The instant familiarity Dina provided made me want to open up and talk about this case. That would be a bad idea, so I searched for something to say but nothing was coming to mind. While I struggled in the blankness of a muted mind, she lingered a little while longer then in the silence walked off to tend to the other customers.

When the second round came, I finally had something to say, "You ever go to Baldy's?"

Dina's lips rippled, and her nose crinkled. "Never."

I shrugged, not the best topic of conversation. My phone was on the bar. I watched it light up with a text message alert from Billy. *Check it out* and there was a link to the website. I clicked on the link and then covered the phone. Whatever was about to pop up wouldn't be something I would want people to see me watching. Looking around, the same couple and the old men were still at the bar. Two more guys had come in and grabbed a table. I decided to go out back of the bar where there was a little patio for the smokers.

White lights were strung from the roof to the wooden fence that bar patrons had gratified. Some of them showed talent. Two wooden picnic tables were empty. I took a seat, looked around and then pressed play.

The video began to play. From the view of the camera mounted on a computer monitor, were just a desk chair and a tan couch in the background. The camera light covered everything with a blue-green tinge. The seconds ticked by with nothing happening. Just as I was about to jump ahead the rounded silhouette of a beer bellied naked man stepped into view exposed naturally from the neck down. He stood in front of the camera, hairy chested, and began to stroke his limp dick. He sat down to reveal a black squared hood. The two-pointed corners looked like the hood was nothing more than a black pillowcase with two eye holes cut out.

The man's breathing increased in relation to the rapid movement of his wrist. Then he just stopped. Sitting still, only the heavy breathing could be heard. He slapped his jerking hand down on the table with a grunt. "This is for you Tara." He said and started up again eventually finishing with a groan. He leaned in close to the camera, still breathing heavy and said, "She got hers. I just got mine and now you'll get yours." Then he shut off the video.

I almost dropped the phone. I didn't want to ever watch that again, but I would several more times, each time focusing on some different aspect of the video. The third time through I noticed a reflection off the glass framed picture over the couch. I could see the monitor had two windows open. One was of himself beating off (what the camera saw) and the other was of a girl. The quality was too low to make out features no matter how tight I tried to zoom in. The fifth time through as the man leaned in to shut the camera off, the hood shifted, the eye holes covered his brown eyes, and I could make out the hairs of a mustache creeping around his nostrils as the hood lowered.

The back door to the bar opened and two guys came out talking and laughing, snapping me back from the bizarre world I entered. They took seats at the other picnic table, and both lit up and started the conversation they were having inside. I, not a smoker, decided it was best to head back in than sit and watch wanking videos while two guys smoked in the low-lit courtyard.

Sitting next to my empty glass was Billy, looking around anxiously. He sipped on a sweating golden ale of his own. His hands were exceptionally clean tonight despite his job of being a mechanic. I had to laugh at that, Billy was all too eager to help by watching porn. I sat down next to my friend.

"Good lead." I said and waved to Dina for another stout.

"Yeah, I thought so. Don't ask how I found it." Billy grimaced then sipped his beer.

"No questions, no lies man. I didn't get a chance to look up the user. I imagine there won't be much on him."

"I couldn't find anything beyond his username, Playtona33."

"*Play*-tona? Sounds like *Daytona*, he's probably a local. Lean runs the site so I'm sure he can get some kind 'a lead on the guy. What a sick little fuck."

"People man." Billy finished his beer. He drank fast and drank cheap. I was nearly embarrassed by my friend's habits. Miller Lite as fast as you can get them. Dina was at the other end of the bar slow pouring a fresh stout and pointed to Billy who nodded for another.

"So, you like that, I got more." Billy swiped his phone open and pulled up a video. I took the phone and cupped the screen pretending it was for the volume or glare when I just didn't want people to see me watching porn. I didn't stop to think about the contradictions in my image. Breaking a leg or nose of some lowlife to get information on a drug dealer was no problem. Doing bad things when they needed to get done was now my reputation. Violence was a way of life for me. Sex was something else. Breaking a jaw and banging a girl weren't the same. Violence and sex didn't mix, placed in separate compartments in my mind. I never thought of myself as a lady's man, though ladies were always in pursuit.

Dina bounced her tits over to us, holding both beers still as she moved. She put the beers down on the coasters just as the video loaded for me. Billy, who truly believed women liked pigs, hadn't turned his volume down. A voice crackled out of the phone, "What will it be tonight boys?" as a gal in a wig climbed on top of a bed. The camera auto focused as the girl in a bra and thong typed into a wireless keyboard. She smiled into the camera, and I held my breath. *Tara.*

"What are *you* watching there, Roger?" Dina tried peeking over the bar top at the phone and catch a glimpse of whoever was speaking in the video. After an eye full of a good-looking girl in her underwear she said, "Well who is that?"

I clumsily closed out the video, dropping the phone. There was no hiding the red all over my grin. A cute girl just caught me watching a webcam video. I wanted desperately to punch someone in the face and walk out.

Dina leaned over the bar all smiles pouring it on in an effort to turn me darker red. "So, your business below the belt does work. We were beginning to wonder about you. I see you sitting at this bar night after night and get hit on by beautiful girls, but you never leave with any of them." She bit her lip while gazing at me with sparkling brown eyes. I looked into my pint glass for support.

Billy piped up, "It's for a case. You little pervert." He smiled big sensing blood in the water. Whenever he came in with me, Dina always paid me all the attention.

"Case? Like casing the joint?" Dina said pressing her round pliable breasts on the bar.

I piped up, "No. Private investigation." I looked over at Billy like I was going to break his neck and Billy knew it.

"Detective work? Like in the movies? Wild. Where's your mustache Magnum?" Dina smiled and walked back to the other customers, looking back over her shoulder one more time.

Billy nudged me with an elbow.

I shook my head. "Don't tell people what I do."

"How the hell are you gonna get work if no one knows what you do? I fix cars, nearly all my work is word of mouth."

"Yeah? Any of that word of mouth mention you used to run a chop shop?" I looked back down at the phone. I pulled the website back up and went back to the video of the very familiar girl. I looked at the face paused in the video and imagined it without the wig. Below were thumbnails of other videos with the same girl in different outfits and sometimes different rooms of a house. I clicked on those and that's when I confirmed the ID.

"Yeah, it's Tara man." Billy said reading my mind then gulped the beer and looked up at the sports highlights playing on the TV.

I flipped through the videos without watching any of them. There were about twenty of them. The earliest was seven months ago. The last one was two months ago. All the videos would have to be watched. Most of the run times were under ten minutes. It would be another long night. Dina might sell me a bottle. Alysa had when she worked here, back when I really needed it. She also showed me I never really needed it.

"Did you go through all her videos?" I asked without looking up. I texted myself the link from Billy's phone and then handed it back to him.

"A few of them, but I decided to come down here and tell you instead of keep watching."

Dina came back over to their end of the bar. "Private investigator, Roger Grimes. Sounds cool."

I said, "Sounds cooler than it is. Mostly cheating husbands and false insurance claims."

"Cheating husbands? I could have used you six months ago, the son of a bitch. Glad that's over. Officially free at last!"

I tipped back the pint glass and finished off the stout. Dina took a fresh glass and poured another without asking. She said from the tap, "This is on me and all the women unlucky enough to hire you to catch their lying, cheating, shit bag husbands. So, you gonna tell me about this case you're on or do I have to get you drunk?" She did that thing with her eyes to make them sparkled and I felt something inside my chest. It was foreign, a feeling long suppressed. After busting up a kid sex ring, the idea of meeting a girl and doing anything together with our clothes off just turned my stomach. I had been a real mess. Alysa tried to help, she got me good and drunk so I could black out and keep the faces of the dead away at night. She thought it would help me, then it was too much, and she thought cutting me off would help more. One day she was gone, and I got through my days without a bottle. Now tonight, for the first time in a long time, I was feeling something I hadn't, myself. I knew I could drink a few pints and be fine to go home and go to bed. I also realized my eyes hadn't left Dina's ass since she walked off. Blood was flowing, warming the cold and dead parts of my body that weren't essential for living.

Must have been the beer, or that Crystal was back in my life. She was always good at curing whatever ailed me with sex, and it was usually her that ailed me. I spilled it. "I can't tell you all of it of course,"

"Oh, of course." She said holding her finger to her rounded lips, letting me know she would keep a secret.

"Basically, I got hired to find a person. And this other person keeps turning up. I'm thinking she's my key. Turns out she is a webcam girl. You know what that is?"

Dina smiled with a grin that let me know she was aware. Was I the only one that just found this out? Could it be the age difference, Dina was nearly ten years younger than me? Kids grow up so fast, I thought.

"Are we gonna find you on this site, young lady?" Billy chimed in.

Dina scoffed, "Sure thing. Keep digging." She looked to me and winked then walked off. I was left wondering if that was sarcasm or not.

Chastity came around to the inside of the bar from making a food run to the table on the floor. She grabbed Billy's empty glass and tossed it in the sink. "Another?"

"Hit me."

Chastity put a fresh golden pint down. "What 'cha talking about over here?"

"Webcam girls." Billy jumped in before I could.

Chastity pointed at me, "I knew you was a freak. I keep telling Dina, don't get to close to that one." Then she let out a big belly laugh and shook her curvy shaped jam filled body.

"How does everyone know about this shit except me?" I finally came clean about my lack of knowledge of internet porn.

"Sugar, a smile like that and you get what you want. Mmmm, I know I'd give it to ya." Chastity laughed again. The irony of her name washed across my face.

She straitened up and grabbed a few dirty pint glasses and began washing them, dipping them in one cleaning sink than another. "Those blue eyes don't need to be watching sex on the internet. I bet you can just flash 'em at a chic and she do what you want."

I shook my head no and sipped some beer.

"You got a favorite cam girl, sweetheart?"

I locked eyes for a moment with Dina who quickly looked away then I put my beer down. "Yeah, this girl." I turned the phone around and showed Chastity. "You know her?"

The bartender's smile faded just for a split second, but it was enough to catch. "Nope."

"C'mon Chastity you know everyone." I smiled and flashed those blues at her.

"Well, not like *know* her in person. I've heard of her. Yeah, she um got messed up in some shit. Then disappeared. Rumor was kidnapped by a fan I heard."

"Hey, how do you know all this?" Billy asked leaning so far over the counter he could suck from the tap.

Her face drooped, sliding away the smile. "Cause I used to do it. It's why I shut down my site. Too many freaks trying to find me. I got recognized one night by this dude, really skinny white guy. Go figure right, beating it to booty like this. I ended up going home with him, it was like we already knew each other. Let me tell you that was the best sex of my life. That skinny dude could go and go and let me tell you he was backed up. All that time just watching and now getting to touch. Whooaah." She wiped her brow with the dish towel.

"So, skinny white guys do it for you now? You should try yourself a red man." Billy sat back from the bar and ran his hands down his long black braid. Chastity laughed and shook her head.

"You crazy. I heard about Tara a week later and decided that was too close. I could be next. I shut my shit down and deleted it. Sorry guy, you can't pay to see this no more." She smacked her round ass.

Billy slapped the bar with an open palm. I didn't say anything, and I was not laughing. Chastity left us to check on her table. I sipped my beer in silence. Dina came to check on me and I only shook my head no. Billy made some crude comments about what he wanted to do to Chastity then said he would get me next time and left me with the tab. I left a good tip and walked out.

Chapter 5

The office was dark. I sat there in the light of the tablet replaying the video over and over and over of Playtona33 jerking off. I clicked on the other videos Playtona posted. They were more of a video diary than porn. He built a fantasy life with Tara that was starting to sound like a twisted Hallmark movie. I checked out the Tara videos and compared the posting times. Playtona was posting a video immediately after Tara posted. Neither of them had posted in a month until now. The post time was only seven hours ago. How did this guy even know Tara was dead let alone so quickly?

Lean's cell went to voicemail. I said nothing and hung up. As I started to type out a text to let him know about Playtona33 my fingers stopped.

Boots clopped on the other side of my office door. With rapid force someone pounded several times.

I slipped the pistol in the small of my back and went to the door. I looked through the peephole and saw the short and tall, odd couple of Sunny and Abby. Sunny had her usual dreary look about her and Abby was just awkward with bad posture.

Sunny banged again, "C'mon I know you're in there you bum. Open up."

I opened the door fast, spooking Sunny making Abby giggle. Sunny shot her a dirty look. "Finally." Sunny said and stepped past me without an invitation. As she passed into the office she kept talking. "This place stinks. What a dump." She sat on the couch with her knees apart, poking out of the rips in her jeans. Abby smiled at me as she came in and mouthed a hello. I hadn't noticed the night before, but Abby was attractive, with high cheek bones and large almond shaped eyes. She had been dressed to appear as a man that night and wore no makeup. Tonight, she had on a little, enough to accentuate her natural good looks.

"Where is she?" Sunny asked.

"I don't know." I stood in the middle of the room and folded my arms. "I figured she'd be at the hospital since her sister just died."

"Well, she ain't. We just came from there." Sunny looked out the window at the river and the lights. "Got any other ideas." She looked back to me, "So you'd do it yet? I mean now he's gone and killed Tara which you could have prevented. Probably killed Crystal too." She went on to mumble some name calling. Abby reached out and touched Sunny's hand. She didn't like Sunny saying that.

"No, and I don't think Lean's responsible for Tara."

Abby piped up, "What makes you say that?" Her voice was gentle and sort of sweet. Her hands were folded in her lap and her back was straight. She didn't belong in Crystal's circle of gutter trash friends. This girl was some sort of educated professional maybe just out slumming it or escaped the vortex of this town only to return to make a difference and fall right back in with the crowd that is going nowhere fast. I just called the kettle black.

Begrudgingly I said, "Lean didn't know she was dead." I turned to Sunny and raised a finger, "Before you go saying some over inflated statement, I have no problem putting you into that wall. I'm not dealing with your shit."

Sunny sat back; her chin dug into her neck cutting off her words.

Abby went on, "So you met with Lean then?"

"Yes. He contacted me and guess why? Someone is trying to kill him. Fancy that. You stupid amateurs. Do you really think you can kill a guy and get away with it? Really kill him?" I paced around and then took a seat at my desk. The girls remained silent.

"So, are you working for him now or what?" Sunny finally found her balls again after I took them.

"Yeah. Listen there is more here than you both realize." I started processing what Sunny had said early and changed course. "What do you mean she wasn't at the hospital?"

"I'm saying Crystal aint at the hospital because Tara aint neither."

I had to think on this one. I watched them take her out of her room. Depending on location, maybe she went to a different hospital, maybe straight to the morgue. I didn't know procedure on things like that. Jennings said the U.S. Marshalls were there, they could have taken her away.

"Did you check all the hospitals? The morgue?"

Both girls shook their head, *no*.

"I watched them wheel her out. It doesn't matter, I doubt Lean is out to get either one of them. Don't get me wrong, the guy is a shit bag, but he doesn't have it in him to kill in cold blood." The room was silent. Both sides sat contemplating the exchange of news and ideas. Working in a team was faster and easier but no way would I want to work with these two. Abby seemed to have a head on her shoulders but not the little one. I wanted to choke that one.

"We gave her all that money to kill Lean because…" Abby didn't finish, she didn't need too. Sunny was thinking it too.

"Yeah, well the world won't miss Oliver Lean even if he ain't a killer." Sunny kept up the tough gal act, though she knew she was played. Crystal was good at that, convincing people to take on her burdens. She never paid a day of rent in her life. Nearly everything she owned came from other people, the men she dated or the women she befriended. It was a nice act, being generous to her new friends, giving gifts, it's easy when it's other people's money. I had gone through her whirlwind years ago. It left me shattered, but I rebuilt. Even now as she blew back into my life I wanted to get carried away in the breeze.

It was late and neither side wanted to discuss it any further. "Look," I said in a low tone, barely above a grumble, "Go home and get some sleep."

I followed them to the door. "I've known Crystal a long time. Selfish is just who she is, she's also a survivor. She'll turn up, maybe you'll get your money back. In the meantime, stop trying to kill Oliver Lean, so I can find the guy who really might do it."

The two girls left. I shut the lights off and laid on the couch. I closed my eyes but couldn't keep them closed. I might have slept but was unsure. In the silence, I stared at the ceiling and watched the glare of a traffic light change between red, green and yellow. I wanted to focus on the case, on who was after Lean and where Crystal went but I found my mind counting the seconds between color changes. Next, I started playing a game of holding my breath between colors and then wondered if I could care for a dog. A dog in the office would be another reason to get kicked out, but it would be nice to have a bitch around that didn't talk back.

BAM! It hit. Damn those magnificent ideas in the dark.

I rolled over on my side and reached out for my phone. 3:34 AM. I wanted to call Billy but couldn't. There were some calls I would have to make but those would have to be in the morning. I set a reminder in my phone for 9:15 am, *TARA ISNT DEAD*.

****

The bright yellow morning sun burned through the window warming my face. I woke up to a sweaty neck collar. I sat up and looked at my phone. The reminder went off thirty seconds later. With that shutoff I used the tablet for something other than those videos and checked my email instead. Your senses can take only so much porn and for a guy that really wasn't all too keen on it, I had seen enough.

I stopped for a large coffee and breakfast wrap at a local drive-thru then made my way out to Whispering Pines. I had to make sure not to leave any trash or crumbs in the Olds or Billy might freak on me.

I watched myself in a pair of mirror-tinted double doors approach the entrance to the home. Inside I found Rosa as she had been the time before, sitting at her desk. She picked apple green scrubs for today.

"Welcome to Whispering Pines," Rosa said as I walked through the door.

"Hi Rosa, George." I paused. "Tara Johnson's brother."

"Hey George, I remember who you are. What can I do for you?" Her tone was cute with an unexpected smile on my end. I studied her rich mocha skin, thick black eyebrows and full black hair. I speculated on what she looked like out of those scrubs. Though I had just seen her the day before, there was something freshly familiar about her now beyond our casual meeting. Perhaps she was just something outside the investigation pushing through now to the front of my mind.

I smiled, "How've you been?"

"Good, good. I want to offer my condolences about your sister."

I took a longer pause than I should have then said, "Thank you Rosa. Say, can I gather her personal affects?"

"Oh sure, well," Rosa clicked on a keyboard and then read something that must have been important. "Let me check the HIPAA. I mean you were just here so..." She didn't finish her sentence.

"Any chance I can at least just see the room. I'm not sure if there would be any keepsakes, a picture maybe."

"Aw that's sweet." The silence after was awkward for the two of us.

"Well, I appreciate what you did for me." I tapped my fingers on the counter. "I know I just met you yesterday, but I can't help but think I've seen you before."

Rosa crinkled her brow, "Hhmm, I have never been to New York." She quickly looked down to her work and avoided eye contact. I realized I went too far and had to back track if I were to get past that door and into Tara's room. Still, I was genuine about seeing her before.

"Oh." I casually took a step towards the door then turned. "They won't just throw Tara's stuff away will they?"

Rosa looked up, "No, well if no one is on a list to claim it…." She realized where I was going. She studied my concerned face. She considered my eyes for a moment, like they were telling her I had seen things, the kind of things that leave a mark. These were eyes of an older man, a wiser man of the world. To her, they were the eyes of a man who just lost his sister.

"You better get in there George." She smiled and buzzed the lock on the door. I smiled back and walked through.

I made it to the room and paused seeing the door was open. I leaned against the outside wall and listened then slowly peered around the corner of the doorway. I could hear shuffling of papers and drawers opening and closing. Then whoever was in there said, "Dammit, dammit, dammit."

I turned into the room. Standing in the doorway I said, "Hello officer Jennings."

The round police officer stood, not moving from where he was with his hands on his hips. "Grimes." He nodded. His eyes darted around the room. The bed was stripped, and the mattress at an angle off the box spring as if he had been looked under. The closet door was open with clothes on the floor.

"Was this you or did the Marshalls do it?" I sat on the corner of the bed. From there I could scan the bathroom. The counter was covered with the contents of a makeup bag.

"The Marshalls? Ah hell, I made that shit up to scare you into talking. Do I have to arrest you for whatever you and Lean are into, yet?" Jennings said matter of fact, almost like he didn't really intend to arrest anyone for that crime.

I moved to the bathroom door. The makeup was scattered as if it had been used in a hurry. Caps were off eye liner, and a compact was open. There was a hair curler still plugged in as well. As I started to look further the 'click' of the room door being shut echoed in the acoustics of the bathroom. I spun on the balls of my feet.

Jennings was standing in front of the door. "What do you want Grimes? Lean aint here and Tara is gone." Jennings sounded stressed. His eyes continued to scan the room, and I being there was upsetting him.

"Okay Jennings. I just wanted to confirm Tara was dead. I think I got what I came for." I said as I exited the bathroom. "Your hair curler is still plugged in."

There in the room Jennings began to breathe heavy. His hands moved out in front of him opening and closing as he talked. "I think there is more you're not telling me, huh. You scummy PI's are all the same. What did you want with Tara!"

"Back off Jennings." I felt my left shoulder turn slightly towards Jennings as my chin dropped just a little. My knees bent ever so slightly just to get a better center of gravity. Jennings was a big guy, at six feet and pushing 250 pounds. He didn't look tough by my standards, but not all men wear toughness on their sleeves.

Sargent Jennings began to sway. "Tara was a good girl Grimes, real good. He crossed a line and I want him." Jennings slammed his hands on the bed. Rage mixed with a plan gong wrong. Nothing he could do was right, and that anger surged through Jennings and out his fiery eyes.

I had seen that look before and was ready for it when Jennings leapt over the bed, reaching out wildly. I, ever quick, stepped back then threw down a right, connecting above his left eye. Jennings fell to the floor stunned. He managed to sit up, leaning against the wall. His arms were loose and resting on his knees. "You bastard. You don't care; you don't care about anyone, just getting paid."

"I think you need to do some talking." I said taking a seat on the corner of the bed again. Tara must have had something special to drive men crazy like she did. Nearly a vegetable and yet this guy fell in love with her. Crystal had me like that once, one of those bad habits I formed. The late nights full of worry and anxiety convinced me of real love for her and then I learned it meant she didn't really love me.

"How did you have a relationship with a vegetable?"

Jennings looked up with a lack of understanding of my question.

"She was a vegetable, right?"

"Who told you that?" Jennings reached his hand out. I grabbed it and together Jennings got to his feet. A lump had formed just over Jennings' left eye. He touched it like it burned his fingertips. "Nah, she was here for rehab, to get off the smack her piece of shit ex-boyfriend got her on. I guess she somehow got a hold of some heroin and relapsed." His once rage filled eyes were now pink and glassy.

Crystal Johnson with the lie. I felt the urge to smack myself in the eye for being so blinded by her plea for revenge. This case was looking more like a bowel of spaghetti. All the players were woven in and out of each other's lives and there was no way to tell where one lie ended, and the next lie began. Was Tara pulling one on her sister? Or was Crystal pulling one on me and where did Lean fit into all this?

"So, you gonna tell me who hired you?" Jennings asked dusting himself off.

"No."

"Doesn't matter, I think I know anyway." Jennings looked around the room, coming to terms with the consequences of his actions. He tried to kill a man because a woman he believed loved him told him to. I couldn't help but see myself as I watched Jennings' self-loathing overtake his face. I was the other side of that coin. Ten years from now I might very well be Jennings, standing alone expecting to die over a dame. He looked so damn pathetic.

"What do you know about the cam life?" I said with eyes glued to Jennings. I needed a reaction with a strong tell.

He pushed his lips together and scratched at his chin, "Not sure what you mean."

"You know, internet porn. Girls with webcams doing live shows." My eyes darted across his large face.

With a big exhale, Jennings shrugged. "I don't know. What's it got to do with Tara?"

"You stay away from Lean and forget about all this. Tara is gone there is nothing to avenge here." I studied the change on Jennings' face. The man's left eyebrow raised a little and then leveled out.

"I guess you'll kill me if I try for Lean again?"

"I'll have to." I said.

Jennings' face sagged. He was a man who was handed a death sentence. To go on living a lonely life or to kill the dragon and win the heart of a young love, those were his options. He wouldn't give up on Tara.

I left him standing there mulling my threat, hoping it would stick and Lean would have one less assassin.

I stopped by to see Rosa before leaving.

"Was her stuff still there or did they clean it out already?" Rosa asked with a smile but no eye contact. Her focus held on sorting manila folders with pastel-colored tabs sticking out of them.

"There really wasn't much. But I feel better for at least checking."

"Sure, I bet." She put the folders down and looked up into my eyes. She held the gaze there and then smiled and looked away.

"I saw Officer Jennings, he was in her room, I guess gathering her things."

"Officer Jennings?" She wore a puzzled look then said, "Oh you mean Sargent. He's not a cop. He's our security guard and his first name *is* Sargent. He struts around like he's a real cop, likes people to think he is." She laughed.

I sheepishly smiled. "I guess I just assumed." My smile was on the outside, inside I wanted to kill Jennings for that.

"He's harmless. He spent a lot of time with your sister."

"He told me all about it. I could tell he cared for her. I'm glad someone was here for her." I rested my elbows on the counter. That familiar look Rosa gave off bounced around in my head. She smiled up at me again with her head turned, like she was waiting for more out of me.

"You want to get a drink tonight?" I played the odds, hoping they were in my favor. Getting to know her could prove stupid.

She thought about it for a second and then said, "Sure. That'd be nice."

I wrote my number down, "Here, call me. I'll be around enjoying the sun and sand the rest of the day."

"Enjoy. I'll call you later." Rosa put the paper in the pocket of her scrubs.

I stood a little taller as I walked out. Asking Rosa out had been to move my investigation along, but it still felt good to have a pretty lady say she would call.

The Olds was parked under a tree in the back corner of the parking lot. I took off the ugly polo I wore and put the top down on the Olds.

A text came through from a number I didn't recognize, it read; *Have fun in the sun while I'm waiting on old people to die.* It was macabre but true, Rosa watched the gurneys wheel out every day. I texted back a smiley face.

Chapter 6

After several of my calls went to voicemail, a text came back from Lean: *Hey bro just landed. Meet me at the marina.* At least he was alive. I could see the marina from the second-floor office window. The distance wasn't worth taking the car, so I walked the few blocks over to the marina.

It was after three and the heat of the day hadn't yet dissipated. I put on a mesh net ball cap I got from the auto parts store I had ordered all my C-10 parts after it was shot up but never installed. I returned the parts but kept the hat. The hat did little to shield my head from the oppressive sun as soon as I hit the street. The walk took about ten minutes.

I stood at the docks looking for a boat I had never seen before. Then among the sea of bright white fiberglass and shiny stainless steel a tanned arm waved me over. Halfway down Dock C, I came to a twenty-seven-foot Sea Ray. The boat was older but well maintained. Lean was standing on the aft deck hosing it off.

"Hey buddy," Lean said through gold rimmed aviators. His shirt was off exposing prickly back stubble that was overdue for a waxing. He wore green and black board shorts and flip flops. I waited for him to finish with the hose and then went aboard.

"Take a tour." He said with a smile and waved me on to the cabin door. I ducked into the cabin and confirmed we were alone. The AC was off, leaving the air warm and balmy. The place smelled of bleach. The small cabin held a head, galley and booth.

I popped back on deck. Lean was standing near me, startling close, and said, "What 'a ya think?" and held his arms out.

"Nice. You just get it?" I slipped past him to a cooler. Inside, were empty green bottles floating in a mixture of ice and water. I fished around and pulled out a full icy one. The first guzzle of beer nearly froze my hot brain.

"I've had it about a month. Only taken it out twice though besides today." The closeness became apparent to Lean who backed up. He sat at the captain's chair and wiped down the dash and controls. "Just giving her a wash down. I went offshore today."

I wiped the dampness from the seat across Lean and sat down. "Catch anything?" I said looking around at the lack of tackle onboard the cabin cruiser.

"Yeah, it was a real blood bath." Lean laughed to himself and went back to wiping things down. On the dash there was a fillet knife. He grabbed it and wiped the blade then stuck it in the plastic sheath. "Sorry I didn't respond sooner to your texts, no reception offshore. What was it you wanted to talk about?"

"Aren't you going to ask if I caught you're would be assassin?"

Lean stopped what he was doing and turned on a smile, "No, I did your job for you." He winked then continued, "I guess you're fired Grimes."

"Okay then." I stood up.

"Whoa, whoa! Don't leave before the big reveal." Lean waved the knife around like a magician's wand. His smile only grew larger with anticipation for another kill. Sweat bubbled along his brow as I watched myself in the man's sunglasses. One bubble broke and a bead of perspiration rolled down the side of Lean's face.

"Tell me your theory." I said matter of fact, feeling the weight of the Glock 30 resting in a holster clipped to the inside of my waist band.

Lean chugged the rest of a beer and set the bottle down in a cup holder. "See, this girl I was dating Crystal, she thought in her twisted head that it was a good idea to have me killed and was in the process of paying off the hitman when I caught her stealing from me. Can you believe that? She was stealing money from me to pay the hitman that was trying to kill me." He gritted his white teeth and used the towel to wipe his forehead.

I sipped beer. Perspiration slipped down my back just as it ran down the neck of the green beer bottle. The bright sun on the white boat was making me nauseous. A salt filled breeze skipped across the harbor and for a second, I was refreshed.

"Did she tell you why?"

"Yeah, she talked, Grimes. She said the guy who was gonna kill me was the baddest and meanest son of a bitch in town. Said he had a big horse cock and would probably use it on me before I was dead. Can you believe that shit? What a crazy bitch." Lean turned to the cooler and flipped back the lid, setting his knife down in the process. With a fresh beer he kept talking. "She liked those trashy types, guys in motorcycle clubs and rednecks with truck nuts hanging off the tow hitch. Total white trash." Knowingly or not, he scratched his crotch with his free hand while tipping the beer bottle back with the other.

Crystal talked before Lean cut her into fish bait, she had to of, she's a survivor. She *was* a survivor? I was never anything more than a tool to her, nothing but a tool to get off and a tool to get a good meal. A tool to not be alone and a tool to scare away tough guys. In a small way, too late, there was something about Crystal I began to miss. My chest swelled by the dead woman's last words. A quick twinge of pain, I'd never see Crystal again. The swelling collapsed as I had to believe not all those comments were about me, there still could be some love crazed cowboy with a long gun pointed this way. I got the feeling I would rather not stand so close to Lean or wind-up collateral damage.

"So, your crazy girlfriend hired a killer to get you but you're not sure why and that's good enough with you to fire me?" I asked directing Lean's attention away from who his assassin might be and more towards a few of his own unanswered questions.

"No, I guess not. She said she was doing it for her sister. I never met her sister. I don't know who she's talking about."

"Think about it." I got up for another beer, they went fast in this heat.

Oliver Lean rubbed the running sweat from his forehead as his eyes darted back and forth, reliving Crystal's murderous interrogation. "She hired someone to kill me man. I had to do it." Lean had his hands up and slowly curled his fingers into fists. The man lived for several weeks with people trying to kill him, his nerves frayed and jumpy, he was convinced killing Crystal was self-defense. He had no idea it was not over for him yet.

"You killed her, and you really don't know why? Seems dumb Oliver, real dumb." I went into the cooler for another beer. Lean was too distracted second guessing himself to notice me move the knife behind the cooler. I could let my guard down and cool off.

After gutting Crystal and leaving her for the fish offshore, he anticipated having to kill me. Without proof of who the hired killer was, I was an accomplice, I was still a loose end. Lean knew I was involved somehow.

I had a new beer to drink down. The heat wouldn't quit, and the breeze was too sporadic to make a difference. The water was a calm brown. Seagulls circled overhead. A few boats down, a radio played classic rock. Other than the crazed killer standing before me it was serene.

"Look Grimes, I'm your client, right? So, what I tell you stays between us."

"It doesn't work just like that but what's your point?"

"You're going to stay quiet about this. I know Crystal hired you to kill me. She confessed it all before I slit her throat." Lean took his glasses off to make sure he looked me in the eyes.

"What's to stop me from killing you right now?" I was not going to let blackmail put me in a corner.

Lean got in real close. The size difference was noticeable now with Lean's eyes peering into my nostrils. "Go ahead do it tough guy, baddest man alive."

My fist pushed deep into Lean's scrotum, sending the porn peddler to his knees. I spun behind the man, wrapped my arm around his neck and stopped short of choking him unconscious. It was a quick jerk and Lean was only out for a few seconds, just enough to daze the man and take the fight out of him.

As Lean caught his breath and regained all function he crawled into the captain's seat. The boat swayed as water splashed lightly off the hull from a distant wake. *Asshole,* he mumbled under strained breath.

Lean's hand went up, "You should know, you can't kill me, I worked it out with the Aziz. I'm protected now." His grin was tough to deliver but he got all his teeth out.

I took a deep breath, the way you breathe when you find your puppy has chewed the TV remote. It's the breath that keeps you from killing the puppy on the spot. Curiosity killed Crystal and now it might kill me. Had I done the job I was paid for it would be over and only Lean would be dead. Doing the right thing got the better of me.

"Okay Lean. There is still another killer after you." I slowly reached in my front pocket under Lean's wide-eyed paranoid gaze. His nostrils flared as if sniffing out what I had in my pocket.

I looked at the time on my phone and made the decision not to let Lean in on Playtona in the black hood. Lean already took matters into his own hands and killed Crystal. His crew sounded like clowns and would only get in the way of me finding him.

I climbed off the boat. I stood on the dock looking down at Lean.

"You better go get him before he gets me, or Aziz will get you." Lean laughed a clever laugh. It might be suicide, but I really wanted to kill the guy right there.

"Five grand."

Lean stopped laughing, "What? You're… "

"No, I'm not. Pay me what I'm owed. You killed my client so pay up or get killed."

"Get the fuck outta here Grimes. That's absurd."

"No, that's your life." I stood there. I was not leaving without my money. Walking away was a wash and a wash was crap. Yesterday I had two clients for one job. Today it was zero. The five grand

Crystal fronted was good but now I know the real cost. Sunny and Abby were right, it just didn't seem appropriate to keep the money that got their friend killed. Lean would have to make up the difference or I would have to steal for Azad Aziz.

"Fine. Dammit. I'll get you your money tomorrow."

"Right now."

"I, I, I don't…" Lean put up his hands as his neck shrank into his shoulders.

"You do." I waved my hand indicating Lean needed to get off the boat and hurry things along.

Lean put his hand out and I pulled him up on the dock. We walked back to Lean's car.

In the parking lot of the marina, Lean's black Mercedes sat absorbing the bright sun. Lean paused at the trunk of the car. He was not sweating as much, and his shoulders were pulled back and squared off. I reached to my lower back and gripped the Glock.

"Whoa easy. It's in the trunk." Lean put his hands up. He pressed the key fob and popped the trunk. As my attention was on the trunk, I missed the sound of the neighboring car doors open and shut. I peered up over the trunk lid and froze, hearing the clicking sound of a semi-auto pistol chambering a round. My Glock was out fast.

I stepped back and tucked the pistol directly to the back of Lean's head. A group of three with the man in the middle holding his pistol proper. I kept a darting eye on the others.

"Drop the gun, Grimes." Lean said turning slowly. I let him go. He backed up to the three men. Lean had talked about his crew before, now I was placing faces with names. There was Kyle, with stringy dirty blond hair, stood in flip-flops and wore board shorts. The guy to his right resembled Lean, Chester, they had to be related with the same Mr. Potato Head shaped body and hairy arms. Juan Carlos, the man in the center with the old Berretta, had black hair cropped short and had an ape face with neck tattoos crawling from beneath his collar of his Tap Out t-shirt. His arms were long for his height, and he had small scars on his face, probably from fighting. Lean now stood a little taller with his balls, just a little bigger.

"I can kill this turd," Juan Carlos mumbled through Spanish lips.

"Drop the gun." Lean repeated, then rolled his eyes to his Latin enforcer, giving him permission to kill me if I moved.

I wouldn't be dropping shit.

I trained the nine on Lean. "Let's not get messy Lean. Just hand over the cash."

"I did my own PI work on you Grimes. I know you need this money to pay back the twenty large you owe Azad Aziz. I sure as shit wouldn't want to owe that guy a dime." Lean pecked around like a real cock.

"It's eighteen actually," I knew that debt would come up to bite me. Aziz was putting my shit on the street. What started out as a small loan was growing day by day. Profit from this job would have kept Aziz happy for a little while. Now Lean was going to use it for leverage somehow. My plan to run to Uruguay was disappearing if Aziz knew Lean was paying me. The weight of rock bottom hung around my neck reminding me how close I am to the ocean floor. Gamblers are all stupid on some level. I didn't want to be stupid anymore.

"I want you to catch the bastard that is trying to kill me."

"Why me? Can't your crew here do the job?"

"They can't be out looking for him and keep me safe at the same time." Lean sneered. His logic worked, though I wouldn't feel very safe with my life in they're hands.

"Okay Ollie but remember I can't find your other would-be assassin if I'm dead." I put the Glock back in my waist. The stink of sweat and blood was in the air, especially around Juan Carlos, but this wasn't the place. Crystal warned me about the guy, but I didn't listen. His pistol was on me but lowered to his waist. The pistol was not a worry, this guy was itching to throw hands with me, and I didn't want to disappoint.

A grin shined across Lean's face. "Everyone has their price." Lean reached inside the trunk, he handed over the same five grand Crystal had attempted to steal. The money felt heavy in a grimy way. Lean rubbed his palms along his thighs as though he agreed the money was tainted.

I made up my mind when this was over, I would kill Oliver Lean. Damn Aziz and damn the pervert in the black hood. Crystal had her problems, but she didn't deserve to die over any of this. Nothing Lean had done or Aziz had threatened that was worth her life.

"I guess it takes a hitman to kill a hitman." Lean said confident a deal had been struck.

Just as tensions began to recede, a black Lincoln came in hot. The large disc brakes stopped the tires, causing them to grab the pavement with a chirp.

My hand went to the Glock while Juan-Carlos turned his barrel towards the car. The window was down and out popped the tanned elbow of Smitty. Tucked in the bend of the old guy's arm was a pistol pointed at Juan-Carlos.

"Put the gun away punk." Smitty grunted. He wasn't looking at me but had Juan–Carlos locked in a stare down. Juan looked away then back. Smitty showed a little more of the barrel poking up from the crux of his arm.

Juan-Carlos backed down. The old man had some salt left.

"Get in." Smitty said to me with the same gruff.

The Lincoln had great acceleration as we sped out of the parking lot.

"What the fuck was that all about kid?" Smitty asked as he put the pistol away in order to light a cigarette.

"Seems I just have one of those faces."

Smitty raised a fluffy white-haired eyebrow at me while exhaling tar and nicotine.

"I came looking for you. Lucky, I found you."

I nodded my appreciation though I thought I handled it well. Smitty was adding this assumed rescue to the list of things he has done for me. A list I was trying to stay out from under.

The black Lincoln was humming along about sixty miles per hour up A1A, slipping in between cars with tags from up norh. Smitty was as cool as if he were going twenty-five. His legendary status in this town afforded him certain privileges or at least he acted like they did. I just assumed not to speed when we were both carrying guns and my pockets were stuffed with cash.

"I want you to pull this job to get out from under Aziz *and* that little shit. I hate that little fucker, Lean. The guy is nothing but a pompous little pimp. Always walking around like he's some kind of tough guy. Oh, I'd like to get my hands around his neck. I'll show'em how we used to deal with tough guys. Did I ever tell you about the time we took care of, what's his name, ah fuck. Anyway, he was the same kind 'a prick. Sal, Sal Luchenzo, yeah, took him out past Tomoka Farms Road. There was more swamp back then. Anyway, it was so hot that day. So hot. When you dump a body, it's best to do in summer. Them gators they don't eat in the winter so much. The bodies, they just float when the gators don't eat em. So, summer is best to dump a body. What was I getting at?"

Smitty could tell stories, stories I remember hearing before about who did what way back when.

"What's the job you have for me?" I failed to connect the dots earlier when Smitty came at me with the proposition. I was eager to make some cash and wanted to do it legal. I hid behind the idea that to do a job right would take a team and take planning and I didn't have either. Days later I was not much better off.

"Lean has something Aziz wants."

"Lean cooks the books for Aziz. I assume that's what he wants."

Smitty shook his head not knowing either, "Aziz wouldn't say until I agreed you were in. Lean thinks he has you in his pocket right now. Aziz wants him to keep thinking that until he gets what he wants from the little punk. He thinks you are going to kill him."

"I am."

"Not yet you aint." Smitty was pointing a finger in my direction.

This time I shook my head.

"What's got into you Grimes? All this killing. You were never like that. Man, you were a great thief, best I ever came across. You say you're out, okay, but then I see you killing 3rd Street punks in a pool hall? And now stealing is beneath you?"

"They were all bad men."

The Lincoln accelerated then Smitty hit the brakes and we cut left up a residential street, whipped some corners then came out on Halifax Avenue, running along the river instead of the ocean. He hit the brakes again and parked alongside the road. We sat across the street from his favorite hangout. An old English taproom called Tully's, with old timbers and white stucco face. The restaurant had been in business over 100 years. Smitty co-owned the place for a long time then lost his half in a card game. They kept his corner-booth with high padded sides reserved for him and his associates. It was where he conducted all his business. I knew the place well. My mom worked there when I was in high school, it's how I got to know the old man.

"My mom used to work there." I said staring out at the place that hadn't changed in 100 years.

Smitty looked over at the restaurant and nodded, "I remember."

We sat silently. The light changed and cars passed us by. When they started to line up again, he said, "Come on into Tully's. Have a drink and let's make a plan."

I shook my head. I hadn't been in Tully's in years. The corner booth, where the jobs came in.

"Look kid, don't kill Lean. There's more going on here than you know. Let me set up a meeting with Aziz, get the details and make a plan. Got it?" Smitty groaned.

"So there is something bigger than Aziz here."

"You just let me worry about it."

I nodded.

"Good. Now get out, I don't want to be seen with no thief." Smitty smiled his grandpa grin to smooth his words, but he meant all of it.

Never one for words, I got out of the car slowly and then turned and walked away. The cash filled all four of my pockets making it a long three miles back to the office. As I walked, I thought about Tara and the hood in the video. She was intimate with the Hood; she should know where he lives. What did Lean have that Aziz wanted anyway? Tara was somehow at the center of these men. The magnetism or charm she must have had to get something from all of them. Why was it taking so long for the Hood to make good on his promise to kill Lean? The man was a coward, that's why. It's why he wore a hood to begin with. Just a love-sick fan of Tara's who, with his dick hard, agreed to do something he didn't have the stomach for. A man who in the moment could act tough but really had no spine. Had I been so different?

I walked straight to my car.

Chapter 7

I parked the car around back behind the nursing home and watched the staff change shifts, leaving a skeleton night crew to tend to the old folks would be asleep in a couple hours. I was there to follow Jennings and learn more about his world. While waiting, I watched all of Tara's videos again.

Rosa walked out of the whispering Pines building and headed for her car, a late model Lexus. That is not the kind of car a front desk receptionist normally drives.

I closed out the videos and sent Rosa a text: *Hey it's George. You're probably just heading out of work but want to grab a drink later?*

I watched Rosa stop before getting into the car. She pulled her phone out, opened the door and got in. She started up the car and blasted the AC. She read the text then typed several responses but seemed to delete them. Then she sent *Love to, gotta knock out a chore or 2. U up late tonight?*

I replied, *Sure just hit me up,* I got back a smiley face.

I watched her drive away when my phone rang with a facetime call coming in. I swiped it.

"Yeah?" I asked not sure what I was looking at for the caller. It appeared to be a parking lot.

"Look carefully." Said the Armenian voice.

There on the screen was the Cutlass with me sitting in the driver's seat looking down at my phone. I looked up and waved at the lifted Toyota.

"What do you want Aziz?" This was no place for another parking lot brawl. Jennings should be coming out any second and he would want to intervene.

"There is a natural order to things, and you need to know your place."

"There's nothing natural about you Aziz." I said fighting to keep my cool.

Aziz laughed, "In time you will learn."

The screen went black. I fired up the Cutlass and chirped the tires getting out of the parking lot.

Rosa was on my mind, where she lived, what she did outside of her job. Those things interested me more than Jennings and his twisted love affair. A long silver Olds Cutlass was not the best car to remain incognito. The black convertible top was up and laying off the throttle was the only way to keep the rumble of the V-8 down. I managed to catch Rosa as she drove through town to a residential area and pulled into her garage. The house was a middle class three-bedroom ranch with wood siding in the heart of a development built roughly twenty years ago. I drove past the house and parked down the street.

The sun was finally beginning to disappear in the west taking with it the oppressive heat. The humidity remained. I sat in the car with the windows down listening to the cicadas sing off key. I leaned forward against the wheel to let the sweat evaporate off my back. I stashed a spare t-shirt under the seat for sweat emergencies. I wouldn't need it yet.

An evening offshore breeze picked up and felt good on my skin. I jumped over to the Playtona33 video once more. The post date on the video was this morning. There must be some sort of review process that takes time after the upload. Lean would have the details on it.

I had a hunch who Playtona33 was now and upset I didn't catch on to it sooner. I left Tara's lover licking his wound in her room. That fire was still burning in him. Tara would have what he needed to reinvigorate his drive to kill Lean.

Playtona's video was enough to kick over to Camp and let her investigate it and scoop up Jennings, but my hands were tied. Lean didn't want the cops involved; it's why he came to me. No cops meant no cops and I needed a pay day. It could have been just curiosity or the fact that I enjoyed my job, but I couldn't shake the feeling there was more to the Crystal, Tara and Lean trio than simply a drug addiction. I wanted to know more before I let Lean know I thought it was Jennings. Lean would send his goons out to shoot first ask questions later. Just because I didn't like Jennings didn't mean I wanted him murdered.

Rosa came out of the house wearing a t-shirt, running shorts and carrying a gym bag. It all made sense until I noticed the bright red lipstick she was not wearing before, which lead to me noticing the heavy eyeliner and blush.

Rosa drove past two gyms and a city park. I tried to work out scenarios that would explain the heavy make-up and gym clothes, but nothing came to mind. Unless she was headed for a personal trainer more than weight training on the schedule.

The silver Lexus turned up Carswell Avenue, a heavy industrial street that ran parallel the railroad tracks. The street was lined with metal prefab buildings and a few older cinder block ones. Though the road was paved there was an ever present fine white dust covering it from the heavy truck traffic. All the workers had called it a day. The street was empty except the two of us, making it hard for me to keep the Olds out of her mirror. Finally, Rosa pulled into the parking lot of one of the tall drab corrugated metal buildings.

I parked the car up the street and watched as she touched up her make-up then puckered for a duck face selfie before getting out. She went up to a steel door and punched some numbers into a keypad. The door buzzed and she went in.

I did an internet search on the address and walked the dusty road waiting for my phone to pull up a map. There was no business name associated with the address and no signage on the building. I kept my distance from the ever-present eye of a security camera over the steel door. I circled the building on foot. Looking up to what would be a second and third level there were a few small windows. On the side of the building that faced the tracks were several two and a half ton AC units. Some gang had tagged the corrugated siding with bright colored letters, *The Dead Ends*. I went back to my car.

I sat there for a minute denying what I knew was going on inside there. That's when the nagging notion of familiarity crashed headlong into unconscious truth. There she had been all along on the screen I recalled, concealed under too much makeup with her hair blown out she had been unrecognizable. It's why I missed it a dozen times before. I turned the volume up.

On a white couch in a large bedroom sat Rosa Sanchez, otherwise known as Rose Pink. She was in a yellow bikini and had on white stilettos. She held the camera with a selfie stick and panned it around her body from left to right. Then lowered it and brought it up along her legs as she spread her thighs apart exposing the tiny yellow bikini bottoms and deep camel toe.

The frame shook as the selfie stick was placed in a stand or tripod off screen. Rosa lay on her back and began the now usual routine of these cam girls, touching and stripping. Over enjoying every fabricated second of the three-minute video. Below were more related videos with more familiar faces. There with an angry look on her dark makeup face was Sunrise Palace. She wore a short black wig and had on shiny black patent leather. I chuckled; of course, her video would be dark and dreary. Linked with Sunny's was the unmistakable lanky body of Abby. Similar to her personality, the background was drab with a tan sheet hanging behind a twin bed. She had an assortment of sex toys laid out and casually went through, using each of them.

Despite her dullness, there was something attractive about her predictable and slightly better than average girl looks who had a little bit of kink. Seemed like a nice combo for a steady girl, not the over actors in the other videos. Usually, the girls I had relationships with were the aggressive types that wore me down and once they had me, they realized there was not much behind my silent demeanor. The chase was over for them.

Sorting through the live feed on the Glory Catz website, I pieced together this murderous gang of webcam stars. There Sunny was in all her dark and dreary shame. She was hanging over the side of a bed, her arms out over her head, free floating in the air. I was not surprised by her armpit hair. I signed out and created a new account to sign in with. I went back to Sunny's stream and sent her a message, *Cheer up*.

A couple other users were on asking her to do random acts of pleasure. When she read my message and sat upright and wrote back, *In the empty abyss of my soul cheer is swallowed by life*

I chuckled. This broad was a cliché. I wrote back, *LOL*. She quickly responded with *WTF?*

I sent out another, *I can pay your half back meet me@ the same place*

Sunny looked right at the camera. The other users were still requesting things and telling her how she should slit her wrists and how they would use her blood, real Sick-O's. Sunny made up an excuse for an early exit and shut off the feed. That was a lot faster than I had expected but I was glad she did.

The sun was beyond the palms and the pines, as the nocturnal creatures began to stir. The early risers were out, mosquitos and other flying bugs began to dart about looking to feed. I had my hand on the key in the ignition when light from inside the building spilled out into the dark parking lot. A small, thin figure walked quickly to a beat-up yellow Caviler and got in. The little car rattled to life and did it's best to peel out of the lot. So, did I.

I slung the long silver Olds into a spot behind Coopers. I started for the door and felt a pair of eyes on me. The man by the back door was smoking a cigarette and staring at me. On the bench was a man half the other's size dressed in all black. He was looking up at the smoker nodding a response.

My pace slowed and I looked around, conscious but casual. I sized up the smoker. He was heavy set and about my height and had a scruffy beard. He wore a baggy t-shirt and baggy jeans. The cigarette was half smoked when he dropped it to the ground and smashed it under his black work boot.

His large hand with thick fingers went up signaling for me to halt. I did but kept a few paces away.

I held my tongue, making him speak first.

"You the one been asking around 'bout me?" He said and brushed oily sandy colored hair from his eyes.

I looked at the skinny guy then tubby. "Probably."

"Well don't." he said. The little guy spit.

"You Eddy?" I asked tubby.

"Nah, see, that's asking about me ain't it?" He looked down at his skinny compadre who chuckled.

I studied the two of them. They looked dirty, even showered they would still look dirty. There was just a constant sweat about them. They stayed up too late and got up too early because they were workers. Their brains just weren't fast enough to figure another way out.

"I'm in a hurry so I'll just ask, why did you tell Oliver Lean to stay away from Tara Johnson?"

Eddy shifted his weight, and he moved his fingers in, feeling his palms. The little guy bounced his eyes from Eddy to me and back again.

"Don't you go asking…"

I closed the gap between us real fast. The skinny guy tried to stand but my hand shoved him back down. Eddy tried to pull back, I stayed close.

"Tell me about Tara now."

Eddy's words slipped and jumped over each other as his cheeks flushed with newly pumped blood.

His hand moved, mine was faster as I slapped him across the face. He stumbled back. His head went down then he charged.

I let him come at me. My arm locked around his neck and the other came from under as I twisted my hips and lifted. Eddy went up and over me coming down on his little friend still sitting on the bench.

Eddy wasn't ready to talk. His eyes sparkled with rage. He was not used to being on his back like this. He was not done fighting by a long shot.

The skinny guy pinned under Eddy began to squirm.

"Tell me about Tara." I demanded still holding him pinned.

Eddy grunted. His large boots slid over the asphalt looking for traction to stand. I kept my weight on the both of them. Eddy's strength was turning, he would rise soon, and the skinny guy would bolt out.

When he refused my second demand to talk, I chopped him in the throat. Eddy's hands released from my arms as he grabbed as his damaged windpipe. It was not hard enough to break it, I still needed him to talk. Now I had time to grab the skinny guy.

"Maybe you know something." I snatched him by leg and drug him out from under Eddy. His arms flailed. He twisted to his back; I held his leg as he kicked. I screwed his leg around at the knee and he yelped. Not the noise I wanted from him.

A young couple came out of the bar, saw what was happening and retreated into the bar.

I let go of the skinny guy and hovered over Eddy waiting on him to speak.

"Okay, shit." Eddy spit pink slime from his mouth. The skinny guy was not doing any better. Eddy climbed the table and sat. He looked around for listening ears then said, "My boss, he, ah, sent me to tell Lean to back off."

"Why?"

Eddy looked at the skinny guy. The skinny guy looked over his shoulder to the parking lot. I shook my head no and told him to have a seat.

"Just who the hell are you, man?" Eddy rubbed his throat.

"I'm looking for Tara. She's in danger and I want to help her."

Eddy squinted and looked around as suspicion clouded his mind. He had every right to be, I was nobody to him.

"I don't know where she is." Eddy's eyes eased at the corners and the crystals of rage melted in his brown eyes. His breathing slowed. I helped him to his feet.

I gave him my card. "Let me know if you find her."

He nodded and shoved the card in his pocket. I didn't have time to waste on this guy when Sunny would know more than he ever would. I left them sitting there.

I walked into Cooper's and looked around. Sunny was sitting at the same booth we had the time before. She saw me, then slashed her eyes away as if I were not worth the contact. Her feistiness made me laugh.

"Come on, I'm in a hurry." Sunny said with nothing to drink in front of her.

"Take it easy, your job can wait." I said and sat opposite her in the booth.

"You're a real piece of shit." She didn't speak again until the server came over, a lumpy looking red headed guy. She ordered a gin and tonic. I told him a beer and a water. He went to get them. When the drinks came, she started talking again.

"What's with the red face?" She studied me with her eyes.

I gulped the water down. After coming up for air I said, "It's hot out."

She nodded and got on with it, "I guess you're not a half bad investigator. You found me, have you found Crystal yet?"

I shook my head yes. "That's why I'm giving it back. Since you and Abby fronted the money for the hit, you should get it back."

"Mighty white of you." Sunny smirked and tossed her drink back. She pointed at the ginger server and signaled a second round. "So, where is she?"

Telling her the truth might cause a seen, "She's split."

Sunny shrugged like she expected that from Crystal, "Then you're not going to kill Lean."

I shook my head no.

"Pussy." She murmured.

A smirk broke across my face. I let it settle then said, "Tell me about Glory Cats."

"What's to tell? You're on the site. So, did your detective skills lead you to it or did you already have it bookmarked in your computer? Let me guess, you just happened across my page and thought, *I know her*." The server dropped off the drinks. "Then you thought, boy I'd like to fuck her now." The redhead waiter paused for a moment and looked at me then back at her.

I leaned forward and said to Sunny, "Frankly you gross me out and seeing you naked will require me to wear special glasses for a week." At that she raised a middle finger. I continued, "I don't care but I'll ask anyway, how'd you get involved in the cam life?"

Sunny shook her head and played with the cocktail straw in her glass. "I'm ordering a double next."

I shrugged.

"Ollie is a real dick. His Crew, that's what he calls them, goes out and recruits girls and couples. I dated one of them, Taylor is his name. You know him?"

I shook my head no.

"Anyway, we dated. He took some pictures and video of us and posted it without me knowing. Then it got, like, a lot of hits and comments. It felt good and we kept doing it. Then I started getting paid and well it's easier than being a stripper. I don't have to touch anyone." Sunny sucked an ice cube into her mouth, swashed it around and spit it back into the glass. She looked up at me, "Too easy? Did you want to hear about rape or some kinda drug addiction? I get paid to masturbate. Image if you got paid every time you jerked your little pecker." She rolled her eyes, "Probably be a millionaire." She said under her breath.

Killing people wasn't a bad way of making a buck either. That's the problem with making an easy buck, there's emotional strings attached. I was a mess after what I did, for good or bad, it doesn't matter to the dead when at night they come back to talk to you. Sunny was no different, she might play a dying girl online but inside she really was dead. I'd wager that boyfriend of hers was gone, maybe not out of the picture, he probably shows up in Glory Cat videos often enough with the new girls. The rudeness in her voice made it clear she didn't like what she did no matter the ease at which she gets paid.

"You knew Tara, didn't you?"

Sunny nodded yes and sipped her drink.

"So, what really happened to her and where is she now?"

"Ollie, he got her into drugs. She OD'd at the studio one night and he was just going to dump her down there by the bus station."

"Then he does use drugs to get some of the girls?"

"Yeah, but not Tara. She was there because she liked it."

"Wait, Tara wasn't hooked on drugs first? You sat right here and went along with Crystal's story of Lean getting her hooked." I jammed my finger into the table as my knee began to bounce. Ollie's story was becoming the true version. Crystal had lied to me.

Sunny scoffed, "We had too, man. Crystal said it would get you riled up to kill him."

I moved on, "And the studio is where you all record?"

"Yeah. It's big inside. He built it out to look like different rooms." Her eyes rolled into her imagination, "You know like a Hollywood studio. With revolving sets and shit. Some of us have our own rooms."

"How does Rosa fit in?"

"Rosa? She works at the funny farm, she convinced Ollie to drop her there and arranged it all for her to get better. Thing is," She paused to take a drink, "Ollie, he didn't want Tara to get better. He was paying Rosa to keep her drugged up."

"Why?"

Sunny shrugged. "I think 'cause she knew what he was doing. I went to see her one time and that's how I met Crystal. Crystal was bringing her around, getting her better. She wanted out of there."

"What did she know about Ollie?"

"Everybody knows. It ain't a secret." Sunny's eyes were large, and she laughed. The booze kicked in over time.

"You mean his ties to Aziz?"

Her eyes shrank, "I don't know who that is." She took a quick chug of her drink. When she came up for air, she wiped her mouth and said, "The cam money is good, but the real money is getting subscribers send us their own dick pics. You know, then Ollie would message them back and blackmail them. They would cancel their subscription but by then he had their home address." Her eyes went down to the table as her neck sank between her small shoulders, "This one guy, Derrick Sills, I'll never forget him, I got him to send me some stuff, it wasn't that bad, anyway Ollie contacted him, and I guess he couldn't pay. After Ollie messaged the pics to Derick's wife the guy shot himself." She shuddered, the first real emotion I saw from her. "I got to know the guy; you know. We messaged a lot; it wasn't all sex. Some of these guys, they're just lonely." Her hands went out and cupped around the glass. Once her palms went cold, she pressed them against her eyes. Right then I wanted to reach out and hug Sunny. The tough exterior that got her through those two-minute videos melted away. The drink was sucked down and this time I waved the server over.

"Why not go to the cops right then?"

Sunny shrugged unable to answer.

I sat back in the booth. I took a deep breath and thought how two days ago I didn't care about anyone but myself and how much whiskey I had. Relationships were hard to come by. I kept strange hours and could never talk about my work. Alysa knew some of it. She had been a good ear. She was gone so, I passed the time alone in thought about pulling off the perfect crime, but I never was able to get away clean, not even in my fantasies.

With her third drink in front of her, the cold exterior was thawed enough to get real emotion out, not the front she wanted everyone to see. "Tara was the tough one. After Derrick, I threatened to go to the cops. She told me to hold on, that Lean was way over his head. It wasn't long after that she went to the funny farm. Now she's dead."

"Tara isn't dead."

Sunrise Palace sat looking into her drink. The golden liquid swirled around the clear water of the melting ice. She pulled the straw out and chewed on it. "Did she and Crystal take off or something? Where is she?"

"No. Tara is alive, but Crystal is dead."

Sunny was the image of stoic, sitting in silence, looking at the other patrons as they socialized, she appeared as if on a date, a boring date as her eyes began to scream to be somewhere else. I didn't have it in me to console her, the kind of comforting words people need always escape me at times like this. So, we sat in silence for a minute that seemed like twenty. Then she cleared her throat and said, "Do you think he knows about us? About Abby and I?"

I shook my head no. Honestly; I didn't know what Crystal told him before he cut her up into fish bait. I didn't want to let Sunny know all the details of Crystal's death.

Then I asked, "What did you plan to do after Lean was dead?"

"We didn't really think that far. Go back to our old lives, I guess. The only money I managed to save went into killing Ollie. I guess I could host my own site and bring my fans with me."

"Tara's been posting videos threatening Lean. Some were from her bed at the nursing home. The videos were pulled quickly, but I managed to save a copy." I pulled the video up. Sunny avoided looking at the phone. I slid it over to her and she looked without touching the phone, like if she did, she would end up like Crystal.

"You know this guy?"

Sunny watched the video and shook her head 'no.' "User upload. Looks like Tara was his favorite, they all go for her. He was smart to wear a hood, Ollie couldn't blackmail him."

"He was in her last video. They were bragging about going to kill Lean."

"Good." Sunny finished her drink. She mumbled something under her breath that I couldn't understand. Then she looked up and said, "Just keep the money and kill Ollie and burn that fucking studio to the ground while you're at it." She slammed the table and stormed out.

"I plan to." I said in a soft tone no one could hear.

I sat there with an empty glass and a paid tab. I thought about what Sunny had said. Blackmail. If Crystal was tortured, she may have given up her friends, I know she gave me up, but we were never friends. It was clear to me Jennings was the Hood. My scuffle with him this morning wouldn't be enough to keep him from going after Lean if Tara was there rooting him on.

Billy texted me, *Look what just posted* with a link to Glory Catz website. I watched the little dial circle indicating it was downloading. Finally, it was done. The video started with a messy double bed then in walked Tara Johnson dressed in a trench coat. She sat down and looked at the camera. I paused it and studied the background. It didn't look like the same location as her twenty or more other videos. This time she was in a bedroom with bare walls and white blinds in a window. I let it play on.

Tara pulled on the belt and the coat fell apart. Underneath she had on a lace bra and underwear. Her posture was near perfect with her back slightly arched pushing her breasts apart as she ran her fingers over the lace and licking her lips. She leaned into the camera, "I want to thank a very dear friend of mine, Playtona33 and what he has done for me."

The man in the black hood stepped into view. He looked at the camera and then to Tara. His white t-shirt was tight with a stain at the collar, and he had on dark blue boxer briefs. Tara's hands began caressing the man's hairy thighs. He leaned forward, his hands shaky as they touched her shoulders and back. Her hand slipped under the blue briefs.

She looked up at the hooded man, "Thanks for bringing me back." Her hand began a swirling motion in cadence to the man's rapid breathing.

I sped things up on the video skipping over action scenes and the finale. Tara pulled her head away from the man's expended crotch and said, "Show them all what you will do for me."

The camera shook as the hooded man pulled a pistol from a desk drawer. The rocking stopped and I could see it was a Smith & Wesson semi-auto, one more similarity to Jennings. He waved it around like he was sighted in on a target. Tara straightened her back and reached out with her hand for the pistol. She brought it to her mouth and licked the barrel. She looked back at the camera, "Bang." She said and turned off the video.

I made a mistake not identifying him sooner reminding me how much a rookie I really was at investigating. Getting to Oliver Lean first wasn't to save his life, it would be to save my own. Otherwise, Aziz would call in my *marker*.

Chapter 8

Another call to Monique got me her password to the skip trace software. I found Jennings' last address. He lived in an all-right part of town. The residential street was lined with single story block homes. You could spot the geriatrics with their fifteen-year-old luxury car still in pristine condition. The driveways with out of state plates were the snowbirds roosting early this year.

I made a pass and saw a light on in the living room, but the driveway and carport were empty. The rest of the street was quiet. Snowbirds go to bed early. I pushed in the headlight switch and coasted the Olds to the curb.

A straightforward approach would work best with Jennings. As I walked to the door, I decided to convince him to back off Lean until I was done. Then, if he were still in love with Tara, he could have Lean all to himself. I wouldn't stop him.

No answer. I knocked and waited. No answer.

Looking through the corner of the window I saw a familiar living room set. This was the Hood's house alright. The desktop computer he used to record himself was there against the back wall. By the couch was a suitcase and large gym bag. The gym bag was stuffed so I could assume the suitcase was as well. It was going down tonight.

I slipped on some gloves and found my way around to the back door. The knob was locked but loose. Using an old garden hose, I tightly wrapped it around the knob and twisted. It took a lot of effort but eventually enough torque broke it. I was in.

The house smelled of old coffee and damp wood. Light from the living room guided me through the kitchen. Under the linoleum, the floorboards were soft, and I nearly bounced as I walked across the kitchen. The dripping faucet kept cadence with each step.

I checked the two bedrooms and bathroom. No one was home.

The gym bag was full of women's clothes and beauty supplies. Since I didn't think Jennings', mom was staying with him, I assumed they belonged to Tara.

In the bedroom a suitcase was packed on the bed, men's clothes. They were going on a trip. Tara wouldn't last long with Jennings on the road. Once he served his purpose she was in the wind. He was a ticket, just a stub for fare paid for with flesh.

There was a duty to warn my client of his impending death. I accepted payment to find the person trying to kill him, now I'm close. A text went out to Lean that I was closing in on his assassin, but it wasn't over yet. He got back to me that he had extra hired guns and to bring Jennings to Glory Catz when I caught him.

In the refrigerator I found a two liter of soda. It was flat. The tap was room temperature, but I chugged back half a glass anyway.

The noiseless living room was an escape from everything but my mind. My legs stretched out on the couch and the pistol rested on my stomach while I waited. Jennings was a sad case, and I tried to work out ways to get him out from under this. Used up and discarded, Tara was showing her worth by getting revenge on every man who took their piece. To do that she had to use the men around her willing to help.

My mind eventually drifted from Lean and Tara. Nine p.m. rolled around, and a text came through from Rosa asking if the Ocean Side Bar was okay with me. I had forgotten about the date. Jennings was my focus, but Rosa had answers too. I replied that I would meet her there.

The bar was on the beach nestled between two large hotels. The whole street was lined with hotels. Parking was a bitch, and I couldn't trust the valet with Billy's car, so I was forced to park a few blocks away on a residential street.

Before I got out of the car, I pulled the Glock and shoved it in my front right pocket. The shorts were baggy enough to conceal the outline of the pistol, but it was still a snug fit. Though my pocket would slow my draw time, in this crowd it was safer there than the grip jabbing out of my waistband.

The Ocean Side was split into two levels. Up top was a nice dining area, a place you could take your kids or converse with your date. Down two flights of sand covered concrete steps was the bar. The large doorman squatted over a stool I couldn't see. His girth covered all but the bottom of the legs. He smiled and nodded, stamping my hand and letting me pass like he knew me. If I asked him from where, he wouldn't be able to answer. I played along, shook his hand and moved on like we were friends.

Inside the red terra cotta tile was slippery with a thin layer of white granular sand. The ceiling was low with a series of dark wood beams. Despite the many ceiling fans on high the place was muggy. The bar was straight ahead, the beach was to my left and there were tables in between.

Rosa wasn't hard to spot. She was at the bar in a tight salmon colored dress that ended mid-thigh. The dress clung to every curve and bump of her creamy skin. Her calves bulged as she balanced on thick wedges. Flanked on both sides by freshly pinked meat heads from up north. She smiled to each and locked eyes with me.

I leaned in between her and the bro next to her. It didn't take long for him to get the hint and give up his seat. The place was full of partying sun burnt and salty tourists with a few locals mixed in. Many of them still wearing their bathing suits. The Ocean Side attracted a good mix. I had always avoided the place due to the tourist priced drinks, the lack of AC and the general noise level. The live band had just taken the stage. It was a group of three middle aged, long haired black guys and a white guy on drums. They kicked off the set with a cover of The Joker, something that was played in bars like this all up and down the coast nightly. At least it wasn't Buffet.

She was drinking some sort of margarita mix. I ordered a fruity drink that came in a mason jar. We clinked glasses and sat without speaking until the band ended their song.

"So, is this your first time here?"

"Yeah, pretty cool." I lied twice. I had been here, and I hated it, but I was on a job.

Three bartenders slung drinks. One was a tall guy, well built with shaggy hair. He cuffed the sleeves on his t-shirt. The other two were women, young but with that that old-time bartender wisdom of you never hit on a bartender at work. Kalie, was covered in fancy ink. She was tall and thin with multi-colored hair and a nice rack pushing out of a custom cut up company tee shirt. She was sexy with a lot of makeup. I figured not so much without it.

The other bartender caused a lump to suddenly grow in my throat and my arms tingling. She had blond hair and the body of a cross fit trainer because during the day she was one. Her skin had a nice natural tan with a dash of freckles. She was in her late twenties and had her own custom-made bottle opener sticking out of her back pocket and wrist full of hair ties. She had seniority.

If I'd have known Alysa was working here, I would never have come. The last time I saw her, in my drunken stupor, I said somethings she didn't deserve to hear. The words were directed at myself, but I didn't know it yet. I know now and hope there would be a chance to tell her.

Rosa finished her drink and pushed it to the back edge of the bar. She signaled to Alysa who looked at me and decided to help another customer. Kalie quickly stepped in and took the order for another round.

"So where else do you like to go?" I said.

"What?" She said slightly louder than the music.

"Where else do you like to go?" I wanted out of there.

"Hold on I gotta pee." Rosa smiled and pointed towards the restrooms. She grabbed her purse and scooted off the stool. Alysa waited until the black-haired Latina was in the restroom before approaching me.

"Business or pleasure?" Alysa leaned over the bar with a white rag and soaked up the condensation from the drinks in the humid bar.

"I'm in the middle of a case."

"That's too bad Roger, you two look good together." She smiled and asked me if I wanted another frou-frou drink. I ordered a shot of Jack. She dumped it in a plastic cup, and I dumped it in my mouth.

"Thanks."

"No problem, Roger. It's on me. Congrats on getting back to work." She winked there at the end, and I watched her walk off to tend bar. I was bewildered. My heart had been racing and hand shaky. My knee was bouncing so fast I might have split the bar in half if it connected. Now, like ice, Alysa wanders in, pours a drink, flirts and leaves. Was that flirting? *Women*.

Rosa came back and took her seat that several others tried to take. I looked around at the crowd and decided I just couldn't take being there. I felt the sweat roll down my back. I had enough of this place.

We shouted at each other, hearing only every third word so our communication relied heavily on smiling and nodding. The music stopped giving us time to catch up on what we already said. After a second round of drinks, more darting stares from Alysa the music started up again.

"Can we go someplace a little quieter?"

"I didn't think you were that old." Rosa laughed. She got up without settling her tab. I tossed thirty down in cash hoping it was enough. We cut through the crowd as the band struck up another song. People got up from their tables and smooshed in on each other as legs and arms went out in sporadic dance.

We exited out the back that opened to the white sandy beach. Rosa took her wedges off and stuck her toes in the sand, still warm from the blazing sun of the day. There was no wind and no waves, just a light water slapping the hard-packed shore of a low tide. We headed south, away from the noise and lights of the pier and boardwalk.

"Now that you got me all alone, what would you like to talk about?" Rosa asked looking down at the wet sand giving way under her toes.

"Tell me more about Tara. Did you know her? I mean did you ever get to actually talk to her?" I felt the tiny grains of sand crunch inside my Vans. I wished I had just taken them off earlier. They were new slip-ons still fresh and white around the soles.

"Um, yeah, I guess. I don't really have contact with patients." Rosa put her hands together and locked her elbows. "How'd you know her?"

"I grew up with her and was always at her house. She was like my sister."

"Hey, I thought you said she was your sister." Rosa jabbed at my ribs. She was smirking to keep it playful, but her voice was sharp, and her shoulders were tense. I was not the only guy to come around asking about Tara. Oliver Lean paid plenty to keep people away and reserve exclusive access.

"Well, no, not by blood. We always would say that about each other, and I said it without thinking."

"Oh, I'm sure you thought it through, you're not stupid George. I can see that in your eyes." She stopped walking and turned towards me, staring up at my eyes. She lingered there and then said, "I've got a pretty good bullshit detector and right now it's going off. So, come out with it." Any forced playfulness was gone. She was all business right now. If I hadn't already checked her hands for weapons, I could have sworn she had a pistol pointed at my nuts.

"I'm a private investigator looking in on Tara Johnson."

"Glad that's out of the way. I was beginning to think you were just some kind of a weirdo." She didn't flinch at the revelation.

Rosa had a strength about her. In both lines of work, at the old folks' home and being a cam girl, there was always that shock value she had to get used to. Either from the old patients wandering around naked in the nursing home to the creepy basement dwelling super fans on the cam-site who try and find your home address.

I couldn't help but chuckle, "Weirdo? What did I say that made me weird?"

Rosa leaned into me, nudging me with her shoulder, then pulled away. "Just your questions. I could tell I liked you, what's not to like?" She ran her hands along my tattoo covered biceps and down veined forearms. "Your story about being in advertising and then the questions about Tara, I wasn't sure, just wasn't sure about you."

"I guess I'm not very good at the undercover work."

We had walked along awhile talking about how the job at Whispering Pines had been a steppingstone in career path until she dropped out of nursing school. Without that degree she couldn't advance. There was no mention of the Glory Cats gig. The typical story of this town, a town that promises all kinds of mediocre rewards if you could just reach the top of the hill, life would coast the rest of the way down. I had been there. Success was always just around the corner for this town. With a handful of the very wealthy and their beach homes lining the dunes it all seemed so easy. Everyone knew someone who had made it and they were next. When I hit a bank and made off with more than five grand, I would hit the town and live like I thought I was born to. Over tipping a bartender would lead to bottle service which would lead to a private party that lead to a house party and then a real house party on the beach. Parties like that, the inevitable *what do you do* question and when I couldn't answer the top tier in this town lost interest. All the while the people changed, I thought I belonged, until I woke up and realized the town is the real thief, taking you for all you think you are. I grew up fast and dropped out of that life, keeping a low profile while honing my skills, making bigger scores, and choosing better targets. The life just got too hot, constantly rounded up as a suspect or under surveillance by cops. I was a prisoner without the bars.

Along the shoreline, hotels gave way to mansions nestled in the dunes. Most of them large black silhouettes against the night sky. It was the wrong time of year to be occupied; these were winter homes. We moved from the water's edge up to the soft white sand and tall grass. I took Rosa by the wrist and sat her down pulling her towards me. She plopped down next to me in the sand. The humidity was high, but the offshore breeze kicked up and kept our skin dry to the touch. I studied her deep brown eyes, sinking into total emersion. I couldn't control my hand as it touched the side of her cheek. Her lips parted as she exhaled.

Rosa grabbed my hips and twisted them into hers, pulling me on top of her. She laid back bending her knees and digging her heels into the soft dune. Her dress slid to her hips. I ran my hand along the inside of her thigh until my fingertip touched her warm center. She moaned and clenched, pushing her pelvis up pressuring my finger to go deeper. She wanted me to taste it. I planted my other hand on the side of her head and locked my elbow, leaning into a deep kiss. Her sharp fingernails dug into my taught, rounded off shoulders. Her fuse was lit; it was only a matter of time before she exploded.

Once it was over for the both of us, I rolled to my side with Rosa's head cradled into my left bicep.

Rosa looked up at my blue eyes, "Damn," She shuttered as a chill went up and down her spine remembering every second, "That was quick."

"Sorry, it's been a while."

"No, no you're fine. I meant me. I don't think I've ever…" She let the sentence hang there as she focused on her breathing. She mumbled something in Spanish that I didn't understand but assumed by her smile it was good.

The moon was out, full and white. The rolling waves had increased as the tide drew closer to us. Tucked in a dune we lay wrapped in each other's arms. I tasted the salt on my lips, caught there from the offshore breeze. Rosa looked up at the stars, the constellations, and asked random questions about them. I did my best to answer but I never was big into astronomy. I needed to ask a few questions of my own but didn't want to ruin this. My body was totally relaxed allowing my mind to lazily wander to thoughts of the Scout and how soon Rosa and I could lay in the back and stare up at the stars. It was the future I was watching and not the case that brought me here. The time came to bring us back to reality, back from off this little island escape, to the reality of the porn peddling blackmailer I was going to kill in the morning.

"George, what's your real name?" She said it so smooth as if asking for the time. Her fingers twisted into mine as she wrapped her little hand around my large one.

My eyes widened taking in more stars in the black sky. "What makes you think it's not?" I asked letting her get us back to reality first.

"When I came back from the bathroom. I saw your long wide back leaning over the bar in that tight tee shirt and I just realized I'd seen you there before." Her other hand came around and rested on my hip.

I didn't say anything.

"So, what is it?"

"Roger."

"Roger? Really? You look like a Sean or something hard, something like… I don't know, Steel."

I laughed. I wasn't sure what this girl saw in me. I didn't feel like Steel, if that was even a real name. "Most people call me by my last name, Grimes."

She repeated the name out loud then said, "Now that fits. Grimes, doing grimy things."

"Pretty much my life story." There was a stretch of silence after that. It was getting late and the sand was losing its appeal, turning from a stimulant to an irritant. I needed to get the information that would end the night.

"Tell me about Oliver Lean."

Rosa sat up. She drew her knees to her chest and bent her sandy elbows over the tops of them. Her chin rested on her forearms. "Who?"

"Now, my bullshit detector is going off."

She covered her face with slender fingers tipped in lavender paint.

Through her fingers she said, "He is just a guy who pays Tara's bills at the home."

"He is more than that."

Rosa dropped her hands but avoided eye contact. Her mouth cocked to the side as she forced a confession of her other job to me, knowing that I already knew.

"You're a real sweet guy. I had lost hope of meeting one of you, the good ones. After going through so many bad ones, I settled on just getting paid for my looks. You know while they lasted." She smiled and looked up at me.

My face was still, numb to her sob story, a story I heard too many times. The other men in her life, so called Alpha Males, used women for all they want and then leaving to plant their seeds in greener pastures.

"Whatever it is you want with Lean; you should drop it." Rosa inserted backbone to her somber warning. "Stay away from him Roger."

"He's in danger and I want to help him."

"That'd be a first. I didn't know he had friends he didn't buy." She looked at me like I had just fed her grandmother a knuckle sandwich. I felt the acid rise in my stomach. I hated to press Rosa after what we shared, but I would have to, to get the answers I needed. Lean was running out of time and that meant so was I. The more I learned about Lean the more I wanted to kill him. Still, I needed to get paid first.

"No, I was bought." I sat up. "Someone is trying to kill him. I just want to find out who so I can get paid."

"Oh." Rosa sat there with a crease between her eyes as wheels turned. The feeling of me inside her was fresh. It hadn't been like anything she has had in a long time. Sex on camera wasn't real, the orgasm was real, but it was just a reaction, like when the doctor hits your knee with a little hammer, your body just reacts. I was in her head. What she just experienced went on more in between her ears than her legs. She wanted it again and again for the rest of her life. Telling the man who sat beside her all she knew, may cost her that.

"Let him die. Wouldn't be the worst thing that happened." Her soft hand went out and wrapped around my bicep.

I stood up and put out my hand. Rosa slipped her hand into mine.

"Do you think the security guard, Jennings, has it in him ..." I never finished my question. Rosa erupted in laughter.

"That lard ass?" She let the laughter die and her eyes thinned at the corners. "He did have it bad for Tara. It's possible, she wasn't always drugged up you know. I guess if she wanted him to do it." Rosa let me fill in the blank. I already knew she wanted him to.

Rosa's laughter at the thought of Jennings actually killing Lean was enough to dial back any urgency to protect Lean. He had guards and his crew, there was no need for me to sit around and wait with them. We walked along unsure how much physical contact was appropriate now that we both knew who the other truly was. I contemplated if letting Oliver Lean get killed was the same as killing him. Finally, when Rosa could no longer stand not being touched, I put my arm over her shoulders and pulled her into me. She nuzzled into my neck, safe and warm.

I took my time with Rosa. I let her enjoy the date she had hoped for. I walked her back to her car, and we made out a little. She kept squeezing me like I was a giant stuffed bear she just won at a carnival. I could feel her appreciation, for what, I didn't know. Without the invite back to her place, I had to ask a hard question.

"Might be weird, but would you mind watching a clip of Tara with Jennings threatening Lean"

"They recorded it?"

"He's wearing a hood, so he thinks he's safe." I reached in my pocket and pulled the video up on my phone.

Rosa leaned against the Lexus. Her hand cupped the side of the phone to amplify the sound. She let it play one time through then slid her finger and backed it up to a certain point. She handed me the phone, "That's not Jennings."

"What?" I took the phone back and watched the end of the video.

"Sargent has a tattoo on his forearm. Your guy doesn't."

I stared into the small screen blocking out everything around me. Deep in my thoughts I waded through the thick confusion and certainty that I had unmasked the Hood. Now I had to start over.

"I wasn't doping her." Rosa said with a slight shudder. My eyes came off the little screen to meet her soft brown eyes. "I just, I had to let Lean in to do it. He would have got me fired. I want to be a nurse not a porn star. The cam life is paying off my outstanding loans so I can take classes again. Once I'm debt free, I'm out, for real." She ran her fingers through pitch black curls. Her face was a shade lighter as nerves twitched in her stomach, turning it over. Guilt consumed her and she needed to purge it.

My arms wrapped around her. I wanted to believe her story, turning a new leaf and all. She had made me feel ten feet tall, a regular Paul Bunyan, I could get used to that. Crystal had burned me out for a long while. The turbulence was constantly making me sick. My circle of friends shrank as Billy and I got more and more into stealing. Now a girl stood before me that made a lot of that go away, but I just didn't buy her student debt story as she pulled back on the handle of the Lexus. A cell phone wrang from her Prada purse and letting me know her baggage was more than I could carry.

She flipped through the messages quickly. I kissed the top of her head and in my heart said goodbye.

Rosa got in her car and started it up. She was all smiles as she waved goodbye. I turned to walk away when the horn beeped. I looked back. She had the window down. The radio was on but turned too low to make out what song played.

The moon that was once full and bright became smeared with thick grey clouds. A soft mist began to fall, covering everything with little diamonds. I wiped off my shaved head and walked for the car. There went another woman in and out of my life in twenty-four hours. Sunny's words lingered, *it's better than being a stripper*. I knew I was better off not pursuing Rosa. The fear of the drama that would ensue, the nights out waiting for a guy to approach our table asking where he had seen her before and then wanting to smash his face when he remembered.

My cell had a text. It was Lean checking in this time to see if I was still alive or if Aziz had made good on his threats. Fun and games for this punk. I decided I wouldn't report that I was about to wrap things up, instead I wanted to let him worry.

It was hard not to break the tires loose on the Olds as I sped out for Jennings's place again. Maybe he wasn't the Hood, but he might know where Tara was.

The light was still on and the back door still easy to access. No one was home. I had gone over the place earlier but didn't know what I was looking for. This time it had to be something small, a detail that will tell me where Jennings was or whom the Hood was.

All the kitchen drawers were checked, under the sink and even in the refrigerator. I moved on to the desk with the computer. It was locked and I was no hacker. I next checked in the bathroom and spotted it. There on white blinds that needed to be dusted was a tight cluster of tiny blood spatter.

The splatter was dried but had no dust on it. I took a picture with my phone and kept searching. Behind the sink, running down the side of the vanity was a pink smear. The light from my cell spotted on the wood floor, down the hall and into the spare bedroom.

I had looked over the room last time I was here, but that was when I was searching for living people. As soon as I opened the closet door, I saw him on the floor. A fixed stare, mouth open, held together by several layers of saranwrap from head to toe. Jennings had his throat cut open. Blood pooled and bubbled in the small bulges under the plastic wrap. His arm was down by his side. I popped open my knife and cut into the wrap. The tattoo checked with what Rosa described.

I snapped a picture with my cellphone. The police would have to be notified. There was no way I could leave Jennings stuffed in his own closet while the killers ran wild and made a play for my only client.

As I began to dial 911, a murmur came from the other end of the closet. It was dark at that end with clothes and boxes blocking any ambient light from the room. I pulled on the chain, but the bulb didn't work. Pushing the hanging sport coats aside, I saw her there wide eyed and bound.

Tara was squirming as I grabbed her by the wrists and dragged her over Jennings's cold corpse and onto the wood floor of the bedroom. The gag came out as I went to work on the electrical cord binding her.

"Who did this?" I asked her.

"It all happened so fast." She was still wiggling, her adrenaline was pumping hard, sparking her nerves into action. I needed her to hold still so I could untie the cord. Her feet were freed. I started on her wrists. The cord was not tight and there were no red marks around her wrists. My hands slowed.

Tara slowed her breathing and stopped shaking her wrists.

"Who did this?" Anger crept in my voice.

She smiled and held her hands out for me to untie. Heartbeat, hair on my neck and all the other little signs scrambling to get a message out from the normally quiet part of your brain. The frightened girl in front of me was jamming the signal as my hands worked independently to unbind her.

Just as her wrists were freed, my attention shifted to a stocky guy about as tall as I came through with his arms extended. Wrapped in his plump fingers was a shiny gun.

I dove before I heard the crack. The bullet impact turned the old plaster to dust. I rolled behind the bed. Another crack and the mattress shook. I reached behind me and slung the Glock out. My hand went out to shoot under the bed when a small foot in a black shoe came swinging into my face. I managed to fire off a round that pinged off the bed leg.

Another crack then a man's voice, "C'mon, c'mon!"

Through one eye I saw little black shoes bounce away. The other eye was a watery blur as tears mixed with blood. I got to my feet keeping the eye pinched shut and scrambled over the bed. Taking a chance, I peeked through the doorway and into the short hall. Tara was grasping for her bag as the Hood pulled her away, telling her to keep moving.

I fired. The bullet missed by an inch and punched a hole through the hollow wood door of the garage.

The Hood shot over his shoulder, as he crashed through the door dragging Tara with him. I returned fire twice, but they were gone.

Tires squealed down the drive as I watched the early 2000's Toyota make a right. I ran to the Olds and hopped in. The V8 rumbled to life and both tires grabbed asphalt, pushing the old steel down the road.

A block down the road ended in a T intersection. I never saw which way they went after that. I chose left. After a few blocks there was no sign of them.

I circled back to Jennings's house and so were the sirens. It was time to phone a friend just in case I left a piece of me at Jennings's.

A voice filled mostly with labored breath pushed through the cell and into my ear, "Yeah, hello."

"It's Grimes."

"Shit." Camp covered the mic and I heard muffled voices then silence until she came back on, "I aint on duty, Grimes. Now what'chu want at this hour?"

"I found a body in his own closet, thought you should know."

"Call 9-1-1."

"Isn't this part of your job?"

"I go on duty in…four hours. Shit don't you ever sleep Grimes?"

"I'll just phone the tip line."

"Now you're talking. 'Night." Camp hung up.

Deputy Camp's apathy for Jennings' murder poked at my insides enough to irritate me. The things I did last year to bust up a child sex ring, all the work, the killing, and Camp got the credit. She admitted it came through a tip, but it was her face on the news, her promotion and all of it without firing a shot. She owed me one for the day shift she was on now. This wouldn't be the one I got from her.

Chapter 9

Tara and the Hood were out for blood and Lean was next on the list. Now that knew everyone's role in this tangled seaweed, I had no problem bringing Tara to Aziz. The only thing left would be to get the black mail to him as well.

A single fluorescent light above a metal door cast white-blue rays down over the concrete slab leading the way to the porno palace. Large moths gathered and chased small mosquitos around the lamp's glass. It was a real turf war for the bugs but isn't it always like that for bugs.

I opened a bright orange can of liquid energy and listened to it pop and fizz. Billy asked me not to drink in his car. He didn't say anything about bleeding in it. I slurped the top and felt an alertness return to my senses.

Now that I knew what Aziz wanted me to steal, I could make a plan. A plan takes time, surveillance, gathering intel on security, bribes to guards or employees and sometimes a good partner. All the things I didn't have time to do.

Lean wasn't answering his phone. I had to make my own way in. The suppressor on my Glock did well as a forty-five round shattered the plastic cover and blew apart the bulb leaving the door covered in darkness. I crossed the street. At the door, I hooked my code scanner up to the keypad. The keypad was low grade with only a four-symbol code required. Quickly the code scanner figured out the correct combo of numbers and the electronic lock buzzed the release.

Inside the place was enormous. The floor was cement with tall plywood hallways that trailed off further than I could see. Dim yellow low watt bulbs hung from metal hooks and joined by extension cords to light each hallway. A tinder box waiting for a tragedy. Lean must pay a pretty dime to code enforcement for a passing grade. Large maroon steel beams ascended into the ceiling.

Along the support walls, metal stairways went up to a second level, leading to more brown doors and plywood walls. Muffled beats accompanied by moans and screams came and went as I stalked the hallways.

At the top of a stairway a soft voice came down. "Grimes? Hey Grimes."

I looked up to see Abby leaning over the railing. Her pleated plaid skirt lifted in the back and her perky breasts pushed against sheer button-down shirt. Typical pigtail schoolgirl, normally a sexy outfit, she managed to make that classic look bland. I went to the base of the stairs. "Where is Lean's office?"

She pointed, and I started walking again. She said something, but I wasn't listening. Mission minded, I pressed on, keeping a clear head but ready to kill Tara and the Hood if I had to. Crystal was dead, Jennings dead and now Lean may be as well. The killing had to stop even I was the one doing it.

The next hallway ended short with a mountain of XXXL denim jacket with shiny brass button. In XXXL hands rests a pistol grip pump action. He swung the shotgun up to hold with both hands.

"I'm here to see Lean, he's expecting me." I said not slowing my pace. My head was low, my shoulders squared as I walked towards the man at the door.

The man towered over me, the shotgun in his hands. He looked down at my shaved head and said, "Roger Grimes, is that you?"

I threw a 1, 2, and 3 fast and sharp. The man went down, his eyes rolling in the back of his head. I picked up the shotgun and broke it down. I pocketed the shells and tossed the two halves down the hall. Listening at the door I heard a TV playing an infomercial on trimming belly fat. Slowly, I turned the knob and was glad it was not locked.

The room was dark with only the TV to illuminate the office. On the left was a desk with a computer commanding three monitors. In the other corner was a couch and end table. The TV was hung on the wall in the middle. On the couch was the black slumberous outline of Lean. His eyes shut, mouth open, he snored away. His shirt was off and so were his pants. He was dressed in just a pair of tight black boxer briefs. I went back into the hall.

With both hands, I grabbed hold of the fat man's denim coat. I slid the dazed man into the room and shut the door. I propped the man up against the couch and turned on the lights. The man mumbled then looked up. That's when I realized I knew Sherman Whitworth.

"Sorry about that Sherm." I squatted a few feet away to be on eye level with a guy I was in county lock-up with.

"Shit." He rubbed his jaw. "Didn't I kick yo sorry ass while we was in county?"

"Sorta. You kind 'a had help." I looked at Lean still asleep. "Why is 3rd Street running protection on this shit bag?"

"He pay cash moneys. I'm here on my own." Sherman rubbed his face with thick fingers.

I put out my hand and helped the big guy to his feet. Sherman sat on the arm of the sofa. Lean kept on sleeping. "Lean said he was in trouble and needed some help. He stopped by Benny's Barber Shop and flashed some cash, I was in there for a fade and said shit, I'll do it. I thought I'd be watching the girls get freaky 'n shit but nah, bitch made me sit on that stool all day."

"Whatever it is, it aint enough. His girlfriend wants him dead, his employees tried to kill him, and so is a guy in a black hood, but I need Lean alive." I started rummaging through the computer desk and paused. Looking back at Sherman I said, "You gonna stop me if I take him out of here?" I asked, hoping Sherman would say no. I didn't want to reignite any beef with 3rd Street.

Before Sherman could respond the door kicked in. A round man in a black hood waved a gun around. "Freeze!" The Smith & Wesson pistol was Jennings's but the man holding it was not. He wore a mesh grey tank top turned inside out and had on black cargo shorts and black work boots.

"Get over there." He barked and waved the pistol.

Sherman and I stood in the corner. Lean cleared his throat and sat up. All blurry eyed from slumber, he rubbed them straight. He looked around and then stood up.

"Who tha …, what tha …" Lean looked at me and then to the Hood. "What the fuck is going on here?" he shouted.

"You," the gunman pointed, "Sit down." He turned back to us, "Get down on your knees."

I had a hard time with this command. The Hood was a wanna be piece of shit and I wouldn't be shot by that coward while on my knees. On the other hand, it would buy time to jump him.

The Hood moved up on me, putting the pistol just out of reach. "Oh, I can't wait to kill you. It's gonna hurt." He turned his attention back to Lean. "You first."

"Listen guy," Lean began to negotiate. He had no spine. Everything he had been trying to accomplish was falling in on itself. To blackmail people affectively, he needed a little muscle behind him. The men he had, the ones I left at my feet, weren't enough. Their tough guy attitudes and threats might have worked on people like Derrick Sills, but it only fueled my desire to destroy them.

The Hood was not having any more of Lean's stalling. He cocked the pistol and pointed it at Lean's head. "You're gonna die for what you done."

Lean stammered and began moving around. The gunman was trailing him with the pistol but growing frustrated at the moving target.

He fired a shot. "Hold still dammit!"

His voice and movements all came together. "Eddy don't." I said getting the pistol pointed at me. I had my hands up and remained calm, "This shit bag isn't worth it, and neither is Tara."

Eddy cocked his head to the side like a dog hearing the word treat. "Don't you say her name. You have no right."

"She isn't worth it, and neither was killing Jennings."

"I, I didn't kill Jennings. She did." Eddy was sweating through his hood.

"That's right," I said, soothing him, "Think man, do you really want to do this? I don't think you do."

"That's where you're wrong dipshit!" Eddy waved the gun around frantically. All the movement from the three of his hostages was giving him a headache. He had been so certain of what he was going to do when he walked through the door moments ago. Now my words had planted a doubt in his weak mind. He looked up as the hood slipped over his eyes and he quickly adjusted it, waving the gun as he did.

"Grimes," Lean said in a loud whisper, "If he kills me, you won't get paid." He looked over to Sherman, "You either." Sherman shook his head; he didn't care this much. It was one thing to sit at a door and scare people away, it was another to take a bullet for some guy you don't even like.

Eddy turned to Lean once more. The hood dipped over Eddy's eyes. I leapt, wrapping my arms around the heavyset bouncer. The gun went off, the bullet ripped through a computer monitor, sending sparks into the air. The man had strong legs and I had gone in too high. Eddy swung the pistol back and forth keeping me on my toes as he turned. He spun us one more time. My grip failed on his sliming skin and rolled across the floor. Lean's eyes were darting from Eddy to the door and back again. He made a break for the door. The gun went off again. Lean fell before getting out.

Sherman stepped up and clocked Eddy in the head. The round man crumpled. I pulled the pistol out of his hand. Lean scrambled along the floor like a toddler learning to walk. He was more nervous now that I had the gun. Disgust pushed the fear from his face, his crew was stupid for going after me so soon. That damn Juan Carlos just really wanted to face me the way Crystal talked about me. Lean had to see me fall. All of that was over now.

"Sherman," I nodded, "you otta go."

Lean yelled about not paying him if he runs and being a coward and some other crap, but Sherman didn't care. He was there for a paycheck, and this was not worth the pay. He nodded to me and left.

Sweat rolled down Lean's olive face and dripped off his jaw on to his neckline. Standing in his underwear near the computers, Lean held his hands up. He said, "Cool it, alright. I'll get you the cash. You did your job."

Lean moved toward his desk, and I leveled the pistol.

"Just cool it alright. I'm getting the cash."

"I need the blackmail." I said moving closer.

"What?" Lean backed up to his desk.

"Don't waste my time. I need the blackmail."

"Aziz." Lean said shaking his head. "Aziz is just using you man. Haven't you wondered why Aziz just doesn't kill me himself? Boghos could snap me like a twig." Lean said trying to back up but running out of floor space. "I told you Aziz was my partner, not my boss. I'm a made man. Aziz can't touch me, neither can you."

With an open hand, I slapped Lean across the face.

Lean threw up his hands, "Whoa, before you go all cowboy, Grimes, remember I hold all the cards. Take a look." He slowly moved his hand down and grabbed the mouse on the desk. A few clicks later and one of the monitors showed a hallway with three men laying on the floor. Chester and Kyle laying still on the floor.

"Shit." Lean said keeping his head low.

"The Hood came here to kill you. This isn't a joke. Those men are dead."

Lean spun around, "The Hood is a myth, a crazy fan who doesn't know when to quit."

"We're leaving and taking the blackmail with us. I know you don't keep the blackmail in the cloud. You're too paranoid about that. So, hand it over."

Lean smirked.

A side door opened and out stepped Juan Carlos. His Nikes sweeping the floor, he floated circling me. His hands circling, climbing higher. "It's about time homie?"

This was the fight he had been waiting for. The tales of me told by Crystal fed his imagination as he became obsessed with throwing hands with the *biggest, baddest man* Crystal had known. Only she won't be here to see it.

"Get him out of here Juan!" Lean spat.

Juan moved fast. My pistol barked, ripping through Lean's knee. I should have shot Juan but keeping Lean in sight was my choice. Betting Juan would flinch was another losing bet on my part as his quick hands grabbed my wrist as I turned towards him. He twisted and had the momentum with him. Another split-second decision was to go with the momentum and let the pistol fly across the room. We tangled like snakes then exploded apart.

Juan was going to get what he came for and it would have to be bareknuckle. With his speed I didn't dare reach in my pocket for the brass I carried. There was no witty banter on my part. We squared off. His hands were up, and his feet barely touched the concrete beneath us. I was breathing heavier than I should have, a result of the months of self-loathing and alcohol indulgence. Uncertainty clenched my muscles taught. Self-doubt began to twist my guts into fear. Now, I had to face off with a guy who has been wanting a piece of me for a while. He's worked it out in his head already. My casual cockiness now left me exposed. Breathe.

His leg jetted; my muscle memory was quick with a block. I flinched waiting for a counter strike that came in the form of a grin across his slimy face.

A flying left came at me, but I was fast to throw up my arm and protect my face. The blow glanced off my arm. I stepped out turning ninety degrees allowing Juan to completely miss the next assault with his right. I retaliated with a fast one, two. Juan Carlos tucked, my blows glancing off his head. He staggered to his left and leaned against the wall. A straight leg kick checked Juan into the wall. The man bounced off and came back towards me. I hit him again with a driving left.

A frozen moment hung in the air as a one second took sixty when both Juan Carlos, and I, thought his knees would buckle, but he held them. I stopped my forward momentum intending to finish him. Regaining his feet, he backed away in a semicircle motion.

He was failing at the one thing he wanted most, to beat me. I wouldn't give him the satisfaction. I knew what he would do before I even got close enough for him to do it. His left came wide, I blocked. His right followed quickly, I blocked. My right leg went out and stuck deep into his stomach. Yellow bile like egg yolk sprayed from between his lips. I felt the splatter on my neck.

He fell, sprawling out on his back. He was quick to roll to his side and start to get up but paused as his stomach spasmed. I stomped the back of his left elbow and heard it snap. He screamed. My knuckles slipped on the brass and so he was out cold.

"Fuck you, Grimes." The porn peddler was on the floor screaming. His hands wrapped around the open wound. Blood and ligaments covered his tightly gripped fingers. Lean grew a sneer that transitioned into a smug smile. "I'm not giving you shit; I'm protected remember. Aziz is gonna kill you anyway. You hear me!" Lean's voice reached an octave I could barely hear.

Lean managed a smile through the pain, "You're too late, Grimes. It doesn't matter 'cause Aziz is gonna kill, gonna kill us both."

A fire welled up inside me, brought on by Juan Carlos and stoked knowing Lean killed Crystal. I had been pulled into a clustered mess of blackmail, double crosses and greed. Everyone was wearing a mask, pretending to be someone they weren't. Lean wasn't a tough mafioso, Crystal wasn't the caring sister and all the girls in this building selling fantasy and friendship to lonely people online. It was time to put an end all the back and forth and tear the mask of all of them.

I knelt and went to work with a fist of brass on his other joints. Brass collided with flesh until it gave way to bone. His elbow popped, ribs cracked, his eyes bulged. Blue and purple veins ran rivers of blood just under the skin of his forehead. The pain was too much. Lean rolled around on the floor moaning. Sweat beaded on his skin, yet he shivered cold. Quick, shallow breaths kept him from saying anything else.

Killing wouldn't solve any of my problems. I eased up and regained a focus on the blackmail. I went through every drawer in his desk while Lean rolled around on the floor. He would cry then laugh as I crawled under the desk looking for a hidden compartment. Then his cries and laughter stopped. I looked up to see Tara on top of him. Her knees were on the ground as she straddled him. Her hands were wrapped around a black nylon stocking, twisted tight around the man's throat. Her mouth was open, and her teeth gritted shut. Drool strung down from her lower lip, nearly reaching Lean's chest. His gurgles filled the silent room.

I shoved her hard. She went tumbling across the room.

Tara spun around and quickly bounced to her feet, wiped the drool from her mouth and stuffed the stocking in her shorts pocket. "What are you doing?" she screeched. Her hair was shorter and curlier. She lacked all the porn makeup I was used to seeing her covered in. She had on an orange sleeveless shirt and khaki shorts.

"I need the blackmail, Tara. Hand it over and you can do what you want with him." I scanned the room for my pistol. It was near the couch. I walked carefully, casually as Tara began doing the same. She stopped at Eddy's lifeless corpse. My foot covered over my Glock.

"What does it matter Grimes? If we don't get out of town, we'll all be dead."

I saw the stab wounds in Eddy's gut. She knelt and touched his face. The nylon stocking came out of her pocket and went into the dead man's hand. She whispered something to him, but I couldn't hear what she said.

"Unless you have nine grand, I'm taking you with me." I said.

Lean was coughing, still lying on the floor, still bleeding from wounds I gave him. He was trying to talk but being choked and in pain nothing came out.

Tara turned and looked up at me. I had a pistol pointed at her. Rage built and she could spit acid. Her hair was tangled and frazzled. She was breathing heavy, and her little fists were balled with hate at the end of skinny arms. She came to kill Lean and I was now in her way, denying her the greatest satisfaction she could think of.

She said nothing to me.

"I'm not going to shoot you, I want you to get out of here, just leave town and never come back, Tara." I moved to position myself between Lean and her. I still needed Lean alive long enough to tell me where the blackmail was stored. She looked past me with those hate filled eyes.

"You'll have Aziz coming for you." I said.

Tara stood with her hands on her hips. "Aziz doesn't scare me."

"He wants you back, Tara."

She laughed, "He only wants me dead. I did the dirty work for him and now I'm just a loose end. If you send me back there, he'll kill me or worse."

"Then now is your only chance. Run, get out of here and forget about Aziz and Lean and all of this."

Tara covered her face with her hands, newly dyed blonde hair falling over her fingers. She looked up and moved closer to me. Her hands went out, "I don't know what to do."

The gun went back into my waist.

"You better move."

"What?"

Tara was fast on her kick sending her foot up to my crotch. I was faster closing my legs, catching her ankle. Next, I dropped my right foot back and blocked a wild right punch. My left went out and four fingers wrapped around her throat with my thumb closing off her windpipe. Her eyes bulged as I lifted her to her tiptoes. She punched, sending small-balled fists to my chest, I took the blows.

Then I grabbed her one arm and letting her throat go, grabbed her other arm.

"You're dead already Tara, killing you won't be a big deal."

"You really don't know shit Grimes. I had it all figured out at Whispering Pines and just needed to get Jennings on the hook. He was in love with me, always coming in my room, in the corner watching. Most of the time I pretended I was asleep because if he caught me awake, he would talk my damn ear off. Ugghh, it was worse than the heroin withdrawals to listen to that fat bastard dribble on." Her body relaxed. I let her go completely.

"So, you got Jennings hooked and then what? Did he back out after his threats got too hot? So, you replaced him with Eddy."

A shrill scream pierced my ears. She was losing and she knew it.

"And you're so different Roger? My sister came to see you and wanted you to do the same and you agreed and for nothing." She smiled like she had one over on him.

"For money." I said flatly.

"Bullshit. You did it for a girl you never got over." She walked over Eddy's body like he wasn't there. Jennings was on his side bleeding out of a hole in his gut. His eyes were half open and one arm reaching out. Lean was on his back, with a bullet in his knee and bruising across his face. Tara was delusional if she thought the cops would buy this scene, Eddy and Lean killing each other. Now that she had tampered with everything, I was left to clean it all up. If Lean died, I may never find the blackmail or get the money to pay Aziz back. All this work wasn't adding up to be worth the payout.

"All this for revenge?"

Tara threw her hands up and smiled out of the side of her mouth.

"No, Roger. The blackmail. It was all my idea. I set it up from Aziz's boss to the average shmoos. It's mine, not his, not Aziz's."

Lean shouted somethings between wincing in pain.

Tara strolled casually through the doorway, as if browsing a sale at the mall. As she sauntered down the plywood hall, she pulled a Bic lighter from her pocket. I barely heard the word as she said, "Run?"

The blue and yellow flame raced towards me, passing through the doorway and to the bodies. The heat was intense as I lifted my arms to cover my face. All traces of this twisted world I found myself in were quickly being licked up by flames. Soon everything would be but ash. And what about the rest of the girls in the rooms?

Lean shouted for me to help him. He cried out he didn't want to die.

"Tell me where the blackmail is!" I shouted as the heat intensified.

"It's not here. Quick, get me out, I can't walk."

"Where is it?" Smoke was blurring my eyes. Breathing was becoming difficult.

"Get me out and I'll tell you." Lean said as he reached out for my hand.

I grabbed his arm and started to drag him, but what about the others? The girls in their rooms unaware of the flames just out their door. I jumped the line of fire and ran down the hall. As I went, I banged on as many doors as I could until I got to Abby's door. I kicked it in and found the staged bedroom empty.

I went back through the wooden halls as smoke chased me, catching me at every turn. I shouted and slapped against the unfinished plywood walls. My eyes stung from soot. Somewhere in the back of the building something collapsed, metal and wood fell as fire ate away their support. I kept running, kept shouting until my lungs could take no more.

Outside the fresh air shut my eyes and filled my polluted lungs. I was bent over, my hands pushing down on my knees coughing out the smoke. Sweat dripped off my head onto the white powdery ground. Behind me the glow of orange flames cast my shadow long into the night. A group of women stood, watching, hands over mouths, as their place of employment came crashing down.

I watched in the radiance of the fire as the smoke blocked out the stars and disappeared into the night. I saw Sunny tucked under Abby's low hanging arms. They both watched their world crumble.

Chapter 10

The first thing I needed to do, was go home, to my actual apartment, and shower and change. Tara can wait. It had been a few long days of other people's problems. I guess that's what you step into when you're a PI. If I didn't know better, I'd say that's where the term 'gumshoe' comes from, other people's problems sticking like gum on your shoe. I thought I would be hired to help one side win, to expose liars and dirt bags. Instead, I was helping keep them alive. Money doesn't care about character, it never has. Money to keep alive a blackmailer like Oliver Lean and money to cover my gambling debts. Money doesn't care that I told Lean I'd keep him alive and then turned around and let him die.

I pushed open the door to a startled roommate who immediately rolled away from me on the couch. There on the coffee table was his laptop with a porn video playing. He reached out and shut the laptop.

"What up bra?" Brock said in a shaky tone.

"Nothing." I came in, kicked off my Vans and headed for the bathroom. He said something, but I wasn't listening. I needed to move out. I was too old and too much of a loner to have a roommate.

The hot water rolled off my body as I stood in the shower letting my skin soak in the moisture. The steam filled my nostrils, draining them. Black soot flushed from my sinuses as I leaned my head forward. I scrubbed the dried blood from under my nails and washed the rest of my body down removing filth and grime of the day, sending it down the drain. The soap stung as it cleansed my open wounds on my face and knuckles. The back of my head started to bleed again. I was tired, I needed a break. I needed that cold beer on Billy's velvet couch in his basement. I needed to get Aziz off my back, and I needed to smash Boghos's face for making me piss my pants. I hadn't forgot about that.

I laid on my bed, fresh from the shower. I was hungry but too tired to get up and all the food in the refrigerator was my roommate's anyway. My hand ran over my buzzed head. I needed to cut it again soon.

Darkness engulfed my mind until my cell phone erupted with texts. My eye lids were too heavy to fully open. My hand flopped around the bed, using my ears to guide in search of the phone. I clicked the button on the side to silence it. With the noise gone, I could escape back to the blackness and run fast towards whatever the next dream would have for me. But the dream never came. My eyes popped open and the rush of thoughts about the case charged in, pushing the sleep from my brain.

I sat up. *Fuck,* I breathed out. Every muscle came alive in fire as I felt my heart thumping in my skull. Exhaustion was the only thing that had silenced my restless mind. I scratched at a prickly jaw. My phone was still flashing alerts. My thumb skimmed through the texts. Rosa then Sunny, back and forth with a group chat. Abby was in the mix as well. There was also a separate text from an unknown number, but the message told me who it was.

The text read: *You failed. Time to pay up.*

Aziz knew Lean was dead and I would be now whether I squared the debt or not. He wanted the blackmail and I failed to find it. There was a chance my relationship with Smitty was on the ups and he could intervene. Sanford wouldn't do it, he never approved of my gambling. Times like this I regret being such a loner. Friends could be useful about now.

I went back to the group text with Sunny, Rosa and Abbey. Sunny knew Tara was still in town and would be trying to get into Lean's personal safe. According to them, the safe held a lot of cash. I was intrigued. The old me could crack that safe with no problems, but I was a changed man or at least trying to be. That's how I crawled into bed with Aziz, he needed to be repaid in blackmail. That was the job he needed me to pull. All this struggle against who I was running from, and it all came back to simply cracking a safe.

Even if the blackmail wasn't in the safe, Oliver Lean still owed me at least five thousand, dead or not. So, I would take my cut and divvy the rest up with the girls. After all they were out of work now. I text back asking if the safe was at the warehouse and got a quick reply. Rosa said she thought it was at his house. A home safe was not much of a challenge, one I have done many times. Lean's safe couldn't be anything special, nothing high-tech enough to keep me out.

It was too much cash to miss out on, I told them I was in, and we needed to meet.

Falling back into my pillow, trying to go back to sleep failed. The sun had broken past noon, a new day was half over. My mind wound with ideas waiting on replies to my texts to come through. They were either talking it out amongst themselves or they had finally gone to bed.

I got dressed and left to find a place still serving breakfast.

I drove with the top down to meet Billy. As the warm air blew over head, I thought about the last few days. The only thing that stood out were my mistakes, things I thought I should have known. The moves I made screwed things up and I was feeling trapped inside myself. My phone lay in the empty black bucket seat of the Cutlass. The light caught my eye as a text came through. I grabbed the phone and pulled into a gas station. As I filled the tank with premium, per Billy's orders, I saw it was from Rosa. She said she was with Sunny and Abby, and they were ready to meet. I text back I would be free shortly and that I was bringing in another guy to do this job.

I called Billy.

The breakfast place was in a strip mall off US 1. It had a cow theme with porcelain cows doing human activities like cooking, driving and flying a kite. There were a few other knickknacks spread around giving the place a country feel. I spotted Billy sitting at a table in the corner. He was in his usual Bike Week tee shirt with the front pocket holding his cigarettes, worn blue jeans and cowboy boots.

This place was always good to eat, and I never had to look at a menu. I sat down and ordered my usual biscuits and gravy with three eggs. Billy ordered a sausage plate with some over easy eggs.

We sipped coffee and chatted about the Olds, he made sure to mention only use premium gas. I asked about the Scout. He said he got the C-10 stripped and was already selling parts. He asked if I wanted to make the parts list for the Scout or just leave it to him. There was no way I was leaving it to him, first, he would order way too much, I didn't need a blown Hemi. Secondly, it was my baby and only I knew what was best for my baby.

The food came and the conversation turned to the case. Billy liked to talk while he ate.

"This, Tara, is still out there, and the girls think she's after Lean's secret cash?" He crunched into some white toast with yellow yoke soaked into it.

I had a bite of biscuit and gravy in my mouth as I nodded, "Yep." I swallowed then said, "If we get her, we get her. I don't think she's a threat anymore, but she might still be worth something to Aziz."

"Shame, she's cute." Billy said noting the only quality he knew of hers. That's all we would ever really know about her, she was cute. If I ever saw her again it would be to turn her over to Aziz.

I took a bite, chewed and swallowed. "Yeah, until she's mad at you. Then usually you die."

Billy shoved more food in his mouth, took a few chews then said, "And what exactly do we get out of it?"

"Depends how much is in the safe."

"Roger Grimes is coming out of retirement for some cam models and some cash."

I frowned, "Not exactly. I owe Aziz and this seems like the best way to pay him."

"Who's money is it?" Billy asked. He wasn't asking because he knew a guy like Lean would have either stolen it or some other ill-gotten gains and they usually had very bad guys attached.

"Blackmail." I shoved more egg in my mouth.

Billy nodded, I was giving him details to a story he already knew.

"Did I tell you Lean was into blackmail?"

"Blackmailing his own customers?" Billy sucked at his teeth and sat back with a full belly from a hardy breakfast. A criminal through and through. He had Lean all figured out, there was no need to explain the process. If there was a fast buck to be made or a way to squeeze another dollar out, Billy was on it. Except when it came to his cars. Car enthusiasts should never run repair shops. All his profits went into his next build, and he never got out what he put in. I was beginning to see a similar pattern building with my own career path.

"Yeah, actually. The cam models would get customers to send in photos and then he would blackmail them."

"And now Aziz is out money. All that trouble for some dick pics."

We sat in silence, the only sounds came from chewing and slurping coffee. When I cleared my plate I said, "Lean said one of the clients was a VIP of some sort. The kind of guy you don't blackmail."

"Like you?" Billy laughed. "Did it burn up in the fire?"

"I've been thinking about that. Lean said he didn't like using the cloud or anything that could be hacked so it's got to be on a flash drive or external hard drive somewhere. The way Tara set the blaze and split makes me think it wasn't there. The blackmail was the only thing keeping her alive."

"Maybe she thinks if it's burnt up, she's in the clear."

"Maybe, but gangsters like Aziz don't think that way."

Billy shook his head in agreement. Then he said, "So, if it's still out there what are we gonna do with it? Do those girls want it?"

The waitress dropped the check. Billy acted like it never happened.

"No. I was thinking I would destroy it. Maybe send the victims an anonymous email it was over or something. I don't know. They deserve to know it's over."

Billy sat not saying anything until a smirk wrinkled his tanned face, "You do gooder."

I showed him the bill and told him to leave the tip then went to counter and paid.

Chapter 11

We met the cam girls at the mall. It seemed like the best place to blend in and have enough people around that Aziz wouldn't try to make a move on me. The food court held plenty of tables. At this time of morning the mall consisted of old people out mall walking. Dressed in white Velcro shoes and sweat jackets, they marched around, pumping their arms, doing laps from one end to the other. The other mall walkers were high school kids cutting class. They walked slower, aimlessly, unsure of what to do with their few hours of freedom. Then there was us. A couple of thieves and three internet porn stars. What a group we made.

Sunny had her boots up in an empty chair beside her, sipping a frozen fruit drink. She was dressed in black tank top with black sports bra underneath suppressing her already small breasts. She was in black jeans despite the raging heat outside. Abby was in a white top, cut short, and a pair of blue jeans with manufacture rips and holes and had sandals on her feet. Across from her sat Rosa. She wore pink short shorts with a designer t-shirt that was purposely cut up and hung loose against her caramel-colored skin. Her black lace bra shown in the cutouts of the shirt, again by design. Black kinky, curly hair was pulled back tight in a hair tie. Despite the tired dark circles under her eyes, there was a raw attraction totally separate from the one I had when she was freshly painted the other night. This was a girl just out of bed, and I wanted to be back there with her.

"Hello ladies," Billy said running a hand over his long black ponytail. He pulled a chair and took a seat opposite Sunny but next to Rosa. Rosa nodded, Sunny scowled, and Abby smiled. Billy returned a smile to each of them.

I took a seat without saying anything, they all knew me. I had my job face on, unmoving, expressionless, like I was in deep thought. I should have been in deep thought, focused on finding the safe and cracking it. I was rusty, hadn't cracked a safe in years. There would inevitably be hang-ups and the threat of Tara hanging around upped the ante. As if that wasn't enough to focus on, including the smell of Rosa near me, I had Aziz on my mind, specifically Boghos and his large hairy hands. My motivation for this job was the cash at the end of this shitty tunnel.

Rosa looked up from her phone and into my eyes. She held the gaze for a moment, studying the new bruises on my face. Still so fresh, it was too much for her to look at and went back to her phone. "So, Abby says she heard Lean talking to someone on the phone about the safe. Abby, fill them in." Rosa looked at me again, this time her eyes were a little softer.

Abby straightened out of her typical slouch, "I heard him talking about it to someone. Lean was screaming about Crystal stealing from him. About how she found his safe and she needed to be dealt with." Abby folded her hands, gave a quick frown then looked over to Billy who was leaning over the table to hear her soft words. This put a soft smile back on her face.

Billy finally took his eyes off Abby and laid them on me, "His crew? That makes three; us, Tara and mystery them." He pulled on his long black braid.

I felt pressured to speak. "His crew is dead." I studied everyone's face, besides avoiding eye contact nothing changed. "Lean killed Crystal for stealing from him and starting this whole thing. That's where she got the extra dough to have me kill Lean. Does anyone know where the safe is?"

Abby shook her head no, then shrugged apologetically. We all agreed it wasn't at the warehouse. Lean was a braggart and foolish, but this was something secret, something he kept from a partner. The only partner I knew of was Aziz. A pit opened in my stomach and began to suck the air out of the room. No matter what, I couldn't shake Aziz off me. If he was a part of it, then he too was looking for the safe. We had wasted too much time talking, and not enough time doing. We were about to become the 'we never sleep club'.

Rosa clicked off her phone and put it in her pocket. Her distraction was over, she had ignored me enough. If she was upset with me, I had no idea why or how I wronged her. We went out, I treated her well, though I lied about who I was, not only did she figure that out, but she was keeping a big secret from me. Had I been genuine from the start, then I should be the one upset. My attraction to her subdued my rejections of her nighttime job on the internet. I wanted it to not exist, to have never happened and let things just start over and play out between us.

"Lean's partner in the blackmail is an Armenian named Azad Aziz. Ever hear of him?" I said and looked around at the three female faces. They were either showing their best poker faces or really didn't know the guy, at least by name.

I looked back at Sunny. "You've been quiet."

Sunny Palace slurped her frozen drink. Her skinny lips let go of the purple straw and her mouth let out an *aahh,* letting us all know she was satisfied with her drink. She pulled her boots off the seat and sat up.

"So, you wanna know what I think? Well, I don't really care. I'm out like a grand a week, not to mention the money I gave Crystal. And while you all are planning some kinda great heist, I'm wondering how the hell I'm going to pay my rent and feed my dog. So, I think, this sucks. I never had a problem with Lean, I'm only here because Abby asked me to."

Rosa and Abby both started in on Sunny at the same time. It was hard to pick apart actual words in all the duck quacking, they called her out on having wanted to be a part of this and committing earlier to seeing it through.

"You want to leave, leave." I said talking over the three women. Sunny just stared at me and snarled but she didn't get out of her seat.

"Then contribute if you stay." I turned back to the other two ladies. "I need Lean's address. Billy and I will case the place and then go in and get what we came for. You guys need to lay low and keep searching for Tara. I have a feeling she's still in town."

"I think we should all go together," Abby piped up. "I mean, when you actually crack the safe."

"You don't trust us?" Billy said flatly though his face held a smile.

"No, it's not that." Abby laid one hand down on the other then pulled the lower one out and put it on top like she was cutting a deck of cards. "I think there is something in there, that well, I would rather get myself."

"Aw shit Abby," Sunny balled her little fists.

"It's not for me, I swear."

"Who is he Abby?" Rosa beat me to the question.

"Well," Abby looked at Billy then down to her hands again, "Tom Burley."

Rosa looked at Sunny. Sunny shrugged.

"I think I know him," Rosa said looking at me then back to Abby. I felt a little queasy after just getting over Aziz being a part of this blackmail scheme. Immediately I thought whoever Tom was messaging with Rosa, probably trying to meet her. Maybe he did, maybe they went to the Ocean Side like we did. The story Chastity told Billy and I a few nights ago in the bar replayed in my mind except instead of her and some scrawny dude, it was Rosa and this Tom Burley.

Rosa was reading my mind, or maybe the look on my face, I wasn't sure, but she cleared the air when she said, "Yeah Tom was a nice guy. He tried to get in touch with me." She looked at me closer, studying every taught muscle in my face, "He sent me a lot of pics and tried to get a date. But I *never dated* a fan."

Rosa turned to Abby and lightened her tone, "I sent the pics on to Ollie like he requested we do and never heard from Tom again."

Rosa's brow crinkled. She looked up quickly at Sunny then to Abby. "Wait a second. He was blackmailing them? All those pics we forwarded? Lean was using it against them." Her smooth mocha face drained into a pasty whitewash. Guilt crept in the corners of her eyes as she shut them tight. Not all the girls at Glory Catz knew what they were doing or bothered coming to terms with it. It hadn't occurred to her; she hadn't thought it through all the way or had the devious mind that Sunny had to reach such a conclusion.

"That's how he did it," I said. "Got you all to get guys to send in the dick pics, find out what they do for a living and then he would go after them."

"Hey, we didn't ask for them," Sunny jumped in fiery as ever.

"Sunny, Grimes isn't saying you did it on purpose." Rosa reached out across the table, but her arm wasn't long enough.

"Well, he shouldn't talk like we did. He can just sit there like he's so above all of us. But really, we know, we know he went after Lean just because dear old Crystal batted her eyes at him. He's no different, in fact I think he's worse." She was looking at me now, her eyes a glow with hate for me, for men in general. Abby reached out and touched Sunny's arm, but she waved the comforting off.

Sunny wasn't wrong. I entertained the idea of killing Oliver Lean to make an old flame happy. Even dressed up and disguised as *protection* or *safety* I knew it was just because I could, I could have killed him a hundred times over. It was make-believe to think I walked away from killing. The faces of the dead still find me in the dark, when I should feel the safest, they appear and tell me of the hell I sent them to. I didn't tell them that, I let them go on believing I didn't care, that it wasn't in me to care. Guilt is a heavy stone.

"Then let's make this right for the others." I said and looked around at each of them. "Billy and I can get into that safe. We're going to have to act fast. Aziz may have already got his hands on it."

"What makes you think the blackmail is in the safe? Wouldn't he just have it uploaded somewhere?" Abbey said. She had a point. All the girls, and Billy nodded as they waited on me for an answer.

"I don't think so. Lean knew how to hide money; he would know how to hide pics. Having Aziz and Tara in on it, he would need it to be tangible, something he could physically hide. The blackmail is only worth anything if the blackmailer is the only one with it. Tara wants it too. That means it's out there somewhere."

That satisfied their curiosity. Billy took over the planning because that is the way we worked. He got Lean's address and started looking at it on his phone. He checked the latest average police response times to that neighborhood along with streetlight placement and a few other things he liked to check off in his mind.

All the girls agreed they were coming with us. We tried to tell them no, but they insisted, partly out of a mistrust of a couple of old thieves and because they wanted more skin in the game. They had all taken part in the death of Crystal and Lean and probably soon Tara. Seeing this to the end, freeing the blackmail captives, would make Crystal and Lean's lives worth something.

I looked at Billy and he shook his head and sighed. Then I said, "Okay, this is how it's going down. We'll meet at my office. We drive over separate, park a few houses down. We'll text you when we're in and then we will let you in."

Sunny started to argue, "Why do you want that blackmail so bad?"

"I don't want it falling into the wrong hands." I shrugged, hoping they would buy the half-truth. My trouble with Aziz was none of their business.

"Will you shoot Tara if she tries to stop us?" Abby said as she reached out and touched Billy's grease-stained hand.

Billy looked up with a blank stare. He repeated her words in his head, having heard them but not listened to them.

"No, we don't like to bring guns with us for a routine B&E." Billy snorted a little and spread a grin across his face. I thought he was going to say some old Florida cracker phrase and turn this moment into an episode of The Andy Griffith Show.

With Aziz on my ass, I didn't like to go anywhere without a gun, but Billy's code was right. If we got caught, the sentence would be a lot shorter.

"We can handle Tara just fine." I said. Billy was deep in thought, and I didn't want this pasty broad to distract him. He could miss something that would get us all in lock up.

"Okay Grimes," Rosa said. "I trust you." her hand went out and touched my shoulder then ran over my chest before she pulled it away. She turned to the rest of them, "I don't know about you all but, I'm going home and getting some sleep. I suggest you do the same."

"And I suggest you all stay together if you can. Tara is still out there and dangerous." I left them with that warning.

Rosa shot me a glance one more time before walking off. Nothing was said or communicated in the glance, not an invite, just a look. It made me feel I still mattered a little more than the guy who was breaking into a safe for her. I liked that.

Billy reached out and shook Abby's hand but skipped on Sunny. As we walked off, he turned back a couple times, the first time he smiled at Abby who was looking back as well. The second time she was nearly out the door with Sunny who no doubt was scolding her for smiling.

"That lanky one is cute. Is Abby her internet name?" Billy messaged his sparse mustache and then pulled his phone but promptly put it back as we passed through a department store on our way back to the car.

"I think so. I really wasn't searching for her."

Billy nodded and made one more mental note.

Chapter 12

Without needing to ask where we were headed next, Billy drove us past Lean's condo. It was on the beachside with a gate but no guard. That was a major plus considering we will have three stragglers. I was surprised Billy didn't try to cut them loose or give me hell for being so relaxed about them coming. I assumed it had to do with the lanky girl, but I never brought it up.

Each condo looked like the next, baby blue with white roofs and white doors with large two car garages in the front. We made a whole lap of the complex and then came back to Lean's condo. We never got out of the car. Billy drove off.

Back at Billy's, under the house in the basement, we reviewed what we saw. Billy pulled on a shelf and swung it open to reveal a well concealed compartment. From inside he pulled a gray duffel bag with backpack style straps. It was his tool bag, not for fixing cars but for stealing them and other things.

"I figured there might be something in here we need." Billy dropped the bag at my feet and went on over to the fridge and pulled two gold cans of suds. He handed one to me and then took a seat on the gold velvet couch. I took a seat on a stool.

"I still have my tool bag." I cracked open the beer and sipped it. "More than once as a PI I've had to pick a lock."

"Yeah, I bet. There aint nothing in there you probably don't have but taking an extra is a good idea."

I nodded and sipped the cold beer. Old times, for me this was a beer commercial. Most beer ads are social settings in bars or clubs, and the great outdoors, but not for me. I was most happy here, before and after a robbery.

Billy knelt by the bag and opened it up. "Two drills, four batteries, titanium bits sharp as hell, four carbide tipped glass cutters, extra gloves, bleach wipes in case you get sloppy. In the red box, are all my electrical odds and ends, jumpers, snips, wire, assorted batteries, tape and stuff."

Billy got to his feet, "Been holding on to that shit for a while now. Wasn't sure if we'd ever use it again." He went back to the couch and just stared at the bag, taking pulls from his beer can until it was empty. When it was empty, he crushed it and went for another round.

"You gonna tell me about this Aziz character?" Billy asked very plainly. He was still unaware of my current debt with the *Armenian Don*. I hadn't told him earlier because he would start cooking his books and suddenly there would a few thousand all wrapped up for me. It wouldn't be enough to get me out of trouble, but his smiling pride would force me to take it. Not only would I still owe Aziz, but a debt to Billy meant no skipping to Uruguay.

"Well, he is the head of some kind of organized crime in town. He runs underground gambling and was mixed up with Oliver Lean on his porn site and the blackmail scheme. He got me for eighteen grand. I'm not really sure how powerful he actually is, but people fear him like it's the truth. Even Smitty has me treading lightly." I crushed my empty can and went for another. There wasn't time to get drunk, but right now I needed the buzz to keep going.

"He's probably already hit the safe then, why even bother?"

"Smitty's our inside man on this. Aziz still wants him to hire a crew to find it."

"That's the job Smitty wanted for us?"

"Yes and no. He wanted Smitty to put together a crew to steal it not knowing I would be a part of it. He wanted me to find Tara for her role in all of it. Remember, Lean was a snake. If Aziz is willing to wipe my debt for whatever Lean had, I have a feeling he never disclosed everything to Aziz. Lean laundered money, he's good at hiding stuff." I sat back down. I felt my phone buzz with a text. I reached in and pulled it out. The number was blocked. My palm covered the screen. With a casual glance, I read the text, 'I like to play with fire too. You've been charged a late fee.'

My face pulled apart around my mouth as an unconscious smile split my lips and showed my teeth. I felt a slight rumble inside, deep at my core. I steadied my hand and put my phone away. My head began to hurt with possibilities. Somewhere a building was on fire and that somewhere meant something to me.

As I considered Aziz's power, I got another text. It was from my roommate, Brock. *Yo bro call ASAP never gonna believe this. Our apartment burned down.*

The Armenian Boss was more ruthless than I thought. I was too busy looking for an out than just buckling down and paying the man. Now that I knew the extent, he was willing to go, I could start making a move of my own. I'm easy going until I'm not. Aziz must not have heard the rumors, stories of the carnage I brought to the human traffickers months ago. Being Armenian, he'd probably grown up with horror stories of genocide. I doubted he had ever lived it. Now as he was going to experience it firsthand.

Going after the safe would have to be tonight. There was no guarantee it was even in the condo, but it was the best place to start.

"You alright?" Billy asked. He knew me, we pulled too many jobs for him to be fooled by that smile.

"Yeah man. Good news. Aziz doesn't have the blackmail. So, what do you say we hit this place tonight?"

Billy sat up from a slouched position on the couch, "Sure we can. Listen, if you can just pay Aziz off, I can probably cover you." Billy said.

"Nah, I got it covered. Listen, let's just get this done tonight. I gotta run." I made it to the steps of the basement before Billy said anything. Instead of responding to his questions I just told him I would call later.

I fired the Olds and sped out headed for my apartment. Driving fast, I scrolled through my phone looking for Smitty's contact.

"Your shits all over the news kid." Smitty said over the phone. Something crunched as he ate.

"Couldn't be helped. The job is still in play."

"Call me when it's done." He crunched his food once more and hung up.

I crossed the bridge and from the top could see the smoke blowing west from the complex. I drove a little faster.

The street was blocked with cop cars and firetrucks and even an ambulance. About thirty people lined the curb on the other side of the street, watching. Some had open mouths saying nothing. Others sobbed. I didn't have much in the apartment, some clothes, a bed and a TV in my room. I felt no loss or tragedy, Aziz failed there. What I was feeling was anger, anger for these poor people in the street who lost everything they owned. This was not a fancy high-rise looking over the beach or river. This was a simple three-story mid-century block apartment complex in a part of town that has been discarded by the tourism board. These were the down and outers, the people who came to Daytona Beach on spring break and never left. These people didn't have renter's insurance or a savings account, they weren't even done paying off their rented furniture. I was angry because it was my fault.

I saw a familiar face holding the yellow tape, telling residents they still couldn't return to see the damage done to their lives.

"Camp," I said walking her way. She turned her round bulldog face towards me. I jogged over to meet her.

"Grimes." Camp said flatly, neither enthused to see me nor bothered at my presence.

"How are you liking your promotion?" I said with a half grin.

Camp smiled briefly, "Yeah. You know the more I run into you, the better I am at my job. So, what do you know about this fire?"

"Oh," I ran a hand over my shaved head, "I live here, or at least I did."

I watched the thick black smoke bellow out of the broken windows in what was once my bedroom.

"Really? You're just a magnet for shit storms. And it stinks." Camp took her dark sunglasses off and wiped the sweat from her brow and face. She squinted up at me then put her glasses back on.

"So far, it's looking suspicious so we're gonna stick around. Which apartment is yours?"

"308."

Camp called out to another officer and asked which apartment the fire started in. He hollered back 310.

"310 was vacant. Squatters? Crack heads?" I offered hoping to take the spotlight off me.

"You'll have to find another place to stay awhile."

"Yep," I said and started for my car. No point in sticking around.

Camp called after me, "Grimes, someone matching your description was seen leaving another fire."

"You better check that eyewitness, I don't play with fire." I smiled. It had little effect on the deputy.

"They recovered five bodies. One was definitely shot; the others being investigated as murder as well."

"So, all the girls made it out okay?"

"I didn't say nothing about gender."

"Must'a read that in the paper." I started backing up slowly.

Camp watched me carefully. She switched hands holding the yellow caution tape from right to left, leaving her gun hand free.

"Maybe I ought 'a drop your name to the detective in charge."

"We're on the same side here Camp. Trust me." I smiled and nodded then turned slowly and walked conscious of every step.

Brock spotted me from the crowd and called out as I neared the car. I ignored him at first, but he kept yelling. He jogged over wearing a pair of basketball shorts and was holding a t-shirt in his hand instead of wearing it. He pulled back his hair.

"Damn man, you see this shit?"

"Yeah. Did you have insurance?"

"Nah, you?"

"No. So what are you gonna do?" I asked but didn't really care. I avoided eye contact in case he asked to stay with me. My eyes scanned the crowd. Then while Brock was talking about his options, my eyes latched onto someone, someone big and broad and hairy. His long black hair was up in a bun and his black beard was shining in the sunlight like tinsel on a tree.

Boghos was looking right at me then he looked up at the apartment and pointed. He withdrew his arm and stepped into the crowd like a sasquatch stepping into the forest. The cyrtid faded away somewhere beyond the crowd.

"So how about it?" Brock asked looking up at me with saucer shaped eyes.

"I'll call you. I gotta run." I jumped in the Olds and sped out of there leaving my roommate standing along the street. I wasn't sure what he was asking, a loan, a place to stay? I didn't know and didn't care. The further he was away from me the better off he was, though he didn't know that, and I wasn't going to tell him that. I just had to give him the cold shoulder from here on out.

Chapter 13

A block away from my office, I found a place to leave the Olds. Walking around the block, I came up behind the building and leaned against a small tree on the edge of the parking lot. My office window faced the river and Beach Street so there was no way to see if there was a light on or anyone there. I waited around a half hour, watching people come and go. There was no sign of Aziz or his men. I went in.

The deadbolt slid back with a twist of the key. I pushed the door open slowly and stood to the side as I did. The office was just how I left it, empty.

In the second drawer of the locked filing cabinet, I pulled out my old tool kit. I reviewed the contents of the bag and compared it with everything Billy had. It was good to have doubles of everything. Nothing can ruin a good job fast like a broken drill bit or dead battery. It's the simple things that cost you the score.

My phone rang. A blocked caller was trying to reach me. I guessed correctly at who it could be when I answered and heard the Armenian on the other end.

"I hope you didn't have eighteen thousand dollars in your apartment."

I said nothing.

"I didn't think so, not because you wouldn't stash it there but because you don't have it. Lean is dead, Crystal is certainly dead, and you've run out of people willing to pay you what you're due. How does that make you feel Roger?"

"Enough games Aziz. I'm close. Tara is alive and more than well. If she hasn't already skipped town, I'll find her." I said.

"The goal posts have shifted. I want the blackmail or more will go up in flames."

I hung up on him. The partial payment program expired. Aziz wanted the blackmail more than cash and it's possible that is all Lean had in his safe. If my office burned, I wasn't worried about it, but Brock could have been killed today. What if Aziz knew my connection with Billy? He knows how I know Smitty and that is a direct link with Billy. The Olds wouldn't be safe back at Billy's shop because the shop isn't safe.

I stuffed the tool bag into a larger duffle bag with a change of clothes. My hand went for the pistol and stopped. No guns on a B&E, it just adds years to your sentence. The pistol stayed. Just as I was leaving, I got a text from Rosa. She was asking what she was supposed to wear tonight, asking things like *mask* or *no mask*. It was a group text and Abbey chimed in with suggestions of what to wear. The burglary was turning into a fashion show. I put the phone on silent and left.

I slipped the key into the lock on the Olds. Something felt off, out of place. With all that was going on and lack of sleep it was easy to think my mind could be playing tricks on me or maybe somewhere buried deep, my conscious knew Aziz wasn't done setting fires. With a step back I looked over the car.

All four red line tires were slashed. Walking around the car under a careful eye, nothing else seemed to be damaged.

Billy answered his phone, "Yeah man?"

"Can you send Jose with the truck to pick up the Olds?"

"Uggh," Billy groaned through the phone. "Shit Grimes, what happened?" Billy said more like a disappointed father than a best friend who lent his classic car out.

"Someone slashed the tires."

"Someone?"

"Yeah, someone."

"Dammit, Grimes."

I waited a moment, "I think Aziz is getting worried."

Billy swore then lit a cigarette. As he breath out smoke, he said, "Okay, Jose is on his way."

Chapter 14

The urgency to hit Lean's place was clouding clear thoughts on planning. I was trying think ahead in case the blackmail was not at the condo. Aziz turned out to be a much harder man than I expected. Either he didn't want to come after me physically or he knew it hurt more to destroy the people around me than actually beat me to a pulp. It was working. Whether he knew it or not, I was busy beating myself up, there was no need to send Boghos. If I was in the hospital or dead, he wouldn't get paid. Having Roger Grimes pay him his due was more important than a beat down. While I was out running from fires and police questioning, Aziz was stocking up on guns.

It was around four o'clock when Jose hitched up the Olds and took me back to the shop. He didn't say much on the ride over and once back at the shop he went in the office and started filling out paperwork, peeling apart the carbon yellow and pink copies of work orders for the day, filing them and leaving black grease marks everywhere he went.

I took a seat in a red vinyl chair. Billy wasn't in the shop and not in the office either. "Does Billy still have the Honda I dropped off?" I said leaning on the counter.

"Nah, we parted that out real quick. Sorry man." Jose pulled apart another work order, looked at which file to put the pink slip in and then looked up at me. "He said you would try for another car, he also said to give you a hard time about borrowing another one. But I won't."

Jose turned to his right and on the wall was a white metal cabinet with a big red cross on it.

"Keys are in there. Red tags are customers. Probably find something on the bottom row." Jose said, going back to his paperwork.

I stepped past him and opened the white metal box. On the bottom row were four sets of keys. Two were stamped "GM" and a third key was not marked. The last key was for a Dodge. The only Dodge I saw on the lot was gun-metal grey 2016 Charger. The beautiful lines caught my eye but what held my gaze were the lack of badges. No indicator of make, model or package. If this was at Billy's shop it was because someone wanted it to go fast.

"Thanks," I said grabbing the keys to the Charger.

Grinning, he said, "Be careful, she smokes brother."

All the bay doors were down. In the darkness of the shop, I pressed the key FOB and found the car from the flashing yellow lights.

Billy's sharp whistle dismantled my smile then he said, "No way. We take the old man truck."

I turned around to find Billy standing there wagging a finger at me. At his feet was a tool bag similar to mine. The handle was frayed, and the zipper didn't close all the way. He was ready to go to work.

Back in the office I said to Jose, "Billy says, take the old man truck."

"I gotcha," Jose turned and put the key back in the medicine cabinet. He pulled out the long silver key with no emblem on it. "White, '96 F-150. Bone stock."

My smile went crooked, "Thanks again."

Chapter 15

Billy parked the F-150 along the street with no one in the world watching. His eyes scanned the street, and he checked the mirror a couple times then nodded at me. That was my que to head in for the condo.

As I got out and perused the street, I realized the Charger would have attracted looks everywhere we went, not something we could afford. There was nothing out of place with a guy climbing out of a twenty-five-year-old pickup carrying a tool bag. Totally normal.

What wasn't normal was the car parked down the street. A silver Lexus with three women in it. The windows up, car running, AC blasting. They were some distance down the street, but that didn't diminish me seeing the angry scowls on their faces. I had to get to the condo before they saw me, but it was no use, all three popped out of the car simultaneously and came marching towards me. I took a deep breath and enjoyed the next few seconds of silence.

"No, no, no," Sunny shouted, leading the three walking fast to catch me before I entered the town house.

"Would you be quiet?" I shouted in a whisper. I stood on the sidewalk and waited for them to get close enough, so no one had to yell.

Rosa stepped out in front of the other two. Her face was calm, and her lips parted but she didn't utter a word.

"Grimes, you double crossing," Sunny went on to call me names. All three followed me to the front door.

The white door was scared up with gouges exposing fresh yellow wood from beneath the paint. The width of the gouges made an obvious impression of a crowbar. Whoever used it, missed the lock a few times, hit the deadbolt, then finally got the bar between the door and the frame. The door pushed open easily.

"Someone beat us to it." Rosa said stepping a little closer behind me, she put her fingers on my back. I could smell her hair, taking me back to the night in the dune. The memory turned me around with a smile. She just looked up with big round brown saucers, there was no smile, no kiss, no indication we were ever more than partners in crime.

Inside, the condo was dark. I waited for my eyes to adjust before going further, apparently none of the women thought about that as they all bumped into me. The burglary was deteriorating fast. Not only was I rusty but these three had no clue how to work a B&E.

Knowing what Lean did for a living I expected more out of the décor of the condo. The condo had tall, vaulting ceilings. There was a kitchen to my left, on the right, a short hall with an open bathroom door and to the right of that, an open door to a bedroom. Straight ahead was the main living area of the condo. All the gaudy black furniture with shiny surfaces and nude art was not there as I expected. Neither was the white shag rug, none of that had ever been here. This place looked like the kind of place your grandparents go to retire.

Instead of the glitz there was wall to wall beige carpet tacked against eggshell white walls. A

dark brown fabric couch matched the love seat with a glass coffee table in the middle. The condo was torn apart. Everything was upside down, broken or cut open. Stuffing from the couch cushions filled the floor, turning it to a winter wonder land. Pictures were torn from the walls and broken, layering the floor beneath with soft white clouds of couch stuffing crackling with shards of glass.

I stood silent, holding my breath, listening for sounds. All I could hear were the three behind me. Frustrated, I pressed forward.

"Hey you." I called out to no one. All three of the girls gasped, I listened, and no other sounds came from the condo. We were alone.

"What the hell Grimes?" Rosa said digging a knuckle into my shoulder.

"It's easier than walking the place, waiting for someone to jump out at us. Now we know it's clear."

"What if they're hiding?" Abbey whispered.

"It's fine." I said and relaxed a little. We milled about the mess. Nothing was left untouched; appliances were pulled from the wall and every drawer was pulled and flipped.

"Any ideas on where the safe is?" I asked.

No one spoke.

"Let's spread out and look for it." I said feeling like Freddy in a Scooby-Do episode. I went on to find my way into the master bedroom.

The ceiling in the master bedroom was vaulted as well. The mattress to the king bed was hanging half off and had been slashed through. All the drawers to the dresser and nightstand were pulled out. The mess continued into the bathroom. I peered into the cabinet drawers but there was nothing to indicate a safe had been in there. The same was true for the closet.

After I had walked the entire condo, I gathered everyone in the living room.

"Anyone find the safe yet?" I said as we all looked at each other.

"Do you think whoever did all this," Rosa said, "could have taken it out?"

"Not likely. This is amateur. My guess is Tara got here last night and tossed the place." I said.

They all started jabbering at once offering up ideas and theories, but no one knew anything concrete. Sinking in the soft sand of unfounded ideas, the jabber quickly turned to frustration as the level of bickering about who was right or wrong and why we were even doing this increased. It was giving me a headache.

I walked quietly into the kitchen. The refrigerator was pulled away from the wall but still plugged in. From inside I pulled a beer and began drinking it.

"Seriously," Sunny said, stopping her arguing with Rosa and Abby.

All three girls had eyes on me. This wasn't my first burglary. I was relaxed knowing that whoever tossed the place was gone and unlikely to return anytime soon. They had moved on, tearing up some other place that didn't concern me at the moment. I pulled the bottle from my lips and said, "What?"

The front door squealed slowly open. A shadow covered figure stood in the doorway. The girls were frozen, each with a hand on the other for stability and assurance.

"What the fuck?" Billy cackled as he stepped through the doorway. "What'd you all do in here?"

I came out of the kitchen, catching Billy a little off guard. He had on blue latex gloves and was holding his tool bag.

"We found it like this." I said.

"Are we too late?" Billy said, his head on a swivel as he stepped deeper into the condo.

Breathing once more, the girls all relaxed. Sunny went over to the wet bar tucked into a side wall and hoisted herself up on the counter. Her boots dangled as she kicked each one out and let it fall. Abby put a couch cushion back on the couch and took a seat. Everyone had their eyes on Billy.

Billy jerked his head around swinging his black ponytail and looked at each one of us waiting for some information.

"It aint here." Sunny said.

"We don't know that for sure." Abby commented under her breath, her eyes down looking at her hands.

"The girl, Tara, I doubt she could 'a hauled a safe outta here, at least not alone." Billy started walking as he talked. "Since she, or someone, tore through this place, tells me she found nothing." His gloved hand pressed against the smooth eggshell white wall, sliding as he walked.

I followed behind.

"Attic?"

"Not that I could find."

He nodded. I could see his mechanical mind turning. His eyes gauging, his mind calculating. He whispered incoherently and counted steps as he walked. He was seeing things I hadn't as he wandered the condo, always with a finger gently touching the wall. More than his eyes were searching, he was using aspects of his brain that would leave the rest of us wondering.

Billy went into the master bedroom then quickly peered out. We were all silent, watching him work. He quickly ducked back in then out again. We watched the master thief at work like a pro golfer lining up a put on the eighteenth.

With a wave he said, "Come here."

We all went into the room. The three webcam girls were lined up behind me, each with their head leaning to the side, heads stacked according to height. Billy dropped his tool bag in front of a return vent for the air conditioner. It was bare aluminum, roughly twenty-four by twenty-four inches and six inches off the floor. There was a green air filter tucked behind the vent.

"I reckon it's here 'cause there's another return out there closer to the unit." Billy stuck a small flathead screwdriver in one of the four screws holding the vent. He twisted on the top screw, then the others until he got them all out.

After the filter was removed, we all bent over to peer in at the square black metal safe with a long handle and digital keypad. Billy reached in and went for the handle. He shook it, it was locked.

"You really think it would be open that easy?" Sunny mouthed off.

"You'd be surprised short stack." Billy said and got a dirty look from the black-haired cam star. The sneer didn't deter the old burglar. With his hand still in the vent, he tried shaking the safe. It was secured somehow, either bolts or possibly concrete. We had seen a variety of ways people had tried to secure their safes; we beat every one of them.

Though still early in the evening the only natural light came into the room from a north facing sliding glass door. I leaned into the small cutout with a flashlight in hand to examine the safe. The black metal box sat on a two by twelve-inch board that was bolted to two, two by fours. More than likely there were two bolts running through the safe and the two by twelve. Whoever installed the safe did a good job securing it.

"What do you think?" I said to Billy as Rosa came back into the bedroom. We locked eyes for a moment, but it passed as she looked away and took a seat on the corner of the hanging mattress. She leaned back, locked her elbows, pushing her shoulders up to her ears. Her long brown legs went out over the edge of the box springs and her feet rested on the carpet. She looked inviting, but I had to decline. I knew she wasn't putting it out there, it's just the raw sexuality expelling from her every pour. The distraction was surprising to me. I thought I was more of a professional. Billy never took his eyes off the safe, not even when Abby came in and joined Rosa on the bed.

Billy's head was buried deep into the air shaft. I could hear him agree with himself as what to do or not to do. He stood up and said, "How about we go through the side?"

"It's best not to disturb the area. Let whoever comes in after us think there is no safe." I said and knelt next to Rosa's tasty caramel legs. I reached under her legs to my tool bag. I could smell the flowery lotion she used on her skin. Out of the tool bag, I pulled a heavy object inside a lead lined box. Inside was a powerful magnet cut like a thick hockey puck.

I stood up over Rosa. She glanced at me with her deep brown orbs and then looked away. I peeled off my t-shirt and that drew her eyes back, focusing on my chest and arms, not my face. I wrapped the magnet in the shirt.

"Simple," I said to Billy who was nearly scratching his head in wonder. He wasn't usually around when I cracked safes. The routine was he drive and get me in a place and get me out, beyond that he waits in the car.

The magnet clinked against the metal, instantly sticking to it. Still wrapped in my shirt I dragged the magnet over the top left of the door, just above the handle until I heard the bolt slide back. I dropped the handle and that was it. The swung open freely.

Billy and I filled the airshaft with our faces in silence. The safe was completely filled with cash. Tightly banded wads were stacked with no room on either side or the top. At the bottom on the furthest edge of the safe were two Rolex watches and a Ziploc bag with two flash drives in it.

With our heads buried in the shaft, I heard the click of a hammer locking back. A pistol was on me ready to fire. I withdrew my head and turned to face Rosa fanning a pistol between me and Billy. Rosa, Sunny and Abby stood with stone cold killer faces. The switch was on, they went from helpless dames in distress to calculating and cunning women who would never be tricked by a man. These were women with jobs that demanded false veneers. Every day they had to sit in front of a webcam and pretend to be loving what they did to themselves at the request of horny viewers. That look of lust, the pinched eyes of passion being released below, just a mask. Nothing penetrated their flesh; nothing reached their hard hearts.

Sunny stepped up holding a blade shiny and sharp. "Thanks dick." She said and pressed the blade high and inside. I didn't know how good she was with a blade but that close I didn't want to take a chance.

She began patting down my pockets and reached high in my crotch. Satisfied I wasn't carrying, she looked at the bed then back to me, "Get a pillowcase and fill it."

I didn't move. Sunny yelled the order once more. I looked over at the black silk pillowcase and back at Sunny. With a nod, I began moving towards it. I pulled the case off and came back to the safe.

Rosa was standing there between me and the safe. She held the pistol at her waist, the black circle of the barrel waiting for me to do something wrong. Her eyes weakened around the edges; her lips parted. She started to say something, but I cut it off with a shake of my head and walked past her. Whatever magnetism that joined us together before, now was depleted with the tip of that pistol.

"You don't have to do all this." I said kneeling before the false air return and the safe filled with cash. "Billy and I can walk out of here right now." My hand was on the flash drives filled with blackmail. The girls came for the cash not realizing the real money they were missing.

"Can it!" Sunny shouted. The steel of the blade pressed against my neck. She looked to Rosa and sucked her teeth.

The money was so tightly packed in there I had to pinch the sides of the stack to the left and slide out the first wad of banded bills. Each banded wad was ten thousand dollars. As I put the money in the silk case Sunny called out another order.

"You two get something to tie up Billy." Sunny held her hand out in front of Rosa. Rosa slowly handed the pistol over.

Abby and Rosa moved about the room, looking in drawers and in the closet for something to tie us up. My hands moved slowly, placing each stack one at a time in the pillowcase.

"Real clever girls." Billy started talking.

"Shut it redneck."

"I'm just wondering," Billy's deep southern cracker accent came out slow and smooth, reflecting where he grew up not his Cherokee lineage, "who else knows about this here stash."

Sunny shook the pistol at him, "No one, no one left alive anyway. Grimes here took care of all that.

I came up with the plan to steal the money, not Abby, not Tara and not Crystal. It was me. Tara set up to the whole blackmail scheme when she was *called away* by Aziz. When she came back, she had the blackmail and both Lean and Aziz wanted in on it. Then Crystal showed up like the big sister and started trying to get Tara to go straight. It would have worked if tough guy here had done his job and wacked Lean like we paid him to do."

Rosa called out from the other room for Sunny to be the one to shut up now, but she would heed no one's advice. The little firecracker just couldn't contain herself any longer. All the shit she took while devising this plan. She was the one who got the ball in motion. She wanted out of the cam life, not for any one reason other than it was boring her. She needed something more, and this stash of cash would be more.

Sunny began to pace. This was really happening for them. The cash was being bagged. Soon they could split and start over with fresh lives. Rosa would go back to nursing school and Abby would meet a nice man and settle down. I had no clue what Sunny would do, it didn't matter anyway.

Abby came out of the closet with a couple of belts. Rosa came in from the living room empty handed. None of them thought to look in my tool bag where they would find rope, but I wasn't going to suggest it.

"We can make do with the belts." Sunny said overconfident, thinking that her pistol was all the advantage she really needed.

"That won't hold me." Billy said with a toothy grin.

Sunny raised the gun to Billy, her eyes turned to slits as she fought to hold the trigger. Her plan was coming together better than expected. Crystal and Tara were out of the picture so there was more in the pot for the three of them. She had blood lust in her eyes. Billy and I were the last of the loose ends. Just a few pounds of pressure on that trigger and BAM! Blood splatter and death.

Abby had a hold of Billy's left wrist. She synched the belt around the wrist and brought it behind his back where Rosa had a hold of his left wrist. They paused, looking at both his wrists. They knew exactly how to bind a man; the only hesitation was which way to do it. Then Rosa grabbed a hold of both wrists and wrapped the belt around them. Abby held one end taught as Rosa slipped the other this way and that. Quickly Billy was bound.

"I'm telling you gals, it won't hold."

"I'm no stranger to tying a man up." Rosa grinned as she pulled tight on the belt. Her grin faded as her eyes fell on mine. She washed the look away and was all business once more.

Abby looked at Billy and silently mouthed, *I'm sorry*, to him. He smiled and winked. A rush of blood flushed her pale cheeks pink. She looked down at her feet and then back up at Billy's tanned face. Billy held the smile long enough for her to watch it fade from his face, with it, her hopes that when this was over there could be something between him and Abby. She was a complete one-eighty from the types he usually chased. The loud ones, the demanding ones, the ones that always messed up his life.

"Hey, cut it out!" Sunny shouted. "You make me sick." She turned her attention back to me with a wave of the pistol, "Get back to stuffing that sack." Her words rolled out of her mouth like she had rehearsed them in the mirror.

With my hands back in the safe I said, "So Crystal got you the actual location of the cash?"

"She found it alright. Lean had left it open one night and Crystal had a chance to take it all but instead she only took what she paid you. Lean killed her for that." Sunny said with a smile like this had all been a game. She didn't care, she was getting rich. I estimated nearly four hundred thousand in cash going into the sack.

I could feel her close to me, the pistol rattling in my ear. It was a cheap brand, something bought on the street. A couple of quick moves and I might get it away from her. I didn't have eyes on Abby and Rosa was too close to Billy for a quick shot. They had us still.

The money continued to shift from the safe to the pillowcase. Billy was synched tight with a belt sitting on the floor with his legs crossed, up and rigid like the Indian Chief he thought he was descended from. Good for him, I knew nothing of my family line.

My father was a sailor and my mother faded away into the vortex of Daytona Beach when I was young. The old man was gone a lot, leaving his only son to kill the time picking locks and stealing cars. All he left me with was a name and a forty-five.

The last stack of cash went into the pillowcase. A quick palm of one of two Rolexes landed one in my pocket. Old habits and not willing to leave empty handed made it happen. If Smitty was interested at all, the watch should fetch a couple grand.

"Here you go." I extended the black silk pillowcase.

I let go of the bag just as Sunny reached out for it. She didn't compensate for the weight of all that cash, and it slipped through her loose grip spilling out onto the floor. Sunny's eyes went down, and my hand went out for her wrist. I snatched and twisted, breaking her grip on the pistol. She cried out, dropping the pistol. My elbow went up and smashed into her pale face. She stumbled back, falling to the floor. Her hands caught bright red blood as it seeped through her finger.

Rosa was quick to throw a right. I blocked it and ducked the left swinging for the back of my head. I grabbed a handful of curly black hair and tossed her head into the wall.

I never saw Abby. She had snatched up the pistol and came down with it, cracking me in the exact spot I got popped thanks to Juan-Carlos. An electrical shock shot through my body and scrambled my brain as the pain overtook me. Down on all fours the stampede of little feet trampled over my body. Then the cold steel of a gun barrel rested on my neck.

"This time *I* will shoot you." Abby's words were full of spit. "Get on your stomach." Her fire was lit, and I believed her.

Bested by three internet porn stars. Without seeing another option, I followed her command. She pulled my arms back together and bound them along with my ankles. She was faster than Rosa had been with Billy. I pulled on the restraints but all it did was cut off my circulation.

Sunny used the bed to hold herself as she got back on her feet, pinching her nose with one hand and holding the pistol in the other hand. The fight was just beginning to rage in Sunny. She scrambled over and began stomping me with her tiny feet. Abby pulled her away and they went to work gathering up the cash.

Rosa too was up on her feet. She looked at the dent in the plaster, the perfect fit for the top of her forehead. The bruise quickly turned purple and round. She used the tip of her finger to lightly touch the bruise then she turned and spit on me while cussing in Spanish.

As the girls finished their double cross, the room was left silent so we could all hear the front doorknob turning. A squeal stopped then started again. The door closed. We all looked around at each other. No one breathed. Someone was coming in and they were doing it slowly.

I was on my stomach, hog tied. My head was turned to the left looking at Billy sitting with his hands and feet bound. I wiggled turning my body slightly, trying to get a look at the door.

Rosa waved at Abby to stand next to the door, she took the other side. Sunny crouched on the other side of the bed, her little black-haired head popping over the comforter, dark eyes waiting for a target.

I made eye contact with Billy and attempted to communicate with just eye movement and facial expressions. My eyebrows arched as my eyeballs rolled around in their sockets. Billy kept shaking his head side to side then jerking his neck to the right. I didn't know what he was getting at any more than he knew what I wanted. It would have made for a great comedy act if we weren't waiting to be executed. Then he saw it, there in my back pocket, the metal clip to my four-inch blade.

Slowly as if he were on the moon, Billy twisted his waist, inching his bound hands towards my ass and the knife that could set us free. Outside the room, whoever had entered was nearing the door. It was about to go down and no one was breathing.

A slender hand with pink painted nails pushed the bedroom door open all the way nearly hitting Rosa where she stood. As the short-cropped brunette peered in, all three girls jumped out yelling different commands. One yelled to freeze, another to drop and a third to put her hands up.

A distorted looking Tara twitched and fidgeted as she figured out who to listen to. Finally, Rosa shouted them all down, gained control and got Tara to sit on the bed.

The room quieted down. Tara sat and ran a hand through her short, dyed hair. She went from long blond to a butchered short brown. All the thick eyeliner, blush and lipstick was removed. No fake lashes or padded bra either. Her wardrobe consisted of a baby blue V-neck cut tee shirt and jeans with holes in each knee. She looked normal.

The gun wielding girls made a semi-circle around Tara. They looked down at her with expressions of condemnation. Rosa started to speak a couple times but never followed her words up with air. Sonny kept saying things like, *We got you,* and shook her pistol a lot. Abby waited for the other two to speak.

Afternoon had given way to evening. The dipping sun pushed through the sliding glass doors forcing the white walls to an orange glow. Billy and I were covered in shadow from the king size bed. My hands were beginning to tingle from lack of blood flow. All of my muscles were tense, my neck was on fire from holding my head up, trying to catch an eye full of the action unfolding. Eventually I had to rest my face in the edge of the mattress.

"You should have run Tara." Rosa said.

"Fuck you Rosa, fuck all y'all." Tara's pale cheeks filled with blood, turning them pink. "This was all mine and you three got Crystal involved to take it for yourselves."

"Girl, you better cool it." Sunny barked.

Tara stood up, "If anyone deserves a share it's me. Now, where's the money?"

"Sit down!" Rosa grabbed a hold of Tara's shoulder. Tara rolled it, deflecting the grab. She pushed back then Sunny grabbed a handful of Tara's new do. Tiny fists of fury began to fly. Even Abby threw some crooked blows down on Tara.

Tara was a tough girl; she wasn't going to let these three amateurs take her down. She threw a right that smashed Abby's nose. Then pushed Rosa back and kicked Sunny in the stomach. The girls all shrieked cuss words. Arms and legs flew with fury. Scratching and screaming reached a peak and the master bedroom could no longer hold the brawl. They tumbled out into the living room.

As soon as they were through the door and crashing into the living room furniture, Billy went for my knife. He got the blade out and started cutting at the leather belts that bound him.

A squeal pierced our ears and broke Billy's slicing rhythm. He looked over his shoulder and out into the living room.

The girls screamed about a knife. Someone started sobbing uncontrollably. Something crashed and shattered. More cuss words bounced off the walls. I wanted to get free, Billy was cutting too slowly.

Just as one of his restraints broke loose, I heard a familiar phrase, *Police!*

My ears filled with the sounds of popcorn popping in the microwave with each kernel exploding in my ear canal. A few seconds later white smoke drifted into the room filling my nose with sulfur. With Billy's hands free, he cut me loose. I flipped over on to my butt and went to work to free my ankles. Rosa leaned in the doorway, her face wilted, the only color came from tiny red splatter. The pistol, down to her side, free fell to the carpet. Her shirt filled with deep brown wet blotches. Her eyes met mine, soft lips parted taking me back to that night on the beach. If she wasn't a cam girl and I not a dirty PI, it didn't matter now. She flopped on the bed, her face turned, still looking at me as she gasped her last few short breaths.

Heavy boots and jangling keys made their way towards the master bedroom. First the black semi-auto Glock then the round bulldog face of Deputy Camp emerged through the door. She looked at Billy and I, and then back to Rosa. Her left hand went out and grabbed the loose gun. Then she rolled the lifeless body over, taking Rosa's brown eyes away from me, now looking up at the ceiling.

"Anyone else in the house?" Camp asked.

"No." I said pulling the belt from around my ankles.

Camp holstered her weapon. Billy was free and helped me up. The blood rushed back into my hands, hot and tingly.

"What the hell happened here?" Camp said checking over Rosa.

I looked at Billy, but he wasn't talking.

"Frenemies?" I smiled. Camp didn't get it. "Workplace violence." I joked again. She wasn't laughing.

Camp put one hand on her hip and the other grabbed the radio.

"Okay," I said, putting my hands up. "I was hired to find one of those dead girls there."

"What does this have to do with Oliver Lean and the fire on State Street?"

"They all worked there. The short haired brunette, she's the one I was hired by to find. Tara Johnson, she's the one who set the fire."

Camp went to the doorway and looked out at the three dead girls. While her back was turned, I made my way to the safe. Camp sensed the movement behind her and looked over her shoulder.

The corner of her eye caught me. My hand was already in the safe.

"Hold it." Camp's right hand slid along her belt then he palmed the grip of his weapon. Her permanent frown gave way to a half grin at catching me in the act. "Let me see your hand."

I withdrew slowly, the Rolex dangling between my fingers.

"What do you have there?" She got comfortably close to me. Trust was building between us but with her hand still on the pistol, proving we weren't all the way there yet.

"Sticky hands." I said.

"Once a thief, uh, Grimes?"

I shrugged. "I didn't think you'd let me leave with that." I pointed down at the black pillowcase.

Camp tapped it with her boot, scattering the stacks of greenbacks.

"Put the watch back, its evidence now Grimes." Camp said and then knelt to look through the stacks of cash.

I dropped the watch back in the safe and snatched the two flash drives. It was tough knowing I wouldn't get a cut of all that cash, but the blackmail material was really all I came for.

Camp got on the radio and called it in. The shots had already been reported by neighbors. She arched her back and came up slightly on the balls of her feet stretching her height to its fullest.

"I'm gonna walk you out the front." Camp said.

I saw Billy's expression change; his eyes grew larger, and he clinched his jaw. He was going to break any second and I wasn't sure what I would do when it happened. He hadn't got to know Camp like I had. Camp was proving to be a good ally in this new career filled with people I can't trust. Still, I held my breath as we funneled out of the bedroom.

The other three women were sprawled out in twisted positions of death. Life draining from each of them, pooling onto the carpet and furniture scattered throughout the condo. Abby and Tara had fallen where they stood. Sunny was face down with her arm outstretched leaving a maroon smear in the carpet from where she had crawled. Her head kinked to the left, eyes half open, staring without seeing.

"I may not be able to keep you completely out of this, Grimes. Just play dumb and answer any questions best you can about your investigation." We walked the rest of the way in silence with each step getting further away from a pile of uneasy questions. Then one last question came from Camp.

"Wait," She said stopping us at the front door. "Who is this guy?" She pointed to Billy.

Billy smiled, rubbing raw nerve endings.

"My partner." I said hoping that would be enough.

Camp nodded. She wanted to ask more but the siren screaming in the distance ushered us out the door.

"Better get going." Camp said. We headed across the street. Camp turned her head, not watching where we were headed and then she went back inside the house.

Just as I closed the door on the pickup the first cruiser came rushing in. The red and blue lights flashed. Curtains moved in windows as neighbors peered out at the commotion. First the gun shots then the lights, these weren't common in a neighborhood like this. A second squad car arrived. Both officers ran for the door. It was a lot of action for this cramped condo community, still no one noticed two men with tool bags climbing into a pickup truck.

Chapter 16

Billy sat in the passenger seat with a frown staring out the window as we drove towards his shop. He didn't have to say anything, I knew already. We missed out on the money, and he missed out on Abby. Bills at the shop were mounting and letting me borrow the Olds didn't help any now that the tires were torn up. A cut of that blackmail money would have gone a long way for Billy, it would have kept him on the straight and narrow. I thought I was on the straight and narrow as a private investigator, but all I was doing was bringing my friend down.

We parked at the shop. Billy slid out and shut the door. The window was down. He lit a cigarette and leaned against the door with his arms crossed.

"Missed it by that much." He said forcing a smile but not showing any teeth.

From my pocket I pulled the plastic bag with the two flash drives.

"Maybe we still have a shot at something."

Billy shook his head and chuckled. I pulled one by him. After all these years he still underestimated how quick my hands were.

"Shit Grimes. I hope there's something on there we can get paid for. Do-gooding don't pay the bills." Billy slapped the door and started to walk off.

I shouted to him and he turned in time to catch the one Rolex I snuck out of the safe. He smiled then it faded as his keen eyes examined the piece.

"It's a fake." Billy said and slipped it on his wrist.

I frowned, the tells had escaped my eye. "Well, it's your fake Rolex now."

Chapter 17

There was no option for a bed tonight other than my office. The apartment was gone, Rosa was dead, and Billy wanted to be alone. I wasn't ready to crash on burlap sofa.

I looked at the time, Alysa might be on tonight at Ocean Side. She would be yelling last call soon. I chose to stop in for one last drink and try to forget the last few days.

The doorman that had greeted me so welcoming the other night was gone from his little stool, the bar was nearly empty. It had been a Tuesday night, now a Wednesday morning. Two guys that looked like they were in the Army sat at one end of the bar, the other end was occupied by an old couple that weren't ready to admit they should quit. Alysa was the only bartender when I took a stool. There was still one server on, she was sweeping up and putting chairs on tables. The band had already left. I saw Alysa smile from behind the bar and stress melted from my shoulders.

"Finally, off the clock or on another case?" Alysa's smile faded. She laid out a cloth napkin and scooped ice into it as if she were pouring a drink. She rolled it up and handed it to me.

"That bad?" I asked putting the napkin on my scalp, still tender I switched to my eye. Those cam girls had left their mark on my face and my soul. he napkin to my eye.

"Yeah, but I'm glad to see you back at the bar and not under it." She smiled and grabbed a plastic cup, the translucent kind, then dumped some ice and poured coke over it. She winked then grabbed a bottle of bourbon and splashed a few drops in. She bounced off to finished capping the liquor bottles. My good eye tended to her backside as she tipped-up on her toes straining and extenuating well-formed muscles. Rosa was gorgeous but she wasn't Alysa.

I sat quietly looking at the drink. Each rising bubble was the face of everyone that died over what amounted to nothing more than some naked pictures and videos. Those nudes represented a large sum of cash. There were other ways of making a buck. Sunny found that out, she liked the cam life. The role playing, the teasing, the being in control if only for a few minutes a day. At least no one died. Not directly anyway.

Alysa finished her count on liquor and started in on the pile of pint glasses and mason-jar mugs waiting to be washed.

"You look lost. Is it the case?"

"Yeah."

"You can talk about it if you want. Those two down there are Army so they have security clearances." A couple of '*Yes Ma'am*' with drunk half salutes came for one end of the bar. She pointed at the older couple sipping red wine, "And they are from Italy, don't really speak English." *Italia* was shouted at the other end of the bar.

I blinked, "You ever watch porn?" I took the drink and sipped.

Alysa was leaning over the sink now hand-washing pint glasses, dipping them in warm soapy water then chemical mix and then a third dip into clean water. She put the two glasses she held down, took the towel from her back pocket and wiped away water the spilled on the edge of the sink. "No. I mean I've seen it. I don't get off to it if that's what you're asking."

"No, not what I'm asking." I sipped some more then said, "I don't care for it much either. I got friends that watch it all the time, girlfriends too."

Alysa was now pulling the nasty, sticky, smelly wet mats off the floor. "Yeah," She said over her shoulder, "I got a girl friend of mine that said she likes to watch tranny stuff. I don't get it."

I chuckled. Alysa was a great bar tender. I had coincidentally followed her all over town for a few years now. A new place would open, and I would stop in for a drink. She would be there serving. The names changed as places came and went. She didn't always live in town and there were years we didn't see each other. The relationship never really progressed beyond that of bar tender and patron. It wasn't until I became a regular at Cooper's that we formally introduced ourselves.

"This wasn't the usual case for me. I took on a lot. I didn't mean to either. I got two clients in one day."

Alysa began wiping down the bar, "And they were related?"

"Yeah." I finished my drink. I began chewing on the ice. Alysa cashed out the two Army guys and then the Italians. I sat at the bar. The server came and tipped Alysa out for the drinks she made. The manager came by. He was a young man who looked old. He wore a white button up short sleeve shirt with a black tie that matched a thin black mustache. He was skinny everywhere except his stomach that pushed the limits of the middle buttons.

He eyed me and said to Alysa, "The drawer ready?"

She nodded it was and he took it. I saw the end of the night, pulled a twenty and put it on the bar. Alysa pushed it back at me, saying, "Gimme a break Grimes."

"Hey, I gotta try."

Alysa started to walk away and stopped. She turned and stood across the bar from me just as I was pulling off my stool. "If you really want to spend that twenty, I could eat."

I shrugged, "Okay."

I drove but she navigated. We went south down A1A to a single strip mall with an old brick exterior. The only light on the strip was at the end for a twenty-four-hour breakfast place.

No other table came in while we were there, so the majority of the time was spent talking to the server. She was an older lady, thick in the middle with white orthopedic shoes on. By the time the meal was over, I knew more about our waitress then I did Oliver Lean or Tara Johnson. I also got to know more about Alysa, and I liked that.

Alysa made a fuss about covering the check. I, not much for arguing let her take it. We walked out to the empty parking lot in silence, neither one wanting the night to end but both afraid carrying on might ruin what we had waited so long to have.

Alysa turned, "I was thinking about your case." An ocean breeze picked up, tossing her blonde hair across her face. She pulled it back into a ponytail. I leaned against the fender of the F150 and folded my arms not expecting much from her summation.

She continued, "That poor guy, he must have really loved that girl to try and kill for her."

"Which one? There were two and both got killed in the process."

"Oh," Alysa looked at her shoes. The black nonskid rubber sole scraped over the asphalt of the parking lot. "So, who's the other guy?"

"The second Hood was a barback at Baldy's. Eddie was his name."

"Who's the big fish you owe? I bet I know him." She said excitedly and reached out grabbing at my tee shirt. "He probably comes to the bar."

"He owns Baldy's."

"I wouldn't go anywhere near that."

"That's what I'm dealing with." I said through a smile.

We leaned against the Olds. I was hunched making us nearly shoulder to shoulder.

"I knew you were back to work as soon as I saw you." She said looking down at her shoes.

"How is that?"

"You cut your hair." She ran her hand over my bristles of my buzzed head. Her fingers slowing as they softly touched lump on my scalp. Her hand slowly retracted and settled on my jaw.

That was my moment, our moment, almost. It wouldn't have taken much, I just needed to lean in a couple of inches, and she would have filled the gap. Fear scrambled my brain, logjammed my actions. She was something I had wanted for so long. The image of Rosa smiling as she drove off wouldn't clear my mind. Then the face of another blond named Chloe that gave me the same churning gut mixed with fire that Alysa was giving. Both dead. Both women I surrendered to.

We remained still while the moment moved past us. The silence that followed was interrupted as the thumping bass of shitty reggae ton filled the 4 am night. Then came the whirling of the tall mud terrain tires. A familiar Toyota Sequoia rolled to a stop perpendicular to the parked Old. The black tinted window on the passenger side went down. A black-haired Hispanic man with tattoos stretching out from under his black tee shirt said, "What up homie? You know where 2105 South Beach Street suit two is?" in his thick Spanish accent he mispronounced suite for suit.

I casually stepped between the car and Alysa. My right thumb slipped into my waistband as I turned my hips, pointing my left shoulder to the car. "Yeah. I can take you there if you want." I said in a low growl. Hearing the address of my office called out like that began my blood circulating at an ever-growing rate. I had to keep calm and not get jumpy.

All the four doors opened at once. I slid my thumb around stopping at the grip of the Glock. Three men stepped out of the SUV. Three of the men had faces of strangers but they all shared a familiar look, a look that said they want to fight. I wanted to give it to them.

The tattooed man climbed out of the driver's seat. He said, "Why so jumpy Homie? Did we interrupt your date here?" He laughed and the other three men laughed. He was the leader. I just had to drop him first and the others would run. Getting Alysa out of the way was my priority. My left hand went behind me and pressed against her, pushing her back between our cars.

She whispered, "Grimes."

They came from all sides, closing in quickly. I went for the Glock, leaving my right unprotected. Tattoo guy had quick hands getting a punch in, popping my head back. I quickly leaned back to miss the incoming right. My left came up to block a punch. I straight leg kicked out at another and threw a right hook back at a different man, knocking him down. The fourth man on the right went for Alysa.

Alysa did her best to fight him off. She put up her elbows and shot a speedy kick at the man's crotch. He was quick to pull back limiting the damage. He charged hard, throwing out his hairy arms, wrapping her up. I turned and threw a hurried off-balance punch to the side of a man's head and then was punched and kicked myself by unseen hands and feet. They kept coming, no matter how many fists and feet I deflected more came. A few punches connected. One man fell back on his ass. I could hear Alysa's screams as solid metal made a crackling sound near my right temple. My head felt heavy like it was about to roll off my neck and bounce on the old asphalt. Stars danced across my black night sky. The screams faded. A Nike shoe stabbed my stomach sending acid up my throat. The car doors slammed shut. Alysa stopped screaming. Someone said, "I have a message for you Piss Pants. The give Aziz what he wants and you get the girl."

I got the pistol out, but it never went off.

I crawled to my feet. The Cadillac was gone. There was no one in the parking lot, no sirens in the distance. I got in the Olds Cutlass and pulled some napkins from the glove box. In the rearview mirror I wiped away the blood and dirt. Blood dribbled down from my eyebrow. A thumb and index finger pinched it shut. The ringing hadn't stopped but my vision was back to normal. The Cutlass laid rubber all the way out of the parking lot and all I could think about was not to get any blood on the interior.

The second flight of stairs was harder to conquer than the first. The stair well was spinning, and I had to go down on all fours to make the last few steps. Each heaving breath pushed the limits of my skull, it wouldn't take much to split it down the middle.

At the top of the stairs the hallway was dimly lit. Overhead every third light was on leaving pale-yellow circles evenly spaced on the pale grey linoleum floor. My head was hung as I shuffled my battered body in.

I stopped abruptly at the office door. There would be no need to get my key out because the two-inch-thick wooden door was splintered at the stainless-steel deadbolt. My rattled mind worked to sift through a list of anyone that would want to kick in my door. All but one was dead.

Listening in the dim light for the sound of movement on the other side kept me in the hall. When I heard nothing, I pushed the door open all the way.

My office looked much the same way as Oliver Lean's condo only without the four dead girls. All the drawers were pulled out, the contents dumped on the floor and anything that could be smashed was in pieces. The burlap couch cushions of my ugly sofa were all cut and scattered over the floor. Through all the mess, what drew my attention was the open file cabinet.

I shuffled through the mess and found a nearly empty bottle of bourbon. I sipped it. There was not time to rest. Under an overturned drawer were Band-Aids and Ibuprofen.

I grabbed my phone and called Billy.

"Yeah man," Billy dragged his words on the other end.

"Hey, my office was hit, they tore it up. You alright?"

He sucked in some air then said, "Sorry man, but ah, nah the shop is all good."

Billy's tone was still down, the events of today weighed on him. He would need time to work it out of his system. Not even the excitement of my raided office snapped him out of his funk. I wanted to ask him to go with me, to tear Aziz apart, and burn down his mansion. He would go if I asked. I didn't want him to see the things I had seen, carry the guilt I carried and live with the lives I took.

"Good man. Get some rest and we'll catch up when this is all over. It's time to lay low."

Billy uttered a few incoherent words that let me know he agreed and hung up. This is where we parted ways until the job was over. There was not time to rest, I staggered to the file cabinet and grabbed a small red and black canvas tool bag. Inside were the tools I would need to get through the security at Aziz's oceanfront mansion. I grabbed the Glock 30 SF and shoved it in my pocket then synched up my belt to compensate for the extra weight. A couple of ten round mags went in my back pocket.

The infinite trip down the hall to the bathroom was the longest of my life. The cold water felt good on my skin. The white porcelain sink turned pink as the blood dripped from the open wounds on my face. A couple of Band-Aids were slapped over my wounds. The booze and pills began to breakdown in my system and go to work. The pain dulled. I needed sleep. That wouldn't happen.

A rap at the bathroom door shot me with enough adrenaline to open my eyes all the way.

"Roger is that you in there? Dammit, I knew it. You been camping out in your office again. I warned you." It was Berta's ear scratching shrill.

I opened the door. She sucked in enough air to play a tuba but stopped short when she saw my face and the blood drooling from a head wound.

"I'm just working a little over time, Berta." I said and brushed past her with my tool bag full of guns and electronics.

She said nothing as she watched me walk the hall to the stairwell.

Chapter 18

The F150 was parked on the side of a 7-11. I crossed A1A and went down to the beach. The moon had passed and was concealed behind silver lined black clouds. It was another 200 yards through the sand before I came to Aziz's back yard.

All the windows were black. Not a light on in the house. I went up a dune to the neighbor's backyard, scaled a low block wall then climbed through some sea grape trees. The fence between the yards was weathered wood boards held by rusty nails. I pried a couple loose and slipped through.

Going on the memory of the poker game that started all of this for me, I maneuvered around the tiki hut bar and then crawled under the wooden deck, through the sand to the other side. Kneeling, I listened. A steady breeze carried up over the yard, splitting around the house. I moved over to fence.

With the rope in my bag, I slung it up over the railing around the balcony. On the third try, the roped slipped through the bars. Gingerly, feeding slack the rope slid down the wall. I tied a simple loop knot and synched it back to the railing.

The last tug hoisted me up enough to grab the base of the railing causing to shriek. I froze. No lights, no sounds. I pulled myself up and over.

The sliding glass door had a simple magnetic sensor wired to the alarm. I cut the glass and jumped the sensor. Then I cut out around the lock and pulled the door back.

The room was large with white marble floors and salmon-colored walls. Except for two cheap palm tree prints hanging, there was nothing else in the room.

Creeping to the door, I crossed the hall and went to the stairs. Then the lights came on.

Sitting in a white leather wrap around couch, sipping a drink was Smitty.

I went down the stairs and met him at the couch. Steam rose from a coffee cup Smitty held. Slowly he slurped black coffee. He pulled on his short sleeve button up shirt. The top three buttons are undone. A gold chain hangs around his neck.

"You should get yourself a cup."

Every second was precious. I was in a hurry, and I was angry. Most of all, I was tired.

"You got time. I have assurance she'll be fine." Smitty smoothly leveled the cup to his lips, slurped then set it on the coffee table.

I came back from the kitchen with a cup of steaming joe. With my Glock tucked under my thigh, I eased back in the large sofa. The coffee roast was dark and rich and opened my eyes.

"Tell me you're not mixed up in this."

"I don't have to tell you, kid." He shook his head with disappointment at my accusation. "I'm buying you and her time."

"Where's Aziz?"

"He's hiding. When I found out about the girl, I told him you'd kill him without hesitation, and nothing would stand in your way. Nothing."

"Then I'll burn Baldy's to the ground."

"I wouldn't do that."

"That's where they've got Alysa?"

Smitty nodded.

I stood up. It was time to light a fire and get Alysa back.

"Sit down Roge, I gotta make a call and then see what he says and play the back and forth, you know." Smitty sipped his drink, leaving the Columbian flavors in his mouth as he chose his next words carefully, with precision to cut me in the right places. To get me down on one knee and kiss the ring. "I'll broker it just like the old days. You hand over the stuff, he does what he does, and we all get happy together."

There went the hook, just like the old days.

My breathing stopped. My eye lids pinched into slits. "No." I said.

Smitty let out a long-held breath. "No, what? I'm doing this for you."

"No terms. There's no blackmail. He took her from my arms and I want her back. I'll pay my debt and then we are done. Make it quick." I stood up.

"Don't do it like this. Don't go off hot headed, running and gunning and risk it all."

"Risk it all? This isn't about money. I'm not keeping the blackmail. He took a woman, he kidnapped her. I'm going to do whatever I have to, to get her back."

"I know what this *is* about, damn it! You're on fire right now but cool it or you burn everyone around you. If you rush in and things go wrong," He shook his head, "you'll hate yourself the rest of your life."

The old man reached down to an honest place to fee me that advice. I didn't know the place, I didn't know the story, but I trusted it. Heat radiated from my swollen bruises and the Band Aids I stuck on were peeling with sweat. It was time to trust Smitty more than I ever had. He had led me through several high-risk jobs and never failed me.

"Do you have the blackmail?"

I nodded.

"Have you checked it out?"

I shook my head.

"Do you have the eighteen grand?"

I laughed, "He still wants the cash? After all this?"

"Aziz is ruthless and worse, you've not only made him look weak; you've scared him, Roge." He made a sour face as he sipped the coffee. "I warned him. I said, you're poking the jackal."

"And I let Lean die. He said he was connected up north. Philadelphia. Do I have to worry about waking up to a bag man standing over me?"

Smitty picked at his fingernails, clicking them, not trying to break them. "No. Lean was full of it. I've been making a lot of calls, checking into all this, preparing to cover your ass. Again."

It might have made him feel good telling me all this work on his part was for my benefit, but it wasn't. It all leads back to him making the only ass he's covering his own.

"Listen kid, go home. Check out that blackmail so you know you have the real deal, get the cash and I'll set up the transaction."

"No. This ends now." I stood.

Smitty stood as well. He jabbed his fingers into my chest, and I fell back into the couch. "Get some rest. I'll take care of it."

My eyes shot fire as my face twisted from rage. "They took her! They kidnapped Alysa. There is no more time."

He stood over me still holding his coffee, "I made assurances with Aziz. She's okay and will remain okay."

"What assurance? He already knows I'm coming."

"I told him, the only thing scarier than a jackal is a lion. Whatever damage he thinks you can do; I would do tenfold." This time Smitty had heat behind his eyes. It wasn't the fire raging that I had but he was making steam and once that locomotive started chugging, I believed he would indeed roll through Aziz and his man Bohgos. With his word, I could rest for now.

We parted ways with little words exchanged between us.

Chapter 19

It was predawn. Going back to my ransacked office was pointless, my tablet had been smashed so checking the flash drive for dick pics was out. The only way to find out what was on them would be to call Sanford.

The call went to voicemail. I didn't leave a message.

I waited.

The phone lit up. I answered.

"Mr. Grimes." His tone was light but short. Willis Sanford was a talker, tonight he listened.

"Do you know Azad Aziz?" I got to the point. Asking how he'd been and what was new, was useless color. All I wanted was in black and white.

"Hhmmm." Again, his tone light and agreeable telling me he did but he wanted to know why I was asking before he would admit it.

"Then you know I owe him."

"Uhhhmmm." Sanford's tone was lower. He knew, he knew everything.

"I need to borrow a computer."

"My office is always open to you, Grimes."

Sanford hung on the line. I said goodbye and he hung up with no parting words. The conversation was cool and short, not the usual manner for Sanford. I had dodged too many of his calls lately and it was beginning to leave him raw. My last job for Sanford had worked out well for him, I thought I got the raw end so when he called back, I ignored it. It was probably something I shouldn't have done because Sanford could light our bridge and burn it quickly, he didn't need me, but I would always need a man like Sanford.

I parked in the parking garage the CBR Building but had to walk around the building to main entrance and rapped on the thick glass doors. A security guard came out from behind the large desk in the center of the lobby. She was round shaped and walked with a slight waddle. Her short cropped curly brown hair spirted out in a perfect globe around her face like she had a dead Chia Pet on her scalp. Her eyes were bagged yet twitched fast to size me up.

She pushed the button on the two-way speaker, "What can I do for ya'?" she had a high nasal voice linking her to her Midwest roots.

"Roger Grimes, Willis Sanford is expecting me." I said.

She nodded, shaking the dead Chia and walked back the desk. An electronic lock buzzed, allowing me to push on the tall glass door.

"Next time, have him get you a key card." She said with a smile and nod, not annoyed in the least to do her job, just offering friendly advice.

The inside of the elevator was mirrored with gold finish. I avoided eye contact with my reflection until the bell dinged at the seventh floor. I finally looked at myself in the mirror. My face had purple blotches from fists, leaving the skin to feel like it had been dipped in butter and then broiled. The elastic collar around my neck was stretched and there was a dingy dark ring around my ankles so that when I slipped off my Vans it looked like I had on a pair of white socks. I wiped my palm across my damp forehead then wiped the sweat off on my shirt.

The elevator doors parted, and I went down the hall to Sanford's office. The familiar African themed art, a zebra hide, and the dim gold carpet, all were a welcomed sight. Monique was not at her desk to nod to, but she seldom greeted me. A nod with eye contact was all I could hope for. She was an attractive girl, and she knew it and it forced her to work even harder at being attractive. A vicious cycle.

Sanford was standing at the mini bar in the large corner office incased in rich mahogany and gold accented furniture. The large desk laid diagonally against the apex of the window joint that formed the corner of the building. I sat down on a freshly recovered faux leather chair, just like I had months ago, but this time, no longer bleeding from a gunshot wound. Time healed that wound, now, I needed it to heal another.

Sanford had his square framed steel rimmed glasses on. The white cotton ball still stuck in the corner of his forehead, surrounded by tight curly black hair. His eyes were wide and whiskey brown, greeted me with soft acceptance. His gold bracelet clinked against a stainless-steel tumbler as he picked it up, tipped it towards me then drank from it.

"Is it too early or too late for a drink, Grimes?" Sanford said clanking the steel against the granite countertop. He pushed up on his white cuffed sleeves, then tugged down on the grey vest he wore. He looked every bit of a bartender you find at a yacht club or banquet hall. He had been tending bar at this private party for way too long.

"Water." My throat was dry, I've sweated out the whiskey. It collected in a dew on my skin. The cool dry air of the AC began to evaporate the moisture.

Sanford dipped his grey stubble covered chin and came up with water in a bottle. The label claimed to be from a spring on the other side of the world. I don't care if there is truth in the label. I drank half the bottle down before coming up for air.

"Thanks."

Sanford walked to the tall leather desk chair. There were manila file folders in three stacks across his desk and one folder open in front of him. The midnight oil had been burning for Sanford, dimming the natural glow he basked in when I first met him. Gone tonight was that pep in his step, on the balls of his feet like fighters do, his hands danced when he spoke. Tonight, his hands were at his sides and each step brought down a heavy heel.

Sanford sat. He closed the file and placed it on top of another. He took a deep breath and let it out forcefully though his nostrils. "How ya been Grimes?"

"Great."

Sanford's right eyebrow arched, "Yeah, you look great. The washroom is there in the wood paneling."

I pulled the plastic bag with the flash drives in it from my pocket and slid it across the table.

"I need to take a look at these. It contains blackmail material from a webcam site. The guy it belongs to is dead but someone else wants it. They trashed my office and kidnapped a friend. I want her back."

Sanford didn't move his hands. He kept his fingers interlocked and stared at the bag. He looked up and said, "What do you need from me exactly?"

"They smashed my tablet."

"Go buy another one." Sanford sipped his drink. He put it down and waited for me to reply.

When I said nothing, he added, "What is it you really want?"

I sat watching the red ember glow brighter between us, setting our bridge into flames that if burned any longer I could never cross. Ignoring his calls had been a mistake. Wallowing in my own self pities had shut out the only man who could have helped me out of all of this. The fire had to be put out before the bridge collapsed.

"We started something," I said. "I sat right here and listened to your speech about cleaning out the rats in this town. We cleaned up alright. Even though I didn't want to, I kept cleaning. I went on a bender to forget what I did, what I became that night. I sobered up and realized it was someone I've always been, and you just held the mirror up to make me look when no one else had."

Sanford's shoulders went back as he leaned against his high-back leather chair. His fingers where still intertwined but resting now across his stomach. The corners of his mouth crinkled downward. His white teeth showed between his lips. It was a look of being happily disappointed, like when you get your bill and its way less than you thought.

Sanford leaned forward, unclasped his hands and spread his fingers wide. "Sounds to me like you found your feet."

The strings tugged on my arms and mouth opened but I refused to speak. The puppet master across from me grinned. My initial reaction was to resist, cut the strings and fight back, thinking about it I knew he was right. I went out on my own this time and ended up fighting to set a bunch of deviant strangers free of their blackmail chains. I killed a rat or two doing it and this town was better for it.

A red tongue went out to wet my lips, "All I've found is hate."

"But it got the job done, didn't it? The fire at the porn place, that you?" Sanford erased any expression from his face. He wanted to read my face before I could read his. He was losing. Then slowly, excitement built in his tired eyes, rejuvenating them. He was more awake now and wanted the details of my exploits.

"Sort of." I shrugged. "I didn't light the match that burned the porn studio down, but I was there. Turns out the guy running the show was blackmailing subscribers to his porn. I think all the material are on those flash drives."

"News reported the guy was Oliver Lean. Did he deserve it?"

I shrugged again, "He wasn't good for the community."

Sanford sprung from his chair. His hands up and loose as they shot and swooped in boxing combinations. "That's what I like to hear." He laughed. "Roger Grimes has still got some fight left in him."

Delight smeared across the old fighter's face forcing the grooves of life to deepen. Instead of making him look older the grooves made him more childlike. Willis Sanford was proud of his work. He had taken a wooden puppet and made it dance. I cut my strings to become a real boy, but the wood never turned to flesh. I killed some bad people and burned down a house of ill repute. Now I was back at the puppet shop trying to reattach my strings.

Sanford poured himself another Remey Martin cognac with champagne on top. He poured some whiskey in a glass then placed it in front of me as he slung a leg over the corner of the large mahogany desk. The hanging leg swung up slowly then dropped rapidly.

"Do I need to prepare a defense for you? Do the cops even know you were there? What am I saying? You're Roger Grimes! Six months ago, you walked out of that pool hall without a scratch." Sanford's smile dimmed as he remembered that bloody night and the chair, I was sitting in had to be reupholstered.

Without a scratch? Laughable if it hadn't hurt so bad. He just avoided the responsibility of pain. If I were invincible in his eyes, then sending me out to do bad things I was so good at, let him sleep at night.

"The police still don't know who shot that place up. That's why I've been working so many late nights." Sanford said and his leg stopped swinging. He looked at the files like tall grass needing a mow, it had to be done and he'd feel better when it was finished.

Back on the other side of the desk again he shoved some manila folders around saying, "I've been putting somethings together. People, powerful people, want answers. Other powerful people want it buried."

We sat in silence for a few moments. Sanford looked up at me, "You know I hate that you don't talk much. Just nothing, you just sit there. These files have been sitting out this whole time. You ever see my desk with this much work? No, you haven't. Not even a look or glance, anything that would make me think you had a question in your head about it. Damn." Sanford never liked to swear. It amused me.

I saw it all, he just didn't catch my look at the folders when I came in. I read names and linked them to names in the news, the names of political figures and business leaders that have been rightfully dragged through mud as the state rips a sex trafficking case open. It was because of me, all because I let Sanford adjust my moral parameters of right and wrong. A kid who grew up a thief suddenly gets a conscious at thirty and changes careers overnight. How could I know if stealing didn't feel wrong then killing wasn't supposed too either? It did. It fucked me up nicely. Now here I am back at the only moral compass I recognized, and it was the source of my killing.

"Are you defending the people I exposed?" My jaw was left open long enough for a fly to lay eggs and the larva to grow into more flies and lay more eggs.

"Hell no Grimes. Do you really think after what we did, what I got you involved with, I would then try and double dip just to make a buck? I would cuss you out for thinking such a thing if my mama hadn't raised me better." He glared at me then let the anger subsided from his face.

"These folders here are just records of their wrong doings, in case the time comes for you to extend a visit. I believe we met for a reason, Roger. You are my *White Knight*. You like the sound of that?"

"Sounds racist."

His arms went up and out like a hawk about to take flight. His face sobered of enthusiastic outrage. After a moment of processing, his finger went out, pointing at my chest as a smile broke across his face.

"You're pulling my leg with that racist stuff."

I smiled and stood up, grabbed my empty glass and Sanford's then went to bar and poured us another round.

From the bar I said, "Oliver Lean was a shit bag who killed a girl I had once loved."

With full pours again I continued, "It really could have all ended with him dying, but then I found out he was blackmailing a bunch of schmucks and I wanted to stop it. To let them know it was over." I put the drinks down on the desk and pulled out the flash drive from the bag.

Sanford reached into his desk and pulled out a thin Mac. He opened it. As it fired up, he spoke, "Seems like a waste of time to me, but not you. No, you want to pull something good out of what you saw on this case. I can see it in your eyes, tired, distant, you want to close them at night and see a little less pain in the world, even if it means a little more for yourself."

"The dead don't bother me anymore." I lied and handed him a fresh drink. I was beginning to buy in to the myth of Roger Grimes, some kind of dark superhero. It helped Sanford too, if I were his White Knight.

A smirk flashed on Sanford's face then faded into a professional straightness as he plugged in the purple flash drive. The computer made a noise every time he tapped through the route to open the drive. Once he got it open, he turned the laptop so we both could see.

The file had many folders. The name on each folder was someone's last name with a hyphen and either *cash* or *account* next to it. Each folder contained dick pics and some short videos we didn't have to watch to know what they contained. An Excel sheet kept track of when payments were made and if anyone was paid off, falling behind or refused to pay.

I just lowered my head into my hands. I was so close, close to paying Aziz back and close to freeing Lean's victims.

"I have no choice but to hand it over to Aziz."

This time Sanford shook his head, "No. This aint all for nothing. There's a lot more dudes on here. You can't just let them keep on paying. We'll get those two when the time is right." He spun the laptop around and started clicking, reading over the information on it.

I like Sanford's words. It was the hard way but isn't it always. All that I had gone through and what all the others suffered over compromising pics. They would remain in captivity, and I would fade into the background. A knight whose sword of justice was broken. I couldn't let it end this way.

"Wait a second, here, Grimes. There is more on this drive and blackmail. Looks like we got the whole money laundering process too." He clicked around then pulled the drive.

"With Lean dead, Aziz will have to find a new way."

"What will you do?" Sanford said. He expected more from me, excitement, anger, revenge. I had none of that.

"I'll just have to set them free and deal with whatever Aziz throws at me." I shrugged.

"You just going to email them and say it's over?"

"Pretty much. I thought I would write something about it all getting destroyed and they no longer have to worry about it."

"What if they want their money back?"

"Nothing I can do about that. The cops have all the money and I'm not breaking into a police station just to pay these jerk offs their money."

Sanford leaned back in his chair. His eyebrows arched wrinkling his forehead then came down.

I remained silent. Sanford raised his brows again and again they settled flat.

"What?" I said.

"That leaves your debt. How are you gonna pay?"

"I don't know."

Sanford nodded but said nothing. He knew what I was about to say.

"Maybe Smitty can work something out for me. He knows Aziz, there's got to be something else I can steal for him."

Sanford nodded uttering something in agreement. He stood up, clasped his hands behind his back and went to the large window facing west. Out there was the 'hood', the hood he came up in, the hood that taught him to box. The hood he escaped for college. The jury in my mind was out on whether Willis Sanford was a saint or the worst kind of sinner, a fallen angel using morals and righteous vindication to quench the blood lust of revenge. There was no doubt I had become his pawn, defiant as I might be, his mission appealed to me.

A sharp brown finger jutted into the thick glass. "Down there is getting better. 3rd Street had a major setback thanks to you. They're all thinned out and a mess. Yes sir, you done good out on the streets.

"Aziz is a different creature. He has money and a standing in this town, a business owner who likes to schmooze with City Council members. He donates to charities around town you know. Yes, a fine Daytona Beach resident if there ever was one." Sanford turned to his left and looked southeast now, towards the ocean and somewhere off in the distance one of many sparkling lights was Aziz's beach house.

"The man will fall like the others, Grimes. I have faith in that. Now is not his time." Sanford took a seat once more. His face was drained, and his arms hung loosely to the sides. Now I had gone from pawn to knight, though not white by any means. Sanford sought me to join him in his quest to be defenders of the realm that is Daytona Beach.

Taking it all the way with Aziz seemed overwhelming. There would be a lot of shooting and that meant killing. Not only did he have bodyguards he had a police department that would come to his aid. An assassination would draw a heavy investigation. They would question everyone associated with those poker games. Smitty would never give me up but Marcus? I didn't know Marcus.

Sanford came around his desk and stood next to me. He grabbed the chair beside me and dragged it, leaving four tracks in the carpet as he went. Standing on the chair, leaning above the wet bar, Sanford opened a cabinet and reached in. His arm twisted this way and that. After a click, the familiar sound of a safe opening filled my ears. He retrieved what he needed and then slammed it shut with a grunt.

Stepping down he had a stack of greenbacks in one hand and began dragging the chair with his other. He placed the chair back in the exact spot and sat. The cash went on the desk.

"Pay him."

I stared at the cash. The heavy truth lay before me, banded in two $10,000.00 stacks. I had failed to earn it myself. Slowly, I reached out and stuffed the cash in my pockets. Anger creeped around my insides, filling the space between my guts. I was mad at myself, mad that I had come to Sanford and mad he was bailing me out. It didn't help that he was right. The choice was clear, Aziz had to be paid, the debt settled, and then I could move on. Like the strings already attached to my arms and legs, this cash would no doubt have strings attached as well.

"Is this a loan or a pay advance?" I said without looking at him.

"I don't know yet. Maybe we call it a favor between friends, but whatever it is, you'll need to stay alive if I ever want to see this money again." Sanford stood up, "Pay him."

I stood and followed him to the door. Our business was done. He handed the laptop over to me and showed me the door.

Before going out the door Sanford took a deep breath that held me in place.

"I'm not entirely certain how your relationship with Smitty works, but you need to think about distancing yourself. There's going to come a time where our agenda and his conflict. And I don't want you second guessing a thing." Sanford put his hand on my shoulder and patted.

I left the CBR building with plenty unsaid and undone. I didn't like it but there were pressing matters. I wanted to free the blackmail victims quickly then free myself from Aziz. The cash would pay the debt but not erase my rage at the sense of cowering. Aziz would think he won, that he dominated me, forced me to pay by destroying my life. He didn't. He was just getting his money back.

Chapter 20

Alysa sat in a desk chair, pulling on her restraints. That smile she had always greeted me with was contorted with her red cheeks wet with tears. Boghos stood over her. The top of his pants was undone, and he was taunting her with his hips. I tried screaming, there was no sound. I tried swinging my fists, but they were slow, like I was under water.

I sat up with such force that my head impacted the roof of the truck, sending blinding pain through my body. Looking around I was indeed in the cab, but every blink took me back to that scene, that nightmare.

The rain had started late last night throwing white electricity over the city as it moved. The clouds broke with rapid fire raindrops shooting down into the soil. Each drop left a one second divot in the rising pools. Slowly the enemy's barrage from above subsided and moved on attacking towns to the north. The sun split the black cloud and returned color to the world around me. I wiped the fog off the driver's window. There was a clear break in the rain, for how long I didn't know. I was awake for all of it, having spent an uncomfortable night in the truck.

After leaving Sanford's, I drove around with nowhere to go. A burned-out apartment and vandalized office left me with nowhere to go. I drove until my eyelids weighed 100 pounds apiece. I had to pull over and sleep. A service road that followed the power lines was seclusion enough. Surrounded by green leafy cabbage palms, elephant ear and small oaks, I closed my eyes.

A local 386 area code appeared on my phone. It could only be Aziz or Smitty.

"Yeah." I said.

"It's me." Smitty said.

"What time?"

"One hour."

"That's too long. I'm going to take Aziz apart." I started shaking, barely finishing my sentence, but I finished my thought. It ended with Aziz becoming nothing but a bright red wet stain.

"Whoa, hey kid, easy with the tough talk."

"No one is listening to our call."

Smitty grumbled at the attack on his status. He was under the assumption the FBI still cared what he did and was always running a tap on his phone. That was a long time ago and he didn't want to let it go.

"Yeah, okay. So, I got the meeting with Aziz today. We'll all have a nice brunch and - "

"Sooner. Make it sooner."

"Yeah, okay. We'll skip brunch. Meet Boghos at Baldy's. I can come with you."

"I go alone."

"Then go prepared." Smitty said flatly and hung up.

Staring into the black screen, all I wanted was a time machine. I wanted to go back before the White Knight and the sex traffickers. Back to right after my first case, insurance fraud. Sanford deposited the money and I hit Coopers. That night, I'd go back to that night and meet Alysa. We would talk then date. She would keep me from my bad news neighbor at the time and the case of a missing girl. All of it would change, I'd change, she would make sure of that. If only I had that time machine.

I circled Baldy's three times. With no activity, I parked a block down. My breathing was shallow and my palms sweaty. Over a dozen heists and several bank robberies under my belt but nothing like this. Even walking into a pool hall facing certain death, I feared no one. There was nothing to lose but my life. Now my biggest fear was losing a life I've barely known.

I pounded my chest to keep my heart beating then left Billy's white Ford pickup there in the street and walked up Orange Ave to Baldy's. My Daytona Tortuga's ball cap was shielding my eyes from the light drizzle as I made my way. The dark green windbreaker and tactical pants protected the rest of my body from the rain. My Vans were left at the office and replaced with a pair of Kevlar boots. I desperately didn't want a fight. The blackmail, the money, my life all turned over to Aziz just to let Alysa out of her captivity.

Azad Aziz had made a fatal mistake. He thought I was a good detective, he thought I could find his Tara. He thought I was a good thief and could steal the blackmail. He thought taking Alysa would scare me into doing his bidding. He thought all those things and all of them were wrong. The time had come to stop rebelling against my own nature and do what I was good at. I had a job do in front of me, Alysa's life depended on it. No time to worry about Smitty or anyone else getting in the way of taking down Aziz. The newest gangster in town had gone too far.

The old glass door to the bar had a black metal frame and black metal push bar across it. The push bar was shiny chrome where sweaty hands had pushed on it time and time again. I pushed. The door was locked. The time on the door indicated the bar didn't open for another two hours.

I knocked.

After a few seconds, the face of Boghos appeared close enough to the glass that his breathing left two circular fog marks. He twisted back the lock and the door became loose. I waited for him to back up a step and then went in.

The bar was dark and smelled of stale smoke. A string of white twinkling lights ran along the crown molding.

Piss and stale beer burned the high points in my nostrils. The AC above the door pushed flat air over me locking in the moisture instead of whisking it away. I stayed where I was with the door to my back. Boghos flicked the barrel of a nickel-plated revolver at me to join the others at the end of the bar.

With the revolver in one fat hand, he used the other to scrape over my body looking for weapons. I pulled back, Boghros jammed the barrel against my temple. My Glock, he laid on the bar. He fondled the cash blocks in my pockets but left them there. Then took a seat at the middle of the bar.

This wasn't me, to lay down my weapons so easily. It wasn't me to get so deep into a gambling dept that I entertained a hit-job to get myself out. Alysa's life was at stake, and I had to make a change. A woman will do that to a man, change them, knowingly or not. It's tied up in Newton's laws of physics, the first law, remaining in motion unless acted upon by an unbalanced force.

The three men that took Alysa stirred along the bar. A woman on the inside of the bar poured drinks. The bartender wore a rainbow striped tube top covering small breasts and had on black spandex shorts. Her light brown curly hair was pulled back out of a face that had no makeup on yet. The men sat at the end with a lit hallway behind them casting their faces black with shadow, but I smelled their desire for a fight. The strongest odor coming from Boghos who was still sore from the beat down I gave him in the parking lot a few days ago.

"I take it Aziz isn't here." I said.

"You come down here."

Boghos really couldn't believe I was that stupid.

"Where's the girl?" My question went unanswered. He waved me down again, but I wasn't budging.

It was time for action. No talk, no conversation. Demands were made and they were not met. The consequences for their actions must be carried out.

I reached in my pocket and three sets of white eyes shined through the dark back at me. Everyone sucked in a breath. Water dripped from the AC to the moldy spot on the linoleum as it had for decades, scarring the tile with its own little ecosystem of mold and mildew.

My hand came out slow with a damp wad of bills and slapped them on the bar with a splat.

From my other pocket, I pulled another stack of bills. They joined the other stack on the bar. The bartender's smile wrapped around her head. Her nipples poked out against the rainbow tube top. She started sauntering towards me, swinging what little meat she had on her hips.

"A round for the bar?" she said with a smile that was missing teeth.

Boghos dropped a hairy arm down on the bar halting the broad in her bar mat tracks. He grunted something she understood and that drove her back. He looked at me and squared his shoulders. I remembered there just how large a man Boghos was. He wasn't any taller than me, his largeness was in the size of his head and the way one of his fingers equaled the circumference of two of mine.

The three men were up from their barstools now. The man in the middle lit a cigarette. Each of them had hard olive skin with dense black hair. The leading man had deep eyes that had seen things and done things. The guy smoking was not as seasoned, but his coolness was convincing that he wanted to see those things done. The guy on the end had shifty eyes. I doubted his commitment to this fight, but fear does strange unpredictable things to a man, making him dangerous. A fourth man appeared in the shadow of the hallway.

"The girl. Now." My voice was steady. My face cold and still. All I could think about was the weak spot of my cracked skull, proving just how out of shape I had been. Alysa deserved more.

Boghos stepped aside, the rest of the men did as well clear a path to the office down the hall. Each step was slower than I wanted, but at any second the parting of the Red Sea could collapse on all sides and drown me under the weight of flying fists and legs.

The shadowy man in front of the office door was the tattooed talker from the night before. His chin up and his arms crossed his chest. He swayed then stepped aside. I swallowed as I entered incase what I found made me vomit.

Alysa sat wide eyed, bound at the wrists to a desk chair and a gag in her mouth soaked by the tears streaming down her cheeks. Fear had not yet subsided from her green eyes, leaving them a red route to her soul.

I pulled my pocketknife from my boot, Boghos wasn't very thorough. Once her hands were free, she ripped the gag from her mouth and inhaled.

She hugged me tight around the neck. Her feet didn't touch the ground while she hung on the man tree. My arms went around her to let her know she was safe, and she was safe. I had to let her go, there were things left undone. I peeled her off me, "I'm sorry." I said. She said nothing as she slid down around my waist and squeezed. Her face buried in my chest as she sobbed. Then one final large breath and she pulled away.

I lead her out of the office. The back door was pad locked on the inside. I didn't want us to pass back through the bar. There was no other way. Boghos never intended for either of us to leave today. Smitty's assurance failed.

"I must check the blackmail." Bohgos demanded. The men behind Boghos drew closer. As we slowly walked for the front door, each one made small movements, inching, creeping their way closer. Then arms hung low, hands disappearing below the bar. A bottle from the bar was missing. The fight was coming, Boghos wanted his revenge. I wanted to set the men free from their blackmail bondage, but the only way to do that now was to go through all four of these men and get Alysa out alive. They would never know the pain I was about to take for them. That didn't matter now, I just wanted it over. Aziz had cost me too much over this debt. His fear and intimidation tactics only made me resolute. Now he was going to know what fear felt like.

The front door was locked.

"You go nowhere." Boghos said.

"I had assurance from Aziz."

"For the girl only." Boghos flicked his wrist, allowing her exit.

I slipped the car keys into Alysa's hands. "The white Ford pickup a block away." I twisted the bolt and guided her out, locking it behind her. We locked eyes through the glass. I spun and knelt, coming up with a hand full of brass, forcing them to stutter in their next step, throwing them off balance and giving me the advantage.

The bartender had held quiet through the fight until now. She began shouting, *Kill'im!,* cheering Boghos on.

All four hoods, plus the bar tender, started breathing heavy. It was obvious they were here to kill me, no need to drag this out.

I kicked out with a right leg, whacking into the side of Boghos's left knee. He buckled but held strong to a tall back barstool. He snorted like a bull casting snot across his lip. The brass buried into the side of his nose. His face was turned just enough that I missed breaking the bone. My other hand was fast to catch him in the throat, he stumbled back on the moldy dark carpet.

The bartender made a move for the cash. I snatched a bottle from behind the bar and threw it at her. She had her arms up as the bottle hit hard but didn't break.

I tried to get over the bar but felt a snag on my right.

The first guy grabbed my leg. I kicked out and he fell back blocking the space between the bar and the tables lining the wall, bottlenecking the other two. The fourth man remained back.

A bottle broke on the bar. Green glass shards scattered across the worn resin surface. The third man held the glass neck. His lip curled in a snarl exposing yellow chalky plaque laden teeth. He pushed the guy in front of him to the side to become the second fighter.

With the bar to the left of me and the narrow room to my right I had to take a southpaw stance.

From somewhere a switch blade popped out with a *CHITCH!* All hell was about to break loose. They would move at once from two sides, looking for an opening.

I tossed a stool at the first guy wielding the blade. My left hand grabbed the wrist of the second guy holding the broken bottle and slammed it against the bar. His grip was strong, he held on. His left grabbed my right shoulder. My right arm twisted around his, tangling our limbs. I swung him to my right, away from the bar to block the swinging blade of the first man. The blade cut the second man deep. He screamed.

I still had a hold of the second man's arm. He was growing weaker due to the blood loss. The broken bottle neck fell to the floor. I threw a hard left into the man's face and his knees finally buckled.

Man One and Three were ready to strike. Boghos was getting to his feet. I got in close to Boghos and threw a couple of combinations, keeping him between me and the other two. The punches were on target, stunning him. The other two wouldn't be denied a fight. I twisted and kept my elbows close as I dodged a few wild slashes from the first guy with the blade. I grabbed a bar stool and pushed back at the blade like a lion tamer. He lashed out again and again trying to make me taste the steel.

Time was against me. The longer I fought one the more the others would regain their strength. I stampeded forward with the stool. The blade screeched along the metal stool leg. The man stopped as he hit the wall behind, but I drove through sticking one stool leg into his chest. His eyes grew large then faded. He dropped the knife.

The third guy needed to make a name for himself. He smashed out the cigarette and came at me wild. His leg went up, I blocked. He kicked again and I blocked. His arms swung quickly, I blocked. Then I saw my opening and got in close jerking a hook with all my wound-up weight. His head hit the bar with the snap of a dry tree limb, leaving a blood smear as he slid to the floor.

The fourth guy was never really in the fight. He gritted his teeth, as drool rolled out of his open mouth. He was breathing heavy trying to build up the excitement to attack. It never came. He backed up then turned and ran to the back of the hall for the exit. He slapped at the lock but couldn't get it open. He had come on his own or not, to kill me today. I wouldn't let him leave without trying.

A couple of half-closed fists backed by weak wrists came at me, pawing like a cat. I slapped them down and grabbed the man by the neck and dragged him back down the hall.

I slammed his face on the bar and a few broken pieces of glass latched on. He shouted again as blood ran down his face. I straight leg kicked him hard in the chest sending him back, toppling over a bar stool, turning it over as he fell, breaking off one of the metal legs.

Scrambling to his feet, looking back as I neared him, he picked up the metal bar stool leg. The swings were wild. I leaned back and to the side, missing both. Getting in close, taking the momentum from his swing, I hit him hard in the ribs, shoving brass up and in. The bone cracked. The stool leg dropped as he staggered back, trying to breath.

I used the stool leg now on him. His skull cracked with each blow.

The heavy rising and falling of my chest slowed. For a moment, the bar was quiet. Then the man with the knife wound stirred. He was trying to roll to his side. His back was stained a deep purple. The cut was deep, filleting the two halves of his back open.

"Hold it!" Shouted the bartender. She held a nickel-plated revolver with the barrel pointed at me. "I want that cash."

We were only a few feet apart, her on one side of the bar, me on the other. Dead and dying men laid all around us. All she wanted was an escape plan and that money was part of it.

I rearranged the cash on the bar and pushed it forward. She smiled.

With a flick of my wrist, I tossed both stacks of dirty bills to her dirty face. She twisted her stringy haired head to the side. I reached out and snatched her by the wrist, the pistol turned away, and I yanked her over the bar. Her crack diseased body was light enough. She spilled over onto a stool already on its side, busting her face against the metal leg. She cursed as she dropped the pistol to hold her broken teeth in their gums. Tears rolled down her sun spotted face and mixed with the blood from her mouth.

I walked around the bar and poured two shots of Jamison. I set them and the bottle on the bar and walked back around.

I sat on a stool. "Yours if you want it." I said to the bartender and kicked back one of the shots. I repeated the process then sat in silence.

She crawled up to the bar and looked at the shot then looked at me. Shaky hands poured back the shot, she decided to take it despite knowing the pain it would cause. She winced. I poured her another.

Through broken teeth and blood, she mumbled.

"What?"

"It's not loaded," she said pointing at the pistol.

Back in the bar a faint cell phone ringing collapsed the silence. I reached into Boghos's pocket and pulled out the phone.

I answered the call but said nothing.

"Hello? Boghos, ... Boghos did he come yet with the money?"

I held the phone away from my ear but could hear everything Aziz said. Some words he shouted in a language I didn't speak, but fully understood their meaning. The phone call ended.

There was a pounding on the front door. I unlocked it, opening it to see Alysa's face shielded by her blond hair. Behind her the F150.

She jumped into my arms and squeezed. "You're alive." She whispered.

Pulling her away, I said, "You shouldn't have come back. We need to get out of here."

She looked past me to the silent carnage strewn over the bar floor. Her arms fell away from my side.

I turned around to see Boghos stand, as a third wind found him. He was calm, his eyes were pinched and had control of his breathing. He hadn't fought a worthy opponent in a while. He had his bearings. He had my speed and rhythm down. He was going to come at me hard.

Alysa started to tug on me, trying to get me out the door. I charged forward, picking up the bar stool leg in the process. The space between the bar and the wall was tight so I took a hatchet swing at Boghos who slapped it away. Then Boghos let loose a barrage. Block, block, punch. Punch, block. Kick. Grunt and breathe. Sidestep and turn. So, the dance went, each of us giving and taking. My hat was long ago knocked off and the windbreaker was filling with steam and sweat.

Boghos grew angry at his lack of success. I was blocking more than punching. His speed was impressive, he caught me just above my left eye. A sting faded to numbness as the swelling started pushing blood down my face.

Filled with frustrating rage, Boghos forgot the mental lessons his training instilled, and he charged. His large hands blew through my defenses as thick fingers clamped down on my shoulder and waist, imbedding themselves into my muscles. He twisted and lifted. My feet left the ground, weightless, I glided. The plaster wall was cold against my sweaty face. My bone slightly denser than the plaster forced a crack. My skin pinched between plaster and bone, broke. Warm blood seeped.

A solid shot in my back ripped my face from the cold plaster and the sticky glue that was my blood holding me there.

An ape like arm hooked around my neck. Instinct to survive took over as I wildly scratched at the hairy arm. Tightening the tourniquet, pinching the air from my lungs, my face beet red matched my bulging eyes. *Tap out!* But this was a fight to the death, one winner, one walks away. I had to carry on.

In a moment oxygen flowing to my brain slowed to a trickle, I began to black out. I weighed the life I lived to the words those would use at my death. A giant scale appeared in which I placed my life against their words. The scale tipped; my life plunged. The things had I done, the crimes I committed, the lives I stole, the weight against the few good things anyone could say about me was too much. I had to correct the imbalances, I had to push back against the weight of who I was and stack the scale with the man I wanted to be. The only way to do that would be to win today and keep winning.

I pushed up on my toes and then dropped my hips, shoving them back. Boghos had his knees locked and his ass against the bar, not wanting to break his hold he toppled over on me. I slipped my hips, spinning Boghos around and me out of the hold but held his right arm taking it with me and bent it behind him and over his head. He screamed as the bone broke in his wrist. I dropped my knee to his neck. Something popped. I dropped my knee a second time and a cracking sound was followed by a gurgle from Boghos's open mouth. The anger faded from his eyes as they grew cold and still.

I wiped blood from my face and looked up into Alysa's eyes. She had seen the whole thing, the fight, and the finish. She was silent, the crying had stopped along with the shaking.

Alysa said nothing, just stared at the dead man on the floor.

The F150 rumbled as Alysa stomped on the gas, taking us far and fast away from Baldy's. We drove along, headed southwest, in silence. She kept the old truck just over the speed limit. Her knee bounced at stop lights, and she whispered, *C'mon, c'mon* at every red light. We passed the bright lights of the gargantuan Daytona Speedway as she laid the pedal down in the home stretch. The city lights of the beach town faded behind us as we made our way west among cow pastures and forgotten orchards.

I didn't know where we were going or why, but she seemed determined to put distance between us and that town. Suddenly Alysa hit the brakes and cut the wheel, sending truck off the road, sloshing onto a muddy road. Passing the pines she hit the brakes, skidding to a stop on a soft gravel service road. She killed the engine.

"What happens now?" Alysa said, her tone flat making it feel like I had been telling her about my day at the office. I couldn't quite make out her expression. The silhouette of her face was draped by shoulder length hair like a hood over her face. Her arms reached out and strong hands callused from opening beers and lifting kettle bells during workouts, wrapped around the wheel. Her arms went taught, her knuckles swelled, I thought she might rip the steering wheel off.

"We go home."

"After all that? After you killed that guy. What about the cops? Evidence? Shouldn't we report what happened to the police? I was kidnapped, damn it!" Her voice was climbing higher with every question I failed to answer. I wanted to reach out and touch her, to console her after what she just went through. Touching was pushing it, hours at the mercy of Aziz's crew left her ice inside. I didn't kill them slow enough.

"I'm sorry." I said to which she scoffed. I continued, "No one will connect you to any of this." I said and kept my hands in my lap. She didn't look at me while processing everything she had witnessed in the last couple of hours.

"You want me to not report my own a kidnapping, and a murder. You killed that man, Roger." Those strong hands of hers began to shake. She looked at me now, half her face was covered in golden hair.

"If you want to go to the cops I understand. When they question you, just say I forced your silence."

"How do you know all this? How are you so confident the cops won't track us down?"

I could hear her voice grow nasally as snot built up along with the tears in her eyes. A high-pitched whine emanated as she let go of the wheel. I reached out and she nearly leapt over into my lap as her arms wrapped around my neck and squeeze. I thought my neck was going to break but I took the risk and let her get it out. Her pain was my fault.

"It doesn't seem like it now, but it's going to be alright." I softly spoke. I didn't know for sure. There was always a chance of a witness, the bartender or a security camera. It was Aziz's mess now to clean up. Some of that pull with the city would come in handy.

She pulled back, sitting with her hands in her lap. The shaking had subsided, and her breathing had slowed to a steady in and out with the occasional nose whistle. She wiped the remaining tears and sniffled.

"Don't worry, I won't go to the cops." Alysa said.

I nodded. We switched seats. I drove us out of there.

I drove along in silence. Alysa spoke only to tell me where to turn. We were beachside headed north along Peninsula Drive. Down a side street was a two-story home that was converted into a duplex, with up and down stairs apartments. The house was English Tutor style with white plaster walls and exposed deep brown wooden beams.

The sun was just coming out of the clouds when I got out of the cab with her, she turned, somewhat surprised I would walk her to her door. She said nothing as her key slipped into the lock.

Alysa paused before going in. With just a quarter turn she said, "Maybe all that back there is normal for you, but it's not for me. You understand, don't you?"

I nodded, "Yeah."

She went in and locked the door behind her. I stood there for a moment then walked back to the truck. Now it was a lonely quiet road back with just my thoughts and the hum of the V-8. I didn't understand her parting words as they lingered in my ear. I assumed much and knew too little.

Chapter 21

In the rearview mirror I removed a wad of blood-soaked gas station paper towels. I could see the swelling above my eye had subsided. The color was deep purple. I sipped a beer from a can nestled in a paper bag. The damp film of humidity covered everything in the truck including my skin. Most of the rain had passed. I was parked under a large oak where the water collected on the leaves until the stems could no longer hold the tiny pools of rain and dumped it on the metal roof of the truck.

There were still fries left over from the drive-thru I hit. I chewed on the warm salty yellow rubbery sticks and sipped the beer with the faces of all I met this week passing through my mind. Rosa lingered in view. Her midnight hair and rose lips stayed just out of reach. The night in the dune played over. I needed it to play longer, but it led to darker images, darker blood smeared faces. Alysa's green eyes and smiling face pushed out the dead. The nights she bounced behind the bar and our one meal together at a diner. I wanted to touch her again, not from a place of fear or relief but to find that connection that always hung in the air between us. I wanted a do-over, a second chance. Aziz made sure that could never happen.

A text came through. *"You have made a serious mess for me. I don't want a mess. We settle up now."*

I texted it back, *I tried to pay up. Boghos had other ideas.*

The beer was almost gone before I received a reply.

"Fuck the money. You know what I want."

I read the text twice and just stared at the phone without typing, without thinking. My mind was exhausted, what I left in the bar was damaging but nothing Aziz couldn't clean up. I killed everyone in that bar but the barmaid. I knew they would all be with me like the others I worked so hard to forget. It would be my job now to erase them from my thoughts, but it is my dreams I couldn't yet control. I had to get this Armenian off my back. Kicking in his front door and going to work on his house was the obvious answer. It was my debt, I earned it.

Chapter 22

There were two business suits and the maintenance man standing around the busted door to my office when I came down the hall. The maintenance man squatted like a baseball catcher to inspect the broken doorknob and the two suits stood leaning and peering into the office discussing whether to call the police or not.

"What if there is a body in there?" said one suit.

"If you go in there don't touch anything." The other suit replied.

"There's no dead bodies in there." I said, "At least not when I left last night."

I brushed past the two suits and stood facing the maintenance man who was fully upright now.

The two suits filled their bug-eyes with the mess that was once my office. Everything was as I left it, same as the guys who tossed the place left it. I stepped into the mess.

"Buddy, you do this?" The maintenance man asked as he pressed a hand against the loose door letting it swing open.

"Yeah." I said and shut the door.

From the other side of the door the man who would have to fix the locks said, "I gotta get new locks. I should have it done by the end of the day. Roberta aint gonna like it." He lingered there for a moment then I heard his work boots shuffle off.

Sitting in the silence knowing what to do next was muted by unstoppable images of Alysa in fear. Nothing had motivated me more than to free her and destroy those responsible for forever damaging her life and now mine. We had our one date, and it was perfect, so perfect, better than any prearranged managed Hallmark

Movie script writer could have done it. Except one thing. I never got to kiss her.

Alysa probably hated my guts.

Blinking brought the mess of my office into focus. Sanford's laptop was unable to find my WiFi connection. I searched through the mess and found the router had been ripped from the wall. The plug was still good and slipped into the socket easily.

At the desk I plugged in the flash drive and began collecting all the email addresses and blind copying them to the same email. I would later delete the email account.

The body of the email would be simple, something to get the point across without being obvious in what I was setting them free from. They would all soon know they were free from the blackmail web that had trapped them. There would no longer be a spider coming if they didn't pay. Their transgressions would be absolved.

As I transcribed the email addresses, copying and pasting, the door creaked open. Deputy Camp's small stature but wide shoulders filled the doorway. She rapped a knuckle against the busted door and then let herself in. I nearly had to rub my eyes when I saw her dressed in civilian clothes, a short sleeved floral blouse showing off toned arms. A pair of salmon-colored jeans tightly wrapped around athletic thighs ending in gold flats. Her face was relaxed, almost calm, a look I knew to be completely forced. Her normally slicked down hair had volume and style accented by gold hoop earrings and what I think was make-up, brightened her eyes.

"Mind if I come in?" Camp said in a soft tone. "I see you had a visitor or maybe this is just how you decorate." Camp circled the room. She was taking mental notes, stopping to inspect and open drawer or cut open couch cushion without touching anything.

"My friends are animals." I went back to copying and pasting email addresses. With only a few left, I finished and closed the laptop, waiting to send the email once Camp was gone.

"Real animals huh? That how you got that lump on your eye?" Camp asked as she turned to face me, her hands resting on her waist just about where her gun would be in uniform.

I put a finger to the lump and the pain brought back the memory of how I got it.

Camp went on, "Another real animal, or animals, ripped apart Baldy's bar early this morning. Killed four men and even the female bartender got the shit smacked out of her. No guns either, all bare hands. You know anyone that could do that?"

I shrugged, "Got any leads?" I leaned back in my wooden desk chair. Now I was the calm comfortable one.

"Nah, the bartender is not talking, and all cameras were turned off like they were expecting trouble. That bar has been a thorn in this city's side for a while. Somehow it stays open." Camp kicked at some of the mess on the floor. I heard glass crunch beneath her shoe.

My phone lit up with a text. I looked at it as casually as I could. *I want that info or you're dead!*

The texts were coming in closer together. He was getting desperate. I knew another fight was coming. This time with guns. Aziz had pushed me all the way. There were things I could have done different, like not care. I can stop caring now and delete this email draft. None of that blackmail shit should bother me in the least, if I keep thinking people get what they deserve. But these saps on this email did nothing wrong but want to talk to a pretty lady. *Lady* may be a strong word, but they needed someone who would talk back. They weren't messaging kids or dealing drugs to addicts. They just wanted companionship, something everyone wanted, and something I wanted.

Here, now, I decided I would risk my life for them and for something new I was learning, principles. As a thief I lived by a code that never extended beyond my partners in the caper. Things were changing. Sanford took on the challenge to fill the void of my indifference for humanity with the principle to care. This emotion had yet to fully develop in me and may never, but I made the decision to care.

I held my phone contemplating the reply, forgetting Camp was now seated across from me.

"You aren't gonna say anything about my look?"

"Yeah." I said without looking at the deputy, the black glass of the cell phone held my focus.

"I did it for you."

That got my attention. I looked up with a smirk breaking through. "Are you asking me out Deputy?"

"Hell no. I don't date white…" She paused and then smirked herself.

My eyebrows went up, I started to laugh, "White boys?"

"That's, I wasn't. Oh, shit Grimes, I wanted you to see me as not just a cop, is all." She crossed her legs, bouncing the top one and folder her hands in her lap.

"You know," She said smiling again, "In case you got any single friends."

"If I had friends, you wouldn't want to date them."

We sat in silence for a moment. Both our minds were too methodical to keep the playful banter going. They had to return to the case, she had questions and I had things left undone.

"That's probably true. You're too busy as a private detective to have friends."

"I do keep busy."

"You know what I think? I think all these cases, the child prostitute ring, the porn place burning and now the bar, are somehow connected. They are connected to someone out there waging a war on crime in this town." Camp said with eyes studying my face.

"Don't you do that every day?"

Camp leaned back. "Not this week. I'm on administrative leave." she grabbed at the heel of her flat, "Because of a shooting I was involved in. Not sure if you heard."

"I read something about that." I said bringing my focus back to my guest and away from my problem on the phone.

Camp's immobile face broke into a smile, "Captain says he'll review me for detective when the dust settles from that. You know, thanks to all the fantastic police work I've put in lately. Yeah, I've been real busy too, everywhere I look there are dead people mixed up in high crimes. The brass is taking notice. They want me to lead a special investigative unit into this vigilante and, this war on crime."

"Good."

"Good?" Her smiling eyes gave way to thin slits as the wrinkles faded from her face. "Are you even listening to me Grimes, to what I'm saying here?"

"Sure, there's plenty of criminals to go around."

"A little less now. Whoever this vigilante is running and gunning around town needs to cool it. This blood bath up the street took out the entire known crew of a local gangster muscling in on the city. Seems this gangster was in the numbers racket and tried branching out. Officially we are looking at rivals, or who have you, put a stop to that. The whole crew beat to death in his own bar. I'd say the work of two or three men." She said watching every pour on my skin for the slightest but of moisture.

When I gave her nothing, Camp went on to talk about the investigation Aziz was now under and how he couldn't let a silent fart out without all of Florida Law Enforcement knowing about it. As she went on, that he was in the wind for now. Her words entered my ears but never made the transition from sound waves to electrical current into my brain. Azad Aziz was finished. He was weak and he knew it. There would be no retribution coming my way. I was safe for now.

The email was still waiting to be sent. I hit the button and all those in bondage were set free, free from the worry of their deepest secrets and fetishes becoming public.

Aziz's death threat was still awaiting a reply. So, I typed one, *I don't think I will let you kill me today.*

I had another email typed out to the police officer sitting across from me. A couple of clicks and all the information on the money laundering from the flash drive was transferred. Then I hit send.

The End

Thank you for joining Grimes on his adventure through the streets of Daytona Beach, FL. Grimes' Retribution is the second book in the Roger Grimes series. For more of Roger Grimes check out @forkermedia on Instagram and read the next instalment, Grimes' Reckoning out now wherever you bought this book.

-H.A.L. Wagner